# WITCHWATER COUNTRY

GARRY KILWORTH

# WITCHWATER COUNTRY

THE BODLEY HEAD
LONDON

**Acknowledgements**

The following books and short story have been used by the author as a source of inspiration for this novel

*The Great Tide* by Hilda Grieve, published by County Council of Essex, 1959.

*Amy Johnson* by Constance Babington Smith, published by William Collins, 1967.

*Oh, Whistle, and I'll come to you, my lad,* a short story by M.R. James.



British Library Cataloguing
in Publication data:
Kilworth, Garry
Witchwater country.
I. Title
823'.914[F] PR6061.I39

ISBN 0-370-30790-9



Phototypeset by
Falcon Graphic Art Ltd
Wallington,
Surrey
Printed and bound in
Great Britain
for The Bodley Head,
30 Bedford Square,
London WC1B 3RP
by St Edmundsbury Press,
Bury St Edmunds
*First published 1986*

*For Annie, with love.*

The sun does descend,
And our sports have an end.
Round the laps of their mothers
Many sisters and brothers,
Like birds in their nest,
Are ready for rest,
And sport no more seen,
On the darkening Green.

From *The Ecchoing Green*
by William Blake

# PROLOGUE

Now and again I catch a whiff of childhood, a feeling as elusive as a hedgerow scent, as I pass a small brook or a greensward where three dead sticks have served as cricket stumps.

Until I was eleven years old, half my world was inside my head. The real and the imagined were so enmeshed I could not separate them. When they were eventually torn apart it was a painful experience and thankfully one I shall never have to repeat. Childhood will normally drift gradually into adulthood over the years of adolescence but occasionally, just occasionally, childhood ends as suddenly as the slamming of a door. They call it 'growing up'.

As a grown man I enjoy being afraid: it gives me a perverse feeling of security. I need the sense of attachment to my youth that fear gives me. Without it my life would revolve around the instant and the future, both of which are unacceptable. My strongest memories are of dark nights and days of rain, when strange beasts lurked in corners and cupboards held supernatural beings behind closed doors. Films and books cannot now stimulate this kind of necessary terror, as they once did. The terror has to come from within. Fear of the dark. Fear of water. Fear of fire. All primal and instinctive. I need my nightmares in a world of mundane comfort and dull rightness, to keep my interest alive.

Children, especially village children, always manage to work themselves to the centre of any incident or tragedy that occurs. Far more things happened to me in the space of a year as a child than they ever did once I became an adult. I believe this is because children are not tied by domestic chores or work to specific places during each day. They have the freedom to roam at will and consequently are drawn to events like iron filings to a magnet. They make things happen too, because they are at the stage of life where experiments are taking place. They are curious creatures, and, unlike adults, they *want* to get involved. And they do.

The following tale I have tried to tell in the voice of a child, though that is of course a difficult, not to say impossible task for a man in his thirties. It is inevitable that certain adult conceptions and thoughts enter into such retrospective recounting of a time when one is developing viewpoints and consciousness foreign to childhood. The incidents may seem many, but as I have already written, children get *involved* — they look for excitement and danger, and they find it. As an adult I find I am too busy with the mundane things in life to be drawn into such affairs and where I know of them I avoid them. Childhood is a journey, and things happen on journeys that never occur when one is settled and living each day like any other. A child's voice then, but not a story for children, for it is *about* adults. A journey into adulthood and one which has left scars that I will carry with me into old age, and perhaps beyond.

# ONE

Before death came between us, to split our ranks and pare our numbers that tragic summer, we considered four to be the perfect group: any disagreements tended to divide us down the middle and the issue could be settled between two equal armies. It was always Oaky who set the rules.

'Only corn in the airguns and crab apples in the catapults.'

'What if we run out of crabs?' Dinger would ask, squinting over puffed cheeks. During schooldays he rubbed lemon juice into the corners of his eyes in order to feign sickness.

'Is plums 'n damsons OK?'

'Plums 'n damsons and any fruit but no half-bricks. First brick that comes near me or Titch gets a lead slug back,' Oaky would reply, patting his air rifle. I wished I had an air rifle. The shotgun effect from filling and firing a barrel of corn was magnificent. We were always searching for realism in our war games.

Once, we had a war using French arrows—pointed sticks fletched with shaped playing cards. You wrap a knotted string around the shaft and use it, sling-like, to flick the arrow into the air. The result is an effective range of two to three hundred yards and if the end is weighted the arrow buries itself point first in the earth with a satisfying *thunk*.

The only accidents we ever had, apart from superficial nose bleeds and black eyes, were a knockout slug behind the ear for Oaky and a hard lump of earth in the groin for me. Oaky was revived before presentation to his family but I could not disguise my ignoble wound from my grandmother. After the doctor had been summoned and the swelling went down the incident was merely one more of those filed away in her memory, to be retrieved when she wished to embarrass me in company. When I was fit again and joined the others, we marvelled at the ingenuity of Dinger who had invented the clod-firing siege catapult. It was a bicycle inner-tube stretched between the fork of a tree trunk. On a day with a favourable wind we found we could get fifty yards out of a one pound sod of earth.

Peter Oaks was as sturdy as his name. He was a thick-set boy, of medium height for a ten-year-old, and the indisputable leader of our gang. His father was a salesman of farm tractors and was almost always away in places like Poland; lands which were only names to us and of which we could form no images. Oaky's mother was a delicate woman who considered her dour, muscled son more a restless bulldog than a boy. When his father was away, Oaky's licence to roam free was, enviably, almost unlimited. He once told us that his mother sometimes went to bed before he got home at night. He could also pee up a wall to a height of nine feet, the force behind his bladder leaving us in awe.

In this activity he was totally uninhibited. He would go anywhere out of doors at any time.

'M'just goin' to have a slash,' Oaky would say, sauntering over to the nearest hedge. Then, head bent and both hands utilized during the operation, he would perform the function.

'Oaky, there's a car comin' down the lane.' On a cold day, steam would be rising from his cupped hands, billowing around his bulky form.

'K,' he would acknowledge, without moving an inch. The vehicle would pass, its occupants registering various reactions, while we carefully examined the growth of the opposite hedge. Then he would shake himself with thoughtful efficiency.

Alexander William Freck was a tall, gangling boy of eleven with a skin as white as milk. We called him Milky. He was the son of a millworker and their terraced house was one of seven that flanked the lane that led to Tenbridge mills. Beyond the back yard was a wilderness of agricultural land. In the early summer of 1952 it was covered in mustard: a stretch of flatland that sung with a bright, yellow voice. It was useless to us. Only corn held any attraction as a playground, because of its height and ability to conceal. Thus the hinterland was struck from our mental geographical charts.

Facing Milky's house were fields, woods and a marshy area of ponds covered in chickweed. If Milky was not in his house we would usually find him watching cricket, up a tree or playing amongst the stagnant, murky pools. On a Saturday shortly before the school summer holidays began, we approached him, Oaky, Dinger and I, as he sat earnestly contemplating the surface of a pond not far from his house.

'Wuppa Milky!'

'Wuppa Oaks!'

'What's up? What'ayer lookin' at?'

Milky nodded towards the water.

'Pond. Mum says there's witches at the bottom. Says if you go too close, they grab hold of you, drag you under and cut you up. Hang bits of you on hooks, like at the butchers.'

Dinger sniggered.

'Ged out. She's potty, your mum.'

'Don't call my mum names. I'll land you one.' Milky's threats were never taken lightly. He said nothing he did not mean.

'Still don't believe it,' Dinger retorted.

'OK,' Milky said quietly. 'Go and stick your arm in then. I don't mind. I'll sit and watch.'

Dinger grinned at Oaky and strolled closer to the pond. There he paused. Unlike the rest of us, Dinger had not been raised in a rural community, a remote village surrounded by salt marshes and accessible only by a single road, or one of the many tidal backwaters that crazed the area between two rivers. We had lived with superstitious, simple country people since we had first learned to ask questions, and their culture was an inherent part of our learning process. Tenbridge was a village that barely acknowledged its connection with the rest of Essex and still bred smugglers, poachers and beachcombers as if they were skilled trades bearing official approval. Witchcraft was more than a local hobby and the vicar had one of the largest collections of books on the occult in the country. Old people with stories to tell could be found down any one of the lonely lanes that veined our brooding playground. And we listened to them. Dinger had come to us from a town and occasionally scoffed at our beliefs but even he was growing into our ways, gradually.

The surface of the pond looked grim and forbidding—it could not have appeared more evil had it been the Devil's face. It was a green, scummy screen that separated us from a horrible fate. Around it the alders crowded like ailing dwarves with crooked, rotting limbs, and willows hung their hair over the dark water. One or two dead branches lay amongst the chickweed, aging into stone.

'Go on then,' challenged Milky. 'Stick it in . . .' But already Dinger had hesitated too long. We knew he was not going to do it. Finally, he snatched up a rock and shattered the still surface with a yell that terrified him as much as it did us, and then we were all running away, shouting at each other.

'Watch it! Watch it! Right behind you Dinger.'

'Come on Titch! Getcher legs pumpin' faster.'

Then, three hundred yards away, in the comforting environs of a cricket pavilion, we fell to the ground gasping for breath. Oaky gripped the back of my neck with his powerful fingers and gave it a painful squeeze.

'Nearly had ole Titch here, she did,' and I squirmed out of his reach, knowing that my grandmother's house had only gas lighting downstairs, with candles upstairs in the bedrooms. I was not allowed to keep my candle alight for longer than it took to get into my pyjamas and slip between the sheets. Where my mother and father had moved to, in Buckinghamshire, there was apparently electric light and blessed, instant relief from the dark when pre-sleep terrors became unbearable. I lived with my grandparents in a house where the darkness rushed in like a black beast, to envelop me in its suffocating folds. Morning was always as far away as death and no comfort could be obtained from looking forward to first light. I used to pray earnestly to God for cars to pass along the lane, so that their headlights would shine briefly on the white ceiling and give me temporary comfort. Occasionally the agony of my fears kept me awake long enough for my grandfather, who slept in the same room as I did, to join me. I loved my grandfather because he had an artificial leg. It took at least forty minutes of adult time to unstrap and unhinge it from his stump and by the time he blew out his candle I would be asleep. My grandfather used to curse his 'tin' leg vehemently but I was sure it was one of God's intricate gifts to small boys who were terrified of the dark, of unknown, unfocused evils, of waterwitches who grip you by the leg, arm . . . neck and drag you down to an underwater slaughterhouse from which there is no return. We were all afraid of witches in our gang. The Essex marshes were full of them and twice during our childhoods we had accidentally witnessed a coven illicitly employing the use of the local graveyard.

John Bellchamber hid firmly behind the nickname Dinger Bell. He had moved to Tenbridge at the age of eight and it had been seven months before the school discovered he had a second half to his surname. I never once saw his full name used in his presence without a scowl appearing on his face. Dinger was moody, erratic by nature and inclined to be vicious. Oaky was feared for his strength, but Dinger, of average height and weight for ten years, frightened me more. He had a twist of cruelty running through him which sometimes appeared on his face, as crooked as the vein that ran across my grandfather's brow. He would argue with venom in his voice, when he knew he was wrong, and was forever inflicting annoying pains on all his contemporaries except Oaky. He would kick someone's heels from behind, so that the victim tripped himself up. Or flick the back of an ear, painfully, with his fingernail. Or stop suddenly, while walking in line, so that the person behind collided with his head. Each time he did something like this to me, I would turn angrily to find him smiling faintly, as if it were all a joke and I was being foolish for not accepting it in good heart. Secretly I hated Dinger, yet I courted his respect. I wanted his approval. I wanted him to accept me. He saw through my falseness and never failed to treat me with contempt.

My name is Raymond Swan but my school friends called me Titch. Tenbridge was the birthplace of my parents and where my grandparents lived until they died. When my parents went to live in Buckinghamshire, in 1949, I stayed behind with nan and grandad because of certain domestic difficulties, mostly financial, in my parents' household. I had two younger brothers, both of whom believed highly in the theory that expending energy was the only way to find joy in life. They went to Buckinghamshire with my mother and father. I loved the days at my grandparent's cottage and hated the nights.

Once upon a time my grandfather had been a field labourer; the cottage was tied to a nearby farm. When he lost his leg in the Great War, they let him remain as a tenant, though not without some mercenary reasoning behind their apparent kindness. His disability pension had been commuted which had enabled him to purchase a horse and cart. With this mode of transport he was able to carry out odd jobs for the farm, and others, and in that way he earned a reasonable living. New horses came over the years but they were always called 'Custard'. Grandad's nickname was 'Rhubub' and any other title for his horse would have robbed the village of a talking point. During my stay with my grandfather he was in his seventies and eighties. My grandmother, white-haired and pleasant-looking, despised my grandfather. The reasons were too complex for a young boy but I understood from my mother that my grandfather had lied about his age when he married my nan and was in fact ten years older than he had said at the time, which put nearly twenty years between them. This seemed to me rather a trivial reason for such a state to come about but I accepted it as one of the many possibilities.

The back pocket of my grandfather's breeches was always stuffed with dirty pound notes, yet he was forever complaining about his poor financial position. He rarely spoke to my nan unless she addressed him first and he ate her food with a look of suffering on his face. She, in turn, had not slept in the same room with him for many years and never ceased to complain about migraine headaches.

They both called me 'the boy' and treated me with a distant kindness that never really developed into love. Often they used me to speak to each other, presumably when they were particularly at odds, but even that did not appear out of the ordinary to me at the time. I was too busy in my own head, with my own schemes, to worry about the antics of old people.

The house itself belonged to the nineteenth century. It owned a coalfired black range, a huge, static boiling copper in the scullery and an outside toilet. Between the scullery and the front room, where nan slept, was the parlour where we did most of our living. It was in this room that the range was situated and this long, black monster formed the centre of our existence. Our water came from a well pump in the middle of the row of terraced cottages. It came up from the depths of the earth very cold, even in summer. The toilet, a place very important to me because I did much of my thinking there, out of the way of the adults, was attached to the house. Hares were hung behind its door until ready to be cooked. The yard itself was full of chickens and a savage dog called Mick, who rejected all my attempts to make friends with him. Peter, the housedog, was part labrador and used to ride with my grandfather on his cart, but he was so gentle and quiet he held no interest for me. There was also a ginger cat that slept a great deal of the time and had the trick of leaping onto the sash cord window, clinging there as it rumbled down to allow him an exit from the house. For our entertainment we relied mainly on an accumulator-powered wireless set, though unlike the adults I read books a lot up in my room. On the last day of term in the summer of '52, my grandad gave me a lift home from school on the cart.

'Hi nan, I'm home,' I called.

She came out of the scullery into the kitchen, wiping her hands on an apron and frowning slightly.

'Don't shout boy, I've got a headache. Well, don't just

stand there, get yourself into the scullery for a wash. Have you wiped your feet?'

'Yes nan,' I lied.

'Hmm. Off you go then. Supper's almost ready—your favourite, mince.'

'Great. Thanks, nan.'

'Dad,' she addressed my grandfather who had been standing behind me all this time, silent and watchful, 'cat caught another mouse in the coal s'morning.' The coal was kept in the cupboard under the stairs.

'Lay a couple o' traps then woman. Why look at me?'

'It's your job, not a woman's. I don't like taking them out. That's not right, a woman doing that sort of thing. You do your jobs and I'll do mine.' With that she swept back into the scullery and I followed.

During supper I contemplated the first day of the holiday. Dinger, Oaky, Milky and I would all be up early. The first day of summer holiday was always the most magical, the sounds at dawn appearing different from those on mornings when we had school: the cock crowing in the yard, the birds in the eaves, the rattle of Mick's chain as he moved around the yard. I would wake up with the sun spilling in through the window, having forgotten completely my night-time terrors. The room would smell warm and musty. Grandad rose at five thirty and would have been long out of the house by the time I opened my eyes. There was one other person who lived with us, on and off: my uncle, Dave. He was twenty-three that year and had a few weeks before rejoining his ship at Tilbury as a merchant seaman. He went to sea only when he was short of money or the police were close to the discovery of some small crime, like the pilfering of some items from the village garage where Dave occasionally helped out. The rest of his life he spent loafing around the house, poaching or riding his motorbike.

To my mother Dave was a waster but to me he was a hero. He owned a 12-bore shotgun and had given me a ferret called Jessica. The gun was one of those marvellous toys of the adult world I was determined to own one day. I cared nothing for my mother's disapproval of my uncle. I cared only that I heard the ferret's bell tinkling as Dave told me to put her down a rabbit hole. I cared only that the gun gave out a noise like Hell exploding and made my knees tremble with excitement. At twenty I would find blood sports totally distasteful but at ten all I wanted to do was own a gun that would spin a hare through a triple somersault and afterwards, legs apart, casually to break the weapon and fill the morning with blue smoke and the smell of cordite. Who else had an uncle who could hypnotize chickens by drawing Vs in the dust of the yard, so that they remained transfixed until he nudged them, minutes later? Who else had an uncle who could play the jew's harp with the speed of an Irish fiddler?

Only *me.*

# TWO

'Grandad, how did you lose your leg?'

'Well, boy, that's a story I don't get to talk on, much. Your old grandad was a soldier in the Great War, 'cept they didn't call it that in them days. They sent us to France on a ship. A frigate, it was. Anyways, we was half-way across the English Channel, what the Frenchies just call The Channel on account of they don't like us English much, when we was chased by a German destroyer. The Hun shelled us good that day. Fire took a hold of the decks and there was I, dousin' with the rest of 'em, when a shell landed slap-bang on the bridge. Piece of sheet metal the size of a tabletop came whistlin' through the air, and spinning like I see those old playing cards you flick around. Took the leg clean off, that metal plate did, as if it was cut through with a bandsaw. Blood spurted out of the punctures. Quick as a flash, one of me mates pressed the stump against the red-hot deck and fried the end, sizzlin' the arteries to stop 'em bleedin' . . .'

Gravel rattled on the bedroom window pane. I knew Dinger was waiting outside but was reluctant to stir for a few minutes. I could hear my grandmother moving around in the scullery below and I knew that soon she would begin frying eggs for my breakfast. The bed I slept in was old and formed a deep, secure pit for my body, and the blankets were heavy. Sunlight cut a shaft for itself directly over my head. I could see the whitewashed wall bulging unevenly where it struck and shone as bright as an angel's wing.

When I looked out of the window, Dinger had gone, so I picked up my book of H. G. Wells' short stories. Dave's girlfriend Cathy had given it to me for my last birthday and I was in the middle of a tale I had begun the previous evening. It was pretty scary—*The Lord Of The Dynamos.* Halfway through, the gas had failed and no one had a shilling for the meter, so we had all sat in a cosy ring around the glow from the range fire. H. G. Wells was one of my favourite writers: his stories were like dreams, worrying yet wonderful.

'Come on, young man!' called my grandmother, some time later. 'It's nearly seven thirty.' There was a sizzling sound as something went into the frying pan, followed by the smell of bacon. I jumped out of bed onto the cool linoleum and shouted, 'Coming, nan.' Looking out of the window again I saw that Dinger was back, kicking the base of a street lamp. I held up ten fingers for him as I caught his eye. Ten minutes. He scowled and moved off in the direction of Oaky's house. They would collect me on their way past.

I dressed hurriedly in flannel shorts and grey shirt, pulled on some socks and shoes and began to descend the barewood stairs.

'Wash!' called my grandmother. I stopped short, then reluctantly retraced my steps to find the china jug and bowl on the bedroom sideboard. I made a great fuss and noise pouring out the water and splashing it onto my face, dried and went downstairs again. Breakfast was on the table but my normal chair was occupied by the cat. I took another place. We had had our differences in the past and I had almost always lost. Ginger was a large beast with a short temper and, though about ten years of age, still very quick with his claws. I used to try to tap him on the head, knowing he was not quite fast enough to prevent me, until he learned the tactic of ignoring my hand and going straight for my elbow. It was impossible to retract my whole arm swiftly enough and he scored several times before I realized he had me beaten. He eyed me now, casually, and it seemed without malice: but who can tell what a cat is thinking? His left ear, badly scarred in a fight, twitched violently and I took my gaze from him. He was quite capable of leaping across the table at me.

Uncle Dave came down, still tucking his shirt into

trousers that were held up with a wide leather belt. He ruffled my hair when he had finished dressing.

'All right, mate?' he said. He was a tall, lean man with thick, black curls. There was a crescent scar on his forehead which he wore like a badge of courage. It was the result of a motorcycle accident. A car door handle, he had told me, had all but winkled his brains from his skull. Uncle Dave and I had the kind of rapport which is only established between an impressionable child and an adult lacking a certain amount of maturity. Dave could still laugh at schoolboy jokes, especially crude ones, and delighted in terrorizing me with ghost stories. I was prepared to believe anything he told me and defended his honour against critics to the point of blind rage and tears.

'Titch, you want a ride on the bike today?' He was pulling on his motorcycle boots by the kitchen range as he spoke. His accident had not dampened his enthusiasm for open air speed. I heard nan say once that they had put a silver plate in his head and he hadn't been right since.

My grandmother stepped from the scullery and pushed a plate of three eggs and four rashers of bacon onto uncle Dave's place at the table.

'Leave the boy alone,' she said. 'He's wild enough without you trying to lead him further astray.'

'*Moth-er,*' cried Dave, in mock distress. 'I'm just trying to keep the lad occupied.'

'He's got plenty to do around here. He could clean up the yard for a start.'

I bent my head over my breakfast, quickly. Nan had not actually told me I *had* to do the chore yet, but she would if Dave kept offering to take me out. I raised my eyes to warn him off but he was engaged in fastening his long bootstraps and seemed to have dropped the subject. It took me only another half minute to finish my breakfast, then I leapt from my chair and rushed out of the back door, yelling, 'Won't be in for dinner, nan.'

Mick came hurtling out of his kennel and ran the full length of his chain, barking like the demented beast he was. The chain pulled him up short about two yards from the toilet. I blew a raspberry at him, showing him my backside, and went into the cool interior of the toilet, leaving the door slightly ajar for light. There was a hare in there, stiff as a board and staring at the floor. It swayed on its hook on the back of the door. Inside, the toilet smelled of disinfectant and dust, and as I relieved myself I searched for newcomers amongst the corners in the darkness of the ceiling where there were webs. I had read somewhere at school that all spiders were poisonous and one day I hoped to find a big one that I could trap and leave in Mick's kennel. One big enough to bite my enemy and hopefully kill him stone dead. All I could see, however, were little red money spiders. I often wondered what they ate: even the flies were twice their size.

I left the toilet to face a renewed outburst of fury from Mick. One or two chickens ran close to him but he took no notice of them. It was my leg he wanted.

I stopped by the garden shed, lifted a brick and checked on my catapult. If nan knew I had one I would not keep it for five minutes longer. She would have had it on the range fire. It was still in the depression beneath the housebrick. I left it there since it was unlikely we were going to war on the first day of the holidays.

Oaky and Dinger were waiting for me in the street.

'Where the 'ell 'ave you been?' growled Dinger.

'Havin' breakfast,' I retorted. 'Don't suppose you came out empty.'

'Some of us get up early enough.'

Oaky had not yet said anything. He normally remained aloof from any bickering between Dinger and me.

'Come on,' he said, 'Milky'll be wonderin' where we are.' Dinger clenched and unclenched his hand, then followed Oaky as the sturdy but placid youth walked off down the lane. There was a pavement on one side only, the side with the cottages, and we walked in single file and in step, one foot in the gutter and the other on the kerb, like three lame military men on their way home from a foreign war.

About a mile from the village we passed the White House, a lone, clapboard cottage set back off the road, with an orchard in front and a stagnant pond at the rear.

The white paint was peeling off the two-storey building to reveal dark, damp patches like black scabs beneath. The house had an air of decay about it. Like the old woman we had seen in its yard, it had that uncared for look which accompanies advanced age. The doors and sills were rotting at the edges and the windows were loose in their frames, and warped. There was a green mould rioting amongst the tiles on a roof which had sunk in several places, forming hollows that trapped the rainwater. One chimney pot had fallen and was lying in the yard below in several pieces.

In the orchard the grass was waist high and the plum trees had been left unpruned, some of their branches disappearing down into the weeds beneath. They were heavily laden with fruit.

We planned a foray for later in the day, though we feared the old woman, whom Milky insisted was a waterwitch. The fact that she was old and had a pond in her back yard was all the evidence needed to reach this conclusion. As for the rest of us, we had seen wet footprints leading to the front door. We feared her but that would not stop us scrumping her plums. Milky's warnings about retribution from the witch only served to add to the excitement of the deed.

A short way past the White House was the lane that led to Milky's house. From the safety of the high spinneys the rooks yelled obscenities at us with cowardly delight. There were lone herons posting the shallow ponds beyond, like druid priests with pagan daggers in their mouths, poised to slaughter the innocent fish. A woodpecker was tapping out its coded messages to the hollow world and a jay, like a piece of turquoise china plate, curved into the trees suddenly from a window in the sky. This was *our* country.

We found Milky in his father's shed, busy stuffing *Spick and Span* magazines back into the flue of an old potbellied stove. When he saw who we were he pulled them out again and we spent the next half-hour studying partly-clothed ladies with disproportionate anatomies. Our studies tended to be clinical, although we gained some excitement from the fact that the magazines were forbidden to us and therefore deliciously sinful. Finally, when the heat of the day had raised the atmosphere in the shed to hothouse level, Oaky suggested we went swimming.

'Haven't brought my trunks,' I said.

'Have to go in skins then, won't we,' said Oaky, ' 'cos I 'aven't got mine neither,' which was fine for someone as careless as Oaky, but for Dinger and myself, shy to the point of preferring death to public exposure, it was unthinkable.

'Keep my underpants on then,' I muttered, and I noticed Dinger nod in agreement.

'We can dry in the sun, after,' he added. 'Milk's OK. He can get his towel and trunks.'

The mill, where Milky's father worked, abutted the edge of a wide part of the river and was separated from the water by a narrow wharf. We used the wharf, tucked away behind a corner and out of sight of the millworkers, as a diving platform. There were other large buildings which we called generally 'the mills' but most of them were probably warehouses. We had only an idea of what went on inside, and in the main were quite uninterested. In some of the yards there were mountains of cockle shells which were replenished from time to time, so we guessed they ground them down for fertilizer or something. Essex is farming country and that made sense to us.

The sound made by the mills was another matter. We liked such noise and used it in our war games. It was the rumble of distant Panzer divisions, or allied tanks crossing into Germany, or the drone of bombers, or fleets of landing craft approaching the beaches of Normandy. There was always a pungent smell about the mills which, with the air always full of brown dust, produced a feeling of familiarity and security in our breasts. Why that should have been, I have no idea, but it did. In the vicinity of the mills we felt like warriors in their own territory, relaxed and easy with one another.

The river itself was not very picturesque. It had a tidal backwash and, like several others along the Essex coast, broke out into the inlets and backwaters of estuary country. At ebb tide, a thin sliver of seabound water ran down the broad, brown back of the silt and the river mud, fringed with saltmarshes of thick poa grass, saltwort and seablite, let out an odour which knocked casual visitors sideways. We were immune to it, of course. At low tide we used to wear dustbin lids on our feet, like snowshoes, and waddle out to the middle of the deep sludge to spear fish in the surviving freshwater stream.

On a summer's day, when the tide was in, the dark, swirling waters were as inviting as a film star's swimming pool. We swallowed gallons of the muck with never a fear of stomach trouble to follow. If the godwits, knots and oyster catchers could drink it in safety, so could we.

On the far side of the river was a salting to which we would swim on the stroke of high tide, but no earlier or later. At that time the currents to and from the sea were as balanced as they ever would be. At any other time there was the danger of the fast central currents sweeping us up or down river. In the shadow of the mills, set aside from the main path of the river, it was relatively calm, with the bars of lock gates to grasp in an emergency.

The day was hot and we stripped down to our underpants, Dinger and I, while Oaky went all the way and Milky put on his trunks. Then we jumped, together, into the muddy waters. The tide was only half in, which meant the wharf was about eight feet above the level of the river. It was about as high as I dared to jump or dive. Oaky seemed fearless of heights, even at low tide when the stumps of an old sunken jetty came into sight.

We had been larking about in the water for about twenty minutes when the girl arrived. She was about our age, perhaps slightly older. Her shoulders drooped a little from her thin frame but there was something very determined about the expression on her face which dismissed any air of meekness from this posture. She was wearing a plain blue cotton frock and her blonde hair had been chopped into a thick fringe.

'Watcha doin'?' she said, in a tone that implied both disapproval and a superior social position.

'Swimmin', what's it look like?' replied Oaky, who was

not to be intimidated by someone just because they were of the opposite sex.

'My dad works 'ere,' she stated.

'So what?' Oaky trod water. 'So does his.' He did not bother to point out which one of us was the son of a millworker and the girl glared at us each in turn, her mouth as thin as a slit in an apple. Despite Oaky's bravado, we knew we would be in trouble if we were caught swimming in the river and I hoped her innuendo was a bluff. I had already had one licking from grandad for trespassing in the same stretch of water. Suddenly, the girl gave a gasp and pointed to Oaky.

'You've got no costume on. I can see your white bum.' We all laughed delightedly at her use of the word 'bum'.

'Goin' to tell,' she snapped, and disappeared from view. This was it! Hurriedly, we climbed up the slippery rungs of the wharf ladder and scrambled into our clothes. A minute afterwards, she sidled round the corner, alone. We all stared at her apprehensively, but it was obvious that she had not told anyone of our being there.

'She wants a thick ear,' said Dinger. He was furious at falling for the bluff.

'Take a man . . .' she said. Then she smiled for the first time and I noticed her two front teeth were slightly crooked and crossed each other. But there was something about her thin, freckled face which I found attractive. Perhaps it was the slight Chinese look to her eyes? They wrinkled at the corners when she smiled and gave her face a look of oriental wisdom. None of this of course would be passed on to the others. I would have been teased mercilessly.

'You're sopping,' she laughed. 'Look at your clothes!'

'Right!' cried Dinger. 'That's it. I'm not taking no more of this rubbish. Time someone gave you a good hiding.'

He was flushed with embarrassment and anger. I think if Oaky had not been in his way he would have leapt at the girl and pummelled her to the ground. Dinger had no schoolboy scruples about fighting girls.

'Leave it Dinger,' said Oaky, calmly. 'She's only a stupid girl.'

'Me name's Jackie, an' I ain't stupid, see. What's your name?' she asked Oaky. When he did not answer, she asked him, 'Can you swim good?' Oaky gave her the slightest of nods.

'Betcha can't swim across the river . . . all the way over.'

'Not now, but I can at high tide.'

'Can you dive good too? Can you . . .' she looked around, then overhead. About thirty feet above a gantry jutted out across the wharf. '. . . can you dive from up there?'

I gazed at the point she was indicating high above us. From below it looked an impossible feat, even supposing one could get up there. I knew that looking down from a height was vastly different from looking up at one. If it seemed frightening from the ground it would be twice as bad when standing on top of the gantry. The river would be a strip of brown ribbon. It would be like diving into a horse trough.

'Think so,' replied Oaky. 'Anybody want to dare me?'

'No!' I shouted, surprised by the loudness of my own voice. Dinger looked at me with a worried expression. 'I don't dare dare you Oaky,' I finished lamely.

'*I* do,' said Jackie. 'But not today. Not enough water. Nex' time, eh?'

*Next time?*

'What nex' time?' said Dinger, voicing my thoughts in a contemptuous tone. I turned my attention to the river. A few minutes ago it had been a source of cool pleasure. Now it had become a dangerous, compelling underworld; a foreign place that held a thousand ugly secrets, a thousand terrible traps. Some of my fears of the river were fanciful and some real: I found it difficult to separate the two. There were strong currents that swept you out to sea and there were monsters that gripped your legs in jaws full of teeth. There were witches and weeds, serpents and cold cramps. There was sucking mud and there were giant eels. I had a mental picture of Oaky, floating face down on the surface, his hair forming patterns in the gentle eddies.

*Rules!*

'Do not swim near moored craft.'

'Do not swim underwater where weeds and currents are known to exist.'

*'Do not dive from high places.'*

I saw, not the dying, but the horrible dead. I saw drifting skeletons. I saw eyeballs in the claws of retreating crabs. I saw fish picking a dead mouth clean of gums. The river was ancient and it carried with it all those superstitions and fears collected in darker ages, distant days. It was not difficult to personify a moving restless thing into a blind but malevolent creature that could hold you deep within its slimy, suffocating folds until your lungs exploded and your heart burst, then carry away your body in its belly to feed it to its parasites.

'Let's go,' said Milky, and we followed him out of the mill yard. Jackie trailed after us, humming tunelessly.

Jackie hung around in the field at the back of Milky's house, while we made our plans for the summer in his shed. By the time we emerged, it was evening. A huge orange sun was stretching the shadows and picking out the rust-red edges to the farmlands that swept away from its face. Jackie tagged on behind, as we crossed the road and climbed the stile into pond country.

# THREE

Jackie followed us back through the pond country, where we played Warlords as we went along. I was always a Norman but never the Warlord: Oaky claimed that role by dint of his leadership. Milky and Dinger were Saxons who refused to be subdued by the invading army. We hunted them down in the marshes and forests of an older Essex, where and when creeping mists were significant elements; where and when trees and rocks had souls; where and when witchcraft was a bare, vibrant art and a religion which was practised with zeal by both Norman and Saxon alike. In our game we demanded absolute authenticity, not through the trappings, for we had no money for such things, but in our acting, our pretence. To maintain the level of belief we required there could be no interruption of the game for twentieth century activities. We therefore ignored the presence of the girl.

Lord Oaks' armour was festooned with bright flashes as he rode his chestnut mare through the occasional patches of sunlight beneath the trees. From his helmet spurted a black plume like a fountain. On his shield was his crest: the black lion.

'How far, my Lord?' I enquired. 'Do you think we shall have them by nightfall?'

Lord Oaks looked around him nervously, his chainmail waistcoat clinking as he turned to the left and right.

'Sooth, I hope we do. These woods are full of evil . . . it would not be wise to be caught in them after the fall of darkness. See, yon ash tree has a wizened look of a wizard's visage. I'll warrant after sunset there is a change—into something not quite human.'

A figure moved in the dark shadows of the forest, a low, sinister shape that had me calling out a warning to my lord.

'Sire, to your flank, a wild boar breaks the thicket.'

Lord Oaks turned in his saddle and at the same moment drew his sword. The boar was almost on him, its sweeping, wicked tusks about to gore the belly of his mount, when he leaned over and thrust downwards at the beast, catching it a glancing blow on the brow. The boar whirled, coming in for a second try. I threw my spear, finding its rump, and Lord Oaks lunged again, this time his weapon entering the beast's neck and skewering it to the ground. Blood gushed along the bright blade . . .

'Why're you hitting that tree stump?' asked Jackie, in a contemptuous voice.

Oaky blinked and studied the yew wand he held in his hand. I stared at her dumbly. After a few moments Oaky muttered. 'We're playin' a game.' I was strangely embarrassed for both of us, almost as if I were ashamed to be caught in the act of creating a fantasy.

'You want to play?' I asked her, fearing the game might be ruined for good if we did not restart soon.

'Don't know. Why doesn't *he* ask me?' she nodded at Oaky.

'Oaky?' I pleaded. 'Can she play?'

I expected him to turn her down with a flat refusal. Our war games had always been sacred and he had done so with many others in the past. Instead he said, 'You'll have to be a squire.'

'I don't mind. What's a squire do?'

Eagerly, I explained. 'He follows the knight on foot. When he calls for fresh weapons, the squire gets them.'

'Where from? Where's the squire get them from?' Her sharp features looked bewildered and I told her that if we lost our swords she should get us more sticks.

'Only never call 'em sticks,' said Oaky. 'Not while the game's still on. They're swords or spears, get it? And you're not allowed to kill anyone. Me and Titch does all the killin', 'cause that's the way it is. You just do our bidding, OK?'

I saw her bite back a retort and then she nodded hard. 'You're the knights an' I'm your squire.'

I retrieved my spear from the boar's flank and we

proceeded through the forest. We had not gone very far when the Saxons ambushed us, dropping down from the overhead foliage and surprising our horses. Lord Oaks engaged the wild Saxon chief Dang Gar, while I sought a purchase on the slippery turf, having been thrown from my mount. The air was full of battle yells and the clashing of metal on metal. A tall, pale Saxon dog called the White Bull aimed a blow at my head with his club, which I managed to wrest from his grasp with great effort. I thrust my dagger into his chest with a cry of, 'Die, Saxon!' when I felt the point of a sword in my back. I fell groaning to the ground, the pain intolerable. With his last dying steps the White Bull staggered towards me and brought his club crashing down on my skull. The Normans had been vanquished this time although their total power in the land was undimmed. Through the haze of approaching death I saw Lord Oaks, sprawled at the feet of the mighty Dang Gar . . .

'Swords anyone?' hissed an eager voice in my ear.

'S'over,' I said, climbing to my feet. 'They won.' She looked deflated, so I added, 'Nex' time we'll probably need 'em. Now we're going scrumping.'

'Oh, hell. She's not comin' is she?' said Dinger. 'Who said she could play anyway?'

'Don't say "hell". It's not good manners to swear in front of a lady,' snapped Jackie, recovering quickly.

Oaky said, 'Why not? She's no trouble.' He was bright red and I knew this was from shyness not anger. If Dinger had challenged him at that moment, I think the gang would have broken up once and for all. There was a period of silence and then Dinger shrugged his shoulders.

He asked, sensibly, 'Well, what's she goin' to do while we're scrumping fruit?'

'I can steal things too,' she said, quickly.

'*Scrumping*,' muttered Milky. 'S'not stealin', not really.'

'Why? Same thing init?'

He glowered at her. 'No it ain't. Lots of it just lies and rots in the grass. If we didn't eat some the slugs would just get more. Anyway, where we're goin', not much gets picked in any case. We're sort of helpin' out really.'

She accepted this argument but still insisted she could do as well at it as us, whatever we liked to call it.

'We're goin' to the White House,' warned Dinger, significantly.

'So?'

'That's the wooden place at the turn of the lane,' explained Oaky. 'The old house. A witch lives there . . .'

'I ain't scared of no witches. My auntie's a witch. They don't do nothin' but have meetings in the living room, an' look at old books and things . . .'

'That's a white witch. This 'uns a black magic witch—a waterwitch. She cuts people up into small bits and feeds 'em to her cats . . .'

Jackie paled visibly but was not ready to accept Milky's word on the subject as final.

'That's a lot of rubbish. Witches don't do that.'

'This one *does*,' shouted Milky. 'Me mum says so.'

I waited for her to call Milky's mother a liar, half-hoping for it, even though I realized that if Milky attacked Jackie it was probable that Oaky would rush to her defence, then perhaps a general free-for-all would follow. I could feel the tension building up inside me and I knew the others were experiencing the same. I could see it in their faces. It was about time to settle old scores. We all stood for a while in a tight circle. Fists began to clench as the tension waxed in the group. I felt all my muscles knotting at the thought of the ensuing fight and my heart began to beat faster. Such an incident was not unknown to us. There had been times when petty frustrations and annoyances wound individuals tighter than steel springs and the only way to effect release was to let fly with a fist. Once that first punch flew, usually in uncontrolled, instinctive anger, the whole group would become involved, savagely hitting and kicking at any target within reach. Only when the collective temper of the group had settled and cooled, like the ashes after a volcanic eruption, would we crawl away from each other, muttering weak accusations and counter-accusations. It would take us at least a day or two to recover from these incidents, of which there had been perhaps five in previous years.

This time it was an external agent that was the potential catalyst for violence. We stood, uneasy with one another, for some time, our eyes unable to meet for more than a second at a time for fear of creating the spark that would ignite the fumes of tension. I was especially anxious about Dinger. I feared Oaky for his heavy fist, which often lacked malice, but my terror of Dinger's blind rages was unequalled by any other source of unpleasant emotion. Dinger's vicious attacks were unstoppable. He was like a machine with a dozen arms and each one of his punches caused intense pain which went through to the pith of my bones. The inner wounds would ache long after the visible bruises had disappeared.

'What're you all looking at each other for? I thought we were goin' scrumping?' said Jackie.

We began to relax, like toys coming to life in a pantomime. While she had been aware that *something* was going on between us, she had no idea what it was. Her intervention had been timely, and suddenly, we all began laughing, Jackie included. The relief was enormous. We were still giggling and in high spirits when we reached the turning which led to the White House.

There was a tree on the corner of the lane which held an old jay's nest. It reminded me of that one spring morning when I had taken home a juvenile, beautiful in its infancy, with colours that belonged to a bird of more tropical climes. Having found it, I wanted to possess it, like an archaeologist would wish to keep a wonderful Egyptian artefact he had uncovered, knowing that it belonged to the world but desperate to hold it for his own. I took the jay home, on my wrist, only to be ordered to return it to nature. My grandmother did not share my enthusiasm for these brightly-hued ornaments of God's household. For one thing, she said, she thought it was cruel, and for another birds had no idea of decorum—they messed where they sat. She was having none of it. The jay was returned to its tree.

We reached the orchard of the White House in the late evening. The fruit was not really ripe enough for eating but we all wanted it, badly. There was a picket fence surrounding the property but one or two slats were missing. We squeezed through one of the gaps and belly-crawled through the high grasses. There was an air of excitement about the venture which did not accompany our forays on, say, the apple orchards of Barnett's farm. On those occasions it was the fun of outwitting Barnett and his bulldog that added the zest to the adventure. This time it was the supernatural element that gave rise to the excitement. We were robbing a waterwitch.

I followed Dinger's backside as he weaved slowly through the tall grass in front. Jackie was immediately behind me. Once, we all paused while Oaky poked his head up and ascertained our position relative to the house. I felt myself pressed against Jackie as we all moved up together to lie in a line. I had a soft, warm feeling inside me and suddenly I felt as if I could stay in that grass-enclosed world forever and be happy. There was security in being close to the earth, folded inside its long, summer coat. Not just that though. It was because it was shared, shared with Jackie. I was brimful of affection for her in that moment, and for all girls of her age. They were creatures who lived on the periphery of my world, like exotic leopards, whom I could view from a distance but have no social contact with. Now one of them had entered and lay next to me, the warmth of her skin melting my antipathy towards her. Around us, the grasses curved upwards, like green sabres, protecting our hide-out. We were safe here.

'She's watchin' us,' whispered Oaky. 'I saw her face at the window. The curtains moved.'

Terror replaced all feelings of security in me. It was getting near to darkness. I suddenly felt very exposed, very vulnerable and realized that the grass only formed a meagre screen against any outside eyes. The waterwitch was in the house. If she caught us we would be dragged to the bottom of her pond and butchered into separate limbs, heads and torsos. Then we would be hung on hooks before being fed to the animals.

'Don't move. Don't move,' whispered Oaky. 'The door's openin'. She's lookin' out through the crack . . .'

My legs were shaking violently and it was all I could do to stop myself jumping to my feet and running away. I wanted to fly, as fast as I could, away from that place. I could hear someone's teeth chattering, noisily. Jackie's leg was trembling against my own.

The next sequence of events is difficult to recall with any accuracy. I know I heard a voice, either Jackie's or Dinger's, and the words were something like: 'Grab some plums! Quick, before she catches us. Run!'

Dinger was instantly on his feet and plucking the fruit from the low branches. Oaky joined him, picking furiously. Finally, Jackie. I was frozen to the ground. Then I thought I heard a shout coming from the house and I panicked. I began running, as fast as I could, towards the gap in the fence. Milky was already ahead of me and I think our retreat must have influenced the other three. Their boldness left them and they took to their heels. Jackie screeched. The next moment all five of us were trying to get through the hole at once.

We did not stop running until we reached the copse and hid amongst the trees. Jackie pressed something into my hand without the others seeing. It was a single plum.

# FOUR

Dinger was full of accusations of cowardice, levelled at Milky and me. He maintained that we had caused the retreat and if he had his way, he said, there should be some form of punishment for being the first to run. Jackie, to my dismay, agreed with him and I saw that Dinger had an ally in her. Someone whose personality seemed to fit his like two halves of a dovetail joint.

'I got a plum,' I said, hotly. 'Here!' I displayed the dark opal to Oaky, praying that Jackie would not give me away. For some reason she kept the secret.

'One,' snorted Dinger, but I was relieved when I realized he had not seen Jackie pass the fruit to me. He must have thought that I had snatched it from a tree on the run. If Oaky knew otherwise he did not say and Jackie had lost interest in the situation. She was counting her own plums in the half light.

'We've always shared 'em out equal before,' stated Oaky, 'an' we'll do it this time. But . . .' he added darkly, 'anybody runs before I do nex' time and we'll stake 'em out in the woods for the night. Don't think I won't do it, 'cause I will, see. We got to have everyone actin' the same or somethin's bound to go wrong sometime.'

A night in the woods, bound hand and foot? My legs went weak at the thought. If the witch had seen us and was out looking . . .

'I think we should do it now,' said Dinger, but Oaky had already turned his attention to the division of the spoils. I was passed three extra plums which I put in my left pocket. The one Jackie had given me, I put into my right. I wanted to keep them separate.

We stood there under the trees, in the fading light, for a few more moments before parting. Dinger and Oaky were going to stay out after dark, one with permission, the other without. Milky was going home one way and I the other. Jackie lived at the bottom of the slope, behind the Cherry Tree Inn and the two stop-outs had promised to see her home. Before we all split up, Milky spoke, and his words were to haunt me for many nights to come.

'She's goin' to get us somehow, that ole witch.'

A true prophet, Milky, but Oaky said, 'Don't talk daft,' with a lack of conviction in his voice.

'Revenge. You'll see . . . I'm goin' home.' Milky turned abruptly and began trotting towards his house. Jackie shouted, 'Scaredie cat,' after him. There was an uncomfortable silence, then without looking at me Oaky said, ' 'Night Titch.' He and Dinger walked off, with Jackie following them. I stood, uncertain, for a few more moments, then made for the road. I had to pass the White House to get home by that route and my fear was almost choking me. On an impulse I tasted Jackie's plum but it had been sprayed with something and for a few moments I felt quite ill. I threw the residue away. A wind had sprung up and was tossing the trees around in the orchard of the White House. It was dark and sinister in their midst and seemed to roll like a ship amongst their leafy branches. Suddenly I knew I hadn't the courage to pass it in the twilight and began to make a long detour round the fields on the far side of the road, following the levee that skirted a backwater of the river.

Halfway round I saw a figure shambling along the high path on top of the levee. My heart jumped in my chest. I stood as still as a post until, finally, I could see that it was a man—not an old woman with vengeance in her soul. The man paused as he drew alongside me and looked down from his superior position. He seemed very tall and arrogant. He was not well dressed: I could see that the crotch of his baggy trousers hung almost to his knees. His jacket was torn and shapeless. There were no socks underneath his shoes, which were white with salt around the laceholes. His hair had been cut unevenly and was unkempt, while his unshaven cheeks and chin glistened with white bristles.

'Hello,' he said, and smiled. Then he scrambled down the bank until he stood beside me. He smelled unwashed and sweaty. In the gloom I could see that his teeth were very long and narrowed at the gums where they were stained brown. They looked like the pegs my grandfather used in his cribbage board.

'I'm goin' home,' I said, quickly. 'Over there.' I pointed in the direction of the cottages. 'Someone's waiting at the door for me.'

'Have you seen anything? Along here?' He indicated the edge of the backwater with a sweep of his arm.

'No. No,' I replied, nervously. 'No one.'

He blinked rapidly. 'Not some *one* . . . some*thing*. Anything.'

'I didn't look. Honest. I just came across the field.'

'Uhhuh,' he grunted. His gaunt features became frighteningly skeletal as he sucked on his teeth, contemplating this lack of information.

'Goodnight mister,' I said, moving away from him slowly, but he continued to stare along the backwater and as soon as I was far enough away from him I broke into a run. I forgot about Mick as I reached the house and went running right into the yard. He almost had my ankle but my nerves were so taut his furious barking put wings on my heels.

Nan and grandad were eating a late supper. I was scolded and the stew and dumplings thrust unceremoniously in front of me. I did not care. I was home and safe. Safe from avenging witches and strange, lean men who were looking for something. Uncle Dave was up in his room. I could hear him punching his wardrobe door and swearing in between the muted thumps. It was a scene I had witnessed several times before. He would probably be drunk.

'Is uncle Dave still in love?' I asked.

'Can't you hear?' grandad growled.

I nodded. I never wanted to fall in love myself. Uncle Dave was always unhappy when he saw Cathy. She kept telling him things that made him angry. Then he would go to the Cherry Tree, get drunk, and come home to hit his wardrobe. It didn't seem a very constructive way to spend one's time. If I were Dave I would be out enjoying myself, hunting or fishing or something. He could stay out all night if he wanted to. That's what he liked best and that's when he was at his most happy. Girls were nice to be with sometimes, like Jackie in the orchard, but not worth spending too much time thinking about.

'Eat your dumplings,' said nan. 'I don't spend all day with a headache making them for my health. Plenty of starving children in China . . .' Her voice tailed off.

After supper I sat and listened to the wireless, hanging out my time as long as possible. The trick was not to speak or make any movement. It was difficult and sometimes very boring but infinitely preferable to the darkness upstairs. If I kept quiet they sometimes forgot about me until quite late.

They remembered me when Peter came in from outside and his black form slunk across the floor towards me. He licked my hand but I could not feel his tongue through the pins and needles caused by sitting so still. Half my body was numb from poor circulation.

'Time the boy was in bed,' said nan. Grandad nodded in assent. I rose from the chair reluctantly and went into the scullery for the candle. Nan lit it with a taper from the range while I got undressed and had a quick cold water wash in front of the fire. Then, with my clothes under one arm and the candle in the other, I climbed the steep, narrow staircase wearing just my underpants.

The shadows followed me, along the walls and on the low ceiling. They flickered in and out of my vision as I tried to ignore the corners. On the mantelpiece of the bedroom were two carved wooden heads which Dave had brought back from a place called the Maldives. They watched me with their small eyes in the candlelight. I thought I saw a skull hanging in the open wardrobe but it turned into a coat when I moved the light. Something appeared to dash under my bed just as I snuffed the candle and I finished pulling on my pyjamas under the bedclothes.

'Is that light out?' called nan.

'Yes.'

'Good. 'Night boy.'

' 'Night nan.'

I kept the bedclothes over my head. Outside, the world had become one single shadow. Blackness enveloped me like a soft, suffocating hand that shaped itself to my body. I kept my eyes closed and my head covered but eventually the air beneath the blankets became stifling. I put my head outside and opened one eye compulsively. There were shapeless forms around my bed which seemed to pulse slowly with the ticking of the mantel clock. Like black, live hearts the size of dwarves. The corners of the room disappeared into dark corridors at the end of which lurked horrible beasts. I wanted to scream but knew that I would only anger my grandparents. This frightening place only existed for children like me. Adults did not experience it, could not believe in it. (*Go to sleep you silly boy. It's only a bad dream. There are no such things as ghosts.*)

It was not the dreams that I feared so much as the turmoil in my mind before sleep; the whirlwind of terrible, fantastic imaginings that delighted in my torment; the repetitive thoughts that turned over and over in my mind and would not leave me in peace. In my world there was little difference between real and unreal creatures. The skeleton that was poised to poke out my eye with its bony finger was as real to me as my grandmother downstairs. I knew it was there. I *knew* it was there. The owl with the features of a man that perched on top of the dresser mirror was as surely present as the thing on which it stood.

A car passed by on the road below. Its headlamps lit the room and allowed a few moments' relief. I could hear its motor growling, its tyres singing on the tarmac. Then it was gone and my private terrors returned.

Memories of the afternoon came back. I tried to concentrate on thoughts of Jackie but soon visions of the dilapidated house began to intervene. There was that white face at the window again. It was almost as if it were disembodied and floating behind the surface of dirty glass. That the waterwitch had recognized us and marked us out for revenge, I had no doubt. We would be punished one way or another. My mind was very inventive on the subject of death and torture. She would pluck out our eyeballs and thread them on a string. She would make garlands of our entrails and hang them from the light fittings. She would melt us like wax and shape us into fiends. Oaky would be a humpbacked demon. Milky a tall, white zombie. Dinger, who for some unknown reason was terrified of feathers, she would skin and stuff with pillow down.

Jackie? She would be the witch's assistant, helping the old woman to deform our bodies. Our screams for mercy would have her screeching in delight. Our whimpered pleas would have her sniggering with pleasure. The worst part of Jackie's involvement was that she only enjoyed our suffering because the witch had put a spell on her. It was an imposed gaiety, all the more terrible because it was false. Her laughter was overlayed with tragedy, her smiles with grief.

Always I was a witness to the plight of the others before undergoing torture myself. Shadows, the sense and smell of death, dead things, stained slabs, draped, unrecognizable organs of the body, dripping meat—these pervaded my waking thoughts.

The rules of survival in a dark room at night were strict: never let a hand or foot hang out of the bedclothes to be gripped by cold, dead fingers; never look towards cupboards or corners for fear of what might be waiting to be seen; listen to your heart beating and concentrate on the rhythm; turn your thoughts to pleasant experiences; never, never hold your own breath in order to listen hard, or you *will* hear someone else breathing in the room.

# FIVE

'Grandad, tell me again how you lost your leg.'

'Ah, that's a story, that is. We was at Wipers, chargin' the Hun, and all along the trenches they had these machine guns blatterin' away at us, as we went over the top. I tell you, boy, the air was so thick with bullets I'm amazed we could even breathe without fillin' our lungs full of 'em. They was like swarms of bees, flyin' straight at us, and I saw me mates going' down, ping, ping, ping, one arter another, fallin' flat in the mud. Like fairground ducks we was.

'One of them machine gunners must 'ave seen what strong, powerful legs I 'ad and aimed straight for 'em. Cut one clean off with a burst of bullets. When I fell over and looked back, there was me leg, a dozen yards ahind. Must 'ave kept on running' without it, I was goin' so fast towards them German buggers with their twitchy fingers . . .'

Sunday. There was the smell of smouldering hickory and oak chips in the house. Dave was smoking eels in the shed at the bottom of the yard. It was an odour that permeated the whole neighbourhood, and nan had had several complaints in the past. I did not see why people objected. I didn't like eating smoked eels but burning wood adds an exciting flavour to the air.

Mick, the yard dog, was lying flat, one eye open for unsuspecting tradesmen. Beyond the allotments, behind the shed, the cornfields were ripening with the prospect of harvest to come and rabbits to chase as their cover was reduced. Gooseberries and greengages. Plums and apples. Late summer still held many promises in its paws.

I walked towards the shed, avoiding Mick as usual. It

was a warm, easy day, full of vague offerings, passionless yet content to remain idle. I asked Dave if we could take the shotgun out into the fields. It was not so much the hunting I craved but a long walk through the wilds with company I enjoyed. The hunting added a sense of purpose.

Soon, uncle Dave and I were knee-deep in corn turning dark and brittle through lack of rain. The air was dry and full of brown dust kicked up by our boots. On the horizon was a smudge of woodland and to our left a circle of still water shining like an offering plate. The sound of church bells floated over the flatlands. Nan would be singing, '*And did those feet in ancient time . . .*' Nan had always been religious, had always gone to the little Anglican church perched on a knoll like a giant stone boot.

(Aunt Elinor, who was dying, had told me tersely during one of our visits to her strange house, that religious people lacked initiative. Their religion, she said, told them what to wear and how to wear it; how to educate their children; what morals to maintain; how to live and how to die; how to spend their money; how to . . . a long list of things that made my head spin. Nan had sat, smiling primly, while Elinor spoke. Aunt Elinor afterwards said that this was because religion told nan how to act towards atheists and heathens.)

The gun was loaded but broken and the sun glinted on the brass cartridge rims. Uncle Dave could snap the breech shut, aim and fire in mid-stride. The pockets of his old grey jacket were stuffed with nets and I carried Jessica, the ferret, in a flour bag hanging from my belt. Jessica was my favourite pet. She would run all over me: up my trouser leg, around the inside of my vest, down my shirt sleeve, her little claws gripping my flesh lightly and her needle-sharp teeth occasionally nipping folded flesh, yet not once had she bitten me to hurt me. She would sit on my shoulder and nibble my ear with fangs that could tear open a rabbit's jugular in an instant. I had seen her sink those teeth into a soft throat, when Dave was too slow to pull her off, the bell around her neck tinkling out her fury as she shook her screaming prey. A rabbit's scream is as loud as a human baby's. I hated the sound and used to block my ears, but Dave always said you shouldn't feel pity at such a scene because a thousand weasels and stoats were doing the same thing out of sight of human eyes.

We paused by a warren in the bank of a ditch. The droppings around the entrances to the holes were moist. The sun was hot on my head as Dave began pegging the nets over the holes then, when he had searched around the bank and for the one escape hatch the rabbits always dug out into the field, we slipped Jessica under one of the nets. She waddled, ungainly, into the darkness below, her little bell marking her progress. When she got within striking distance of a rabbit she would move fast enough.

We waited in the fly-infested open air. Suddenly the net flew outwards as a rabbit hit it like a cannonball in its efforts to escape Jessica. Dave ended its terror with one sharp chop of his hand. Then two more nets became bolts of struggling fur, flying out into the field. I dived on one and held it fast but I did not have the stomach or strength to kill the animal. Uncle Dave took care of that. A minute later Jessica appeared, the bell telling us from which hole, her red, beady eyes shining.

'Time we started back,' said uncle Dave. 'Blasted farmer will be getting back from church soon.'

'We've only got rabbits,' I protested. 'They're supposed to be pests.'

'He'll still think we're after his pheasants,' said Dave, 'and he's right too. If I could see one of the bleeders I'd have 'im.'

He snapped the gun shut.

'Here, you've been wanting to have a go all morning. See if you can hit this.' He put our empty water bottle on a post and took me about fifteen yards back. I lifted the heavy twelve bore and, trembling slightly, lodged it in my shoulder. I spread my legs, one before the other, as Dave had taught me, and pressed my cheek to the polished stock. Then I sighted along the warm barrels.

I squeezed the trigger and the whole world exploded. A puff of dust went up to the right and just beyond the post. My eyes watered with the pain in my shoulder but I kept my feet for the first time.

'*Nearly* got the bugger, Titch,' said Dave, and I felt as proud as any nephew could do, of an uncle that let me fire his gun and praised my failures as if they were successes. One day I would prove myself.

Dave strung the three dead rabbits together and threw them over his left shoulder. Jessica, after being stroked affectionately, was again placed in the flour sack dangling from my belt. The nets were gathered in. Dave replaced the spent shell in the shotgun.

'You'll get that bottle next time, Titch,' he said to me. 'Don't you worry about that.'

'You've got blood on your shirt,' I told him.

He looked down. One of the rabbits was bleeding slowly from the nose.

'Man on the flying horse won't mind,' said Dave. It was an expression we used in the family to denote an insignificant incident.

'He might not but nan will,' I retorted.

Dave smiled, ruffled my hair and set off across the cornfield. The wheat rustled around our legs as if it were made of tinfoil and the warm air was electric with dry heat. In the far distance trees shimmered like mirages under a foreign sun. Occasionally we stopped and gave shrill whistles before scanning the lettuce and other low cropped fields for signs of hares. A whistle will have them pricking up their ears above the level of the crop.

We still had over two miles to go and my throat was feeling parched. I asked Dave for a drink from our second bottle in the knapsack and he motioned for me to help myself, turning his back on me. As I fumbled with the strap I accidentally knocked the shotgun from his grasp. He made an attempt to catch it but only managed to grasp the butt, so that the gun snapped shut and the barrel struck the hard, grassy bank of a ditch. It went off and kicked upwards. Dave swore, shrugging my hands away.

'Sorry,' I stammered.

'Quick. Get your shirt off,' ordered Dave. 'Mine's caught in these straps.'

The blast from the barrel of the gun had set the crisp grass on fire and it was spreading faster than a man can run. I whipped off my shirt and Dave began beating at the flames with it. I found a branch nearby and set to helping him but the wood was so dry it caught fire within minutes and I had to throw it down, adding to the conflagration.

The heat was appalling and the bracken beside us was soon crackling, flames dancing down its stalks with light feet. The fire swept along the hedge like a wave curling down the length of a beach. We were soon covered in sweat and after a few minutes uncle Dave said, 'Let's go, Titch. Before we're seen.'

'But . . . but the fire. We can't leave it. We have to try and put it out.'

'We can't. Anyway, they'll have me for trespassing and poaching. I can't afford no fines at the moment. Pick up your shirt.'

'But . . .'

'Do as you're told, Titch,' he shouted, angrily. 'Hurry up. I haven't got no time to argue with you.'

I did as I was told and we began walking quickly towards a copse.

'Shouldn't we sound the alarm or something?' I said.

He stopped suddenly and glared at me, making me avert my eyes.

'Get it into your head boy, these people don't like us. The farmer'll have the law on us quicker than that . . . and I have a ship to catch soon. Forget the fire. It's not our problem, it's theirs.'

'OK,' I mumbled.

'It's an accident,' he added, still boring me with those dark eyes. We both looked back then at the blaze. There was a lake of fire behind us, flooding into ditches and washing over bushes. I wanted to run back, throw my energies into stemming the flow. I was also aware of a disturbing sound at a pitch much higher than that of burning wood and grass. It was the combined note of individual animals expressing terror and pain. There were creatures being drowned in fire. It was different from hunting rabbits: that was for food.

'Why can't we . . .?' I began, my voice cracking, but

Dave gripped my arm and steered me towards the footpath, skirting the copse, that led homeward. I felt vaguely frightened of the holocaust from which we were running but worse than that was the leaden feeling of irresponsibility and cowardice. Oaky would never have walked away from such a scene, even if he had caused it, even if his uncle was ordering him home. He would have ignored both restrictions and would have thrown himself into fighting the blaze with no thought of the consequences to himself. I felt terribly guilty.

Dave warned me not to say anything when we got home. I went straight upstairs, into Dave's back bedroom, and watched the distant pall of black smoke gather over the fields like a storm cloud. My heart was pounding. We had done something terribly wrong. I knew it was an accident but I still felt we should be punished for it, especially since we had not raised the alarm. I would have felt much better had I been punished. When the call came for help, Dave joined the neighbours in their race to the blaze and I was told later, threw himself into fighting the fire with an energy that earned him high praise from the farmer. Mr Fenlin, who owned the land, was heard to remark, 'He might be a bad 'un but we owe him for today.' Little did he realize just how much he did owe Dave.

That night, in my bed, I heard Dave talking to Cathy in the pool of light thrown by the street lamp below my window. He told such lies I was ashamed of him, because I still loved him then. Cathy worked in the post office and was much brighter than uncle Dave. His exaggerated accounts of his own prowess she treated lightly, bringing him down to earth. His outright lies, when she recognized them, she accepted with an amused chuckle, as if to tell him that she enjoyed his fairy stories but only for what they were.

'Got to go away again soon,' I heard him whisper.

'I know.'

'Well, what are you going to do?'

'About what? I'll be here when you get back. I'm always here, aren't I?'

'Don't suppose you stay in every night,' he said, with a sullen note to his voice.

'No, I don't suppose I do. But then I soon come to pull the thorns out of your paws when you come home, don't I?'

'Don't understand what you mean by that,' said Dave, which made me glad because I didn't either and I wanted her to explain. We were both disappointed. Cathy merely sighed.

'Why don't you stay in?' complained Dave.

'Why should I? Don't tell me when you get to some foreign port you lie on your bunk thinking of me Dave, because I shan't believe you.'

'It's different . . .'

'I know what you're going to say, so don't say it. It's only different when it's convenient, when it suits *you*.'

'Keep your voice down.'

'. . . just because I'm a woman doesn't mean I can switch myself on and off like a light. We're the same sort, you and I, which is probably why I love you.'

'Look Cathy, please. When I'm away all I ever think about is you. You think it's fun on those rusty old tubs? With waves the height of trees coming at you every two minutes? The air full of salt water for days on end, getting into your eyes, your mouth, every crease of your body. Wearing wet clothes that rub your skin raw?'

'It's a hard life in the merchant navy,' she said in a wireless voice. Then her tone changed, became lower, 'But it's bloody boring behind the counter of a village post office. I think I'd swap your life for mine, any time.'

'I don't understand you. I just don't understand you. We have a good time when I'm home, don't we?'

'You're a fool, Dave, a lovable fool but nevertheless . . .'

His voice had a ploughshare edge to it.

'Don't call me names.'

' 'Night, Dave.' The sound of a quick kiss.

I heard her high heels clicking on the pavement as she walked down the high street. Then a muffled groan from uncle Dave. It was too late to go to the pub so he could not get drunk.

Grandad came up to bed an hour later, filling the room with candlelight. I watched him undress then roll up one leg of his long underpants. The flame from the candle was reflected in the shiny metal of his artifical limb. *Snap, snap, snap,* went the catches. Then the slow slide of leather through buckles. Finally, a *plop* as the leg was pulled away from the stump and puckered skin the colour of old bread came into view. It horrified and fascinated me, that stump. I couldn't take my eyes from it, yet it was ugly, revolting, untouchable.

To me it was not the remains of a man's leg but an external growth. A fungus sprung from a rotten log or a blunted stalactite formed on the ceiling of a lightless cavern. I sometimes wondered where his real leg was. Had they buried it? It was, perhaps, twenty per cent of grandad. Didn't it deserve the same sort of sacred rites the rest of his body would receive when he died? Was it any less important than a heart or a head? Perhaps they had burned it? Or were the bones, even now, standing in some college for surgeons? Perhaps it still lay deep under the mud of France, its boot still loosely laced to the foot?

Its metal and leather usurper stood by the bed, armour-like in its pose. Strong, unfeeling and inflexible. Would they bury this hollow, robotic replacement with grandad now? It had been with him longer than his real leg and had given him the same faithful service as the first.

He rubbed some foul-smelling ointment on the end of his stump, which seemed to stare at me blindly, like the exposed root of an old oak tree. Then he lifted the monstrosity, farted, and rolled into bed. I heard him scratching his chest, the nails on white, coarse hair sounding like sandpaper on wood. He coughed. Nan always said she was glad he was not a phlegmy man. Big-boned, solid and heavy, grandad had spent his life in the open air and his thick torso was as sound as a ceramic boiler.

After these attentions to his body, the rituals before settling down for the night, he blew out the candle. I gave a little shudder which coincided with the sudden descent of darkness.

'Get some sleep boy,' he said.

Soon I heard his mouth dragging in the air in noisy draughts.

Shortly afterwards I heard the key in the front door. Nan was back from her usual Sunday evening visit to Southend. It was her only night out each week, but was as much a ritual as her churchgoing. The house was now full again and I drifted off to sleep with the sounds of nan shuffling around in the front room below. It never occurred to me to question what she did on those weekly jaunts. Whatever it was, it must have been boring. She was an old woman.

# SIX

'Look, here's a frog!'

Dinger plucked the amphibian in mid-hop from the edge of the pond. As was his wont he practised cruelty with an inventiveness close to mad genius. Snapping a hollow reed with his free hand he inserted the end into the frog's rectum and proceeded to blow the unfortunate creature into a small balloon. I watched with fascinated revulsion the torture he inflicted upon animals, always hoping Oaky would intervene, but each trick Dinger's twisted imagination produced mesmerized us with horror long enough for him to get away with it.

The frog became a ghastly, translucent bubble of pale-green skin. Its face was distorted into something resembling those pagan gods carved by primitive tribes, the widening mouth drawing into a horrible, sickly grin.

'Pack it in Dinger,' I heard myself saying.

'He's right, Dinger. That's a rotten thing to do,' Oaky said.

Petulantly, Dinger threw the frog onto the pond, where it floated and would no doubt become a meal for the dagger-faced herons. Having made his judgement, Oaky walked on ahead, talking to Milky about football. Dinger punched me slyly on the shoulder and whispered, 'I'll get you for that, you weed.'

I was still very angry about the frog and for once I turned on him.

'I'll fight you whenever you like,' I said, unable to keep the tremor out of my voice.

He smirked. 'Yeah? Getting' brave, aren't we Titch? Remember last time? Or maybe you've forgot already?' Two weeks previously he had given me a bloody nose in a similar incident. In all the stories I read bullies were supposed to be cowards but Dinger did not conform to this pattern. I had seen him fight much bigger boys than himself and beat them through sheer determination and cool rage. I stared at him and eventually he turned away, not because he was frightened of me but because, I think, there was no one to witness the conflict. The other two had gone too far ahead. For some reason he liked an audience, even though he knew that those who watched were unsympathetic towards him. It was almost as if he invited contempt. At home he was always getting the strap from his father or a hiding from his older brother, Ted. Not many people knew this but Cathy, who was distantly related to the Bellchambers, told Dave that Dinger led a miserable home life.

I caught up with the others.

Oaky said, 'Did you bring the smokes, Milky? I brought my gun 'specially.' He held up his air rifle for us to inspect.

We were going to play Afghans today. My idea. I had read a book about gun runners in the Khyber Pass. All Afghans smoked hashish, so Milky produced a sheet of corrugated cardboard from beneath his jersey which we tore into strips and rolled into cigarettes. We had found they smouldered like the real thing, and stayed alight if we puffed them frequently enough. The smoke was harsh enough to give us sore throats for a day or two, but it was worth it for the realism. Our roles having been decided beforehand, we got on with the game, which I had outlined for them all when we had first met up in the morning. It was a new game and we were looking forward to it. Even Dinger seemed enthusiastic.

Hassan smoked the weed with relish.

'There is evil in the air tonight,' he murmured. Then he turned to look out into the wilderness and take a sip of coffee from a tin can converted into a cup.

It was a yellow night, with the moonlight splashing on the dust and rocks and the stars so bright they seemed near enough to touch. Somewhere near a pi-dog howled, possibly smelling the food, and the horses rippled along their line. They were that wild and hairy breed that have neck muscles of iron, and needed arms of steel to hold them at full gallop. Most of them were stallions. They fought all other stallions that came within reach and would even kill a brother because their instinct was to be the only stallion in the herd. Hassan owned one of these savage creatures and he rose, mumbling something about restlessness, and walked away towards the horses. I shrugged and took his coffee. It was while I was sipping at the black dregs that the Imam and the infidel came to my fire. I could see by the Imam's hooded eyes that something was wrong, something bad.

'Where is Shami?' asked the Imam. 'Where is Hassan Shami?'

'My friend is with his horse,' I answered. 'His horse called to him for company.'

The Imam turned slowly towards the horses. Hassan was nowhere to be seen.

'Hassan Shami is a traitor,' the Imam said softly. 'He sells himself to the enemy. Here is a man,' he indicated a stranger, a European, standing by his side, 'who sells himself to *me* and is disloyal to his own leader.'

The man did not look at all perturbed and continued to suck on a cigarette. I stared at him, hating him. A white scar on the stranger's neck forked like lightning to his ear as the light from the fire caught it.

'He would expect no mercy if his faithlessness were discovered by his master. Such a crime deserves only death. You are Shami's friend—you know what you must do,' finished the Imam.

There was no thought, no deliberation. I rose and ran towards the horses, pausing only to pick up my rifle. I reached the spot where Hassan had tethered his mount and found it empty. Taking the nearest stallion by the mane I threw myself on its back and the horse bucked sharply; the weight was unfamiliar and it knew that I was not its master. I crooned softly to the beast and leaned over, cutting the hobble. Then I turned its head towards the desert and dug my heels into the steed's flanks.

We were one. We split the wind and the stars flowed over our heads like rushing water.

I rode until the dawn came over the hills and dissolved the darkness. The rocks suddenly built themselves shadows and the scorpions and camel spiders crawled from their night abodes to sun themselves in the morning's warmth. The horse was wet and slippery with sweat. I ached with fatigue. My mind was also weary. Hassan's tracks had turned to the north-west and I was troubled. Why should the traitor turn away from the pass to the place where he could reasonably expect sanctuary? Perhaps he had some other hide-out? A family that was loyal to him or that owed him some favour?

I thought what a terrible thing it was that I should have to kill my childhood friend. We had grown up together, had been inseparable.

I halted my horse and swung myself to the ground, jarring stiff legs on the hard earth. The muezzins' voices would be floating lyrically from the minarets in the towns and villages now and Islam would be turning its face towards the Holy City, Mecca. I knelt in prayer, keeping hold of the horse's rein in case the stallion should desert me.

Hassan's tracks led me close to a road at one point and I narrowly missed blundering into two English soldiers who had stopped their transport for a rest on their way to their camp. The soldiers were lounging arrogantly on their rifles, smoking and talking in loud voices and I itched to be squeezing the trigger of my own rifle and to watch them rolling in their dishevelled uniforms in the dust. I curbed my lust for violent action and circled them, dragging a horse blanket behind to obliterate my tracks. Not that those pigs could follow a trail if it were stamped on their noses.

By noon my tongue felt like a snake through lack of moisture and my lips were crusted with dry saliva. I had not been prepared for such a long journey and my hasty departure had necessitated taking only my rifle. Even if I found a well or oasis I had nothing to use as a container for the water to get me over any further stretches of desert. I regretted not killing the British and stealing their supplies. Three days was the longest I could survive without water. I would have to rely on getting Hassan's bottle.

My horse had collapsed. I left it where it fell, to run forward and flatten myself against a sand dune. There was a figure in the distance which had gradually been growing larger since morning. I levelled my rifle until I had him in my foresight. I squeezed the trigger, slowly, and the figure toppled from the horse's back and lay still. I felt the jubilation which follows success—then I remembered it was Hassan, my friend and brother, whom I had killed. A traitor was dead, a friend was gone, all in one action. He was more than a brother because brothers are joined in blood not in spirit. Who was the traitor? Hassan or I? My eyes were wet as I stumbled towards his body. Reaching it, I straddled it with my legs, pointing the muzzle of my rifle towards his head. The face was buried in the grey sand and I knew my caution was unnecessary. With a heavy heart I drew my knife and bent towards the head: the Imam would require proof. As I stooped forward, Hassan's mount stirred and buckled at the knees. I was puzzled. Then I realized and smiled grimly. Hassan would have company in death: the company of his brother. Except for a blanket, his horse was unladen. He had been carrying no water either . . .

We saw him from a long way off, an adult of the real world, and the game ended without conclusion. He was searching for something in the rushes and reeds of the saltflats, parting them with a stick and rummaging amongst the jetsam, the old tyres and empty chemical drums that littered the river's edge. The smell of newly disturbed sludge wafted over. Occasionally he would bend, like a grey heron, to peck amongst a tangle of rubbish that had been knotted together by the river eddies. We followed his progress with resentful eyes. He was invading our privacy. As he drew alongside I saw who he was: the same man who had stopped me by the dyke, the evening we had stolen the plums from the White House. I said nothing to the others.

Dinger called out, 'Whatcher lookin' for mister?'

The man looked up, sharply. His shabby clothes hung

loosely from his thin frame like the rags of a scarecrow. He had about two days growth of beard on his chin and the whites of his eyes were as yellow-brown as if they had been stained by nicotine.

'Whatcher lookin' for?' Dinger repeated.

'Dead body. Have you seen any? I'll give you five bob.'

Milky shuffled backwards a couple of steps at these words, getting Oaky in between himself and the newcomer. We were in any case suspicious of offers of money from lone, strange adults but that aspect was completely dwarfed by the monstrous idea behind the offer. The man wanted a dead body. I felt uneasy and frightened by his eyes that were never still. They rested on each of our faces for only a moment before looking up at the sky, out over the marsh, and then back to our faces again, with the rapid darting movements of something mechanical rather than human.

To me his face looked even more sunken and hollow-cheeked in the daylight . . . and yet there was something in his features which I recognized, something that put him apart from the adult world. I knew instinctively that he would not, as some grown ups would, have laughed at our game.

'What sort of body?' asked Dinger at last. 'Not a real one?'

The man nodded solemnly. 'A woman's body . . .'

Oaky laughed nervously.

'No. No.' The man appeared concerned. 'Not *any* body. This is a special one. Amy Johnson's body. I been lookin' for it a long time now. Find it soon, got to. I've looked all over.'

'Who's she?' asked Oaky.

'She was an aeroplane pilot,' I replied for him quietly. 'Used to fly small planes. She's dead now.'

The man nodded enthusiastically.

'He knows, see. Amy Johnson. Know how she died?'

I shook my head. I had heard Cathy talk about her exploits. She flew from England to Australia in twenty days. Nan always said that Cathy really wanted to do something like that.

'Why'd you want to find her—if she's dead?' asked Oaky. 'She's probably buried somewhere. Can't see how you'd find her in the mud. Nobody gets buried here, not that I ever heard of. Milky's mum buried a dog here once but that was ages ago . . . last summer. Crabs'll 'ave got it by now.'

'Tell you why,' came the answer. 'Over there,' he pointed vaguely at the horizon, 'the Thames estuary, see. These backwaters, they all link up, all tidal. Things find their way up here . . . things the liners drop going up the mouth of the Thames. Currents pull them up and down. That old tyre there. Could'ave come from one of the Thames barges—maybe used as a buffer?'

Oaky said impatiently,'What's that got to do with anything?'

'Ah. That's where she drowned see, in the estuary. Jumped out of her plane and never been found. Forty bodies they've said was her, but they never was. Waiting for me to find her, see? Plane ran out of fuel. Had to parachute. Treacherous, those currents. Pull you down quicker than that. They found the plane all right, but Amy's been hidin' ever since '41'

Milky made a noise with his mouth; not words, just a sort of guttural grunt. He wanted to say something but was too shy. I knew what it was. The waterwitches had got her. I told the man what Milky was thinking.

'Naw, witches don't like rivers,' he said.

I wanted to argue with him but those strange, swamp-water eyes were flickering before my face and I just muttered something which would have been inaudible to him and looked away. What did he know about witches anyway?

'Shall we help him look?' said Oaky. 'We know most of the swamps around here.'

The thought of finding a dead body sent a chill through me but at the same time I did not want the others to know I was afraid. The tide was out and the creeks revealed to the world in their greys, browns and slime-green. I could see some swans further down river but they added no beauty to the scene. It was as if some private, decaying place had just been uncovered to human eyes after being hidden since the days of prehistory. It was always like this, when the waters had rolled back into the north sea.

'What if we find her, what then?' I asked.

He showed us those long, peg-like teeth.

'I'll be famous. Get my name in the books.'

'But if *we* find her . . .' persisted Dinger.

'Give you five bob. Then she's mine. You lot are helpers, see. Under my directions. Like the leader of an expedition.'

'Surely she'll just be bones by now?' said Oaky. 'All her flesh'll 'ave rotted.'

The man turned on him with a smile.

'Not really. Bodies can last for years in the mud. Preserves 'em, see. I read about it. The silt keeps 'em fresh.' A dragonfly, a splinter of some rare, blue mineral, landed on his cheek. I watched, fascinated, as it crawled to the corner of his mouth and he made no move to brush it away. It was as if he did not know it was there. My own face began itching in the same spot and I scratched it vigorously. How could he stand it? Finally, it flew away again, darting low over the reeds.

The man said, 'You could pretend it's the Amazon. Like those films. Searching for treasure.'

Now the game had a purpose! The alligators and piranha fish were not just waiting idly for unsuspecting victims, they were there to protect Amy Johnson's body. We had to overcome forest Indians and snakes in order to reach the river. We had to kill panthers and squash giant spiders . . . and she, she was the prize at the end, the reason for our quest.

We made our way in a line, like grouse beaters, over the salt marshes littered with the remains of rotting hulks and jetty posts, digging among the eelgrasses and bladder-wrack for signs of Amy Johnson's body. Maybe it would be just five fingers poking about the mud? I looked as hard as the others but I did not want to find her. I hoped it would be someone else. Each time a pale crab scuttled from beneath a patch of saltwort, my eyes saw a hand moving across the silt and my heart froze for an instant.

An old rubber ball was a white skull and bleached driftwood the legbones of our lost lady aviator. As evening fell, the marshes came alive with insects: gnats, mosquitoes, mayflies. The insects brought the frogs and birds and our land did indeed take on the hues and sounds of a South American river. Shadows began to flow between the waterless banks. It gave the jetsam, the debris of the river, sluggish movement and slow life. I would be searching the reeds with a stick when, suddenly, a black form would catch the corner of my eye and make me start.

The man who wanted Amy Johnson's body talked incessantly.

'Snakes. See any snakes here?'

There were always smooth snakes near the marsh ponds but I knew Milky hated snakes so I told the man that there were none.

'Found a nest of adders in the churchyard the other day,' he said. 'One of 'em bit the warden. Eentsy little thing it was. No bigger'n a worm. Arm swelled up like a balloon. Blue at the elbow and pus-yeller at the fingers. Nasty beggars, snakes. Even the babies got a bite like a succubus.'

I said, 'What's a succubus?'

'Female devil. Don't you know your Bible boy? Should do. I know my Bible back to front.'

A rat came through the eelgrass, stopped, tried to stare me out and then vanished again. Sometimes I could walk right up to them, if I was alone. Dinger looked at me, then at the stick I carried. There was contempt in his eyes. I should have hit it on the head, or so he believed. We never did agree on these things.

When it was dark we headed for the lane and said goodbye to our new friend.

'Remember,' he said, 'if you find her I'll pay you the money I promised. Don't give her to no one else.'

We promised, then made our way wearily home. When I got near the house I made sure the back window curtains were closed then climbed stealthily onto the yard shed roof from the back. I lowered myself gradually onto the top of Mick's kennel. My legs were shaking as I could hear him snuffling below me, his senses alerting him to the fact that something was amiss. Before he had it worked out I reached down and snatched his food dish and pulled myself onto the shed roof again. He went berserk. Barking and snapping his jaws, he leapt at me, almost reaching my ankles even though I was eight feet off the ground.

'Up yours,' I said, softly.

I jumped from the shed and made my way circuitously to the house. Peter was on the back step and I pushed the dish under his nose and watched him wolf down Mick's supper. Mick had to watch too, from six feet away, and he made enough noise to bring nan to the door with her copper stick.

She saw me and said, 'Hello. You home? What's the matter with the dogs?'

She peered out into the darkness. I hid the dish with my foot while Peter took the opportunity of the open door to slink into the house. Mick still growled but the sight of nan and her stick had had a sobering effect on him. Finally, he too crept away, but in the direction of his kennel, grumbling softly.

'I think he's got rabies,' I said. 'Ought to be put down, really.'

'You get in and wash. You're late for supper again. You need a good smack. Rabies. I'll give you rabies, my boy . . .'

'A smack won't do it,' I replied. 'You have to bite me for that.'

I ducked and ran inside the house as a large, calloused country-woman's hand barely missed my ear.

# SEVEN

Grandfather was born in 1871 and, not unnaturally, he understood animals better than machines. Not that he *liked* them better, in fact he was forever cussing them: dogs, horses, chickens, whatever else moved around our yard. He just knew better the way a pony functioned than a motor car. He would have dearly loved a car, though they would never let him drive one with his artificial limb and advanced years, but the way one moved would always be magic to him. He liked his wireless better than the cat but when it came to tuning it in or replacing a valve he was lost. Dave did all that. When the cat failed to eat, why, that was a different thing. Grandad understood the reasons behind worms, fur-balling, distemper and feline stomach complaints, and knew the cures if they were at all possible. But there was no love lost between grandad and his animals. It was all a functional thing—they had jobs to do and if they did them he was satisfied with them, if they did not, why, then he cussed them.

Grandad was well-known and probably well-liked in the village. At any event, he was a 'character' and villagers are proud of their eccentrics, using their stock of stories about them to amuse visitors from the cities. There was one particular anecdote that Alex Goodman, the butcher, enjoyed telling, even at the expense of his own dignity.

Tenbridge is close to the mouth of the Thames and during the Second World War waves of enemy bombers were seen passing overhead on their way to London. Just occasionally one of these black crosses in the night sky would drop its bomb load above Tenbridge in order to lose weight and gain height suddenly, in an attempt to avoid the flack of the coastal batteries. One such incident resulted in the death of the choir mistress cycling on her way home from choir practice. Grandad chanced upon the body, still in its white surplice, in Three Oaks Lane. He put the corpse of Alice Parton in his cart and made his way to the village.

As so often happened, a second air raid took place immediately after the first and most of the villagers were in the shelters on the green. Grandfather, unperturbed by the bombers, was anxious to get home for his supper and seeing the door to Goodman's shop standing wide open, decided to leave the body inside the large freezer at the back.

When the air raid was over, of course, none of the Goodman family bothered to check the freezer and by that time grandad had gone to bed. Alice Parton was forgotten until the next day, when there was a delivery. The lad who brought the fresh meat was a townie from Southend and Mr Goodman opened the freezer door for him as he carried in the carcass of a sheep to hang it on one of the hooks inside. Meat was obviously very scarce during the war and this one carcass represented the weekly ration for the whole village. The young delivery boy came out of the freezer looking decidedly pale and shaken and hurried past the butcher without the good grace to reply to that man's cheery farewells.

By the time grandad got round to telling Mr Goodman that he had got a corpse in his freezer the Southend police were on their way to Tenbridge to investigate reports of cannibalism in the village. The local newspaper was already setting the type for their startling headlines and the whole of Southend was rapidly passing the grisly news from mouth to mouth with horrified delight. Grandad loved the story and although he never told it himself, because his modesty prevented him from introducing an anecdote in which he had had a major role, he somehow managed to steer the conversation in the direction of the tale whenever strangers were present, by mentioning the scarcity of meat during the war and how Tenbridge was a village that could very well take care of its own in emergency situations.

★

The day before I visited my aunt Elinor, I went with grandad on the cart to Mathews, the confectioner, where he bought his chewing tobacco. We chatted to Mr Mathews, leaving the horse tied to a lamp post further down the street. While we were in there a stranger entered and after buying some cigarettes asked for the correct time. Neither grandad nor Mr Mathews carried a watch, so Mathews went into the back of the shop to look at his mantel clock. While he was away grandad treated the stranger, who appeared to be in a bit of a hurry, to a story of his youth.

'When I was ten-year-old,' he began, 'we 'ad a hot summer what burned the corn a deep brown, more the golden brown of a good baccy. It made us all a bit slow, that summer, like them fellas in Spain and such. Too hot for movin' around lively, and things got left what normally was done without too much fuss. We 'ad five clocks in the village then . . . the one on the church—you could've got your time from that on your way out the other end of the village—had got itself busted in 1870 or thereabouts. Never 'ad no mind or money to get it put right in those days. Some of the well-offs 'ad pocket watches as well as clocks . . . the squire an' Jenkins what owned the Cherry Tree pub. The vicar too, I think. Anyways, come one Saturday mornin' we found we was without a timepiece in workin' order. All of 'em stopped, they was.'

By this time Mr Mathews was back but grandad paused only long enough for him to give the stranger the time before continuing with the story. The stranger kept nodding politely but occasionally glanced wistfully at the doorway.

'So we 'ad no right time among us. Well, it didn't worry us none, what worked in the fields . . . sun was good enough for labourers then. Up at dawn, down at dusk, and a bit of bread and cheese at noon. Didn't need no minutes in them days. Worried the old squire though. Wanted the time right badly, he did. Needed it for the cricket match, next day bein' Sunday. Seemed like the world wasn't runnin' proper for the squire 'less he 'ad the time to the dead minute. Sent me runnin' round the houses askin' what o'clock . . . damned if anyone knew. Not a clock in the whole village was stirrin'. Almost as if the heat'd got to their parts and made 'em as lazy as the rest of us.'

The stranger appeared to be getting agitated and mentioned that his wife was in the car outside.

'Well, I'm about finished now,' apologized grandad, 'so it ain't worth calling her in to hear the end, 'less you think it's worth startin' again?'

The stranger blinked rapidly and shook his head. Mr Mathews had a tiny smile caught in the corner of his mouth.

'Anyways, I 'ad to take one of the shires . . . wouldn't trust me to a bred horse, the squire, bein' as I was only a little 'un at the time . . . rode 'im in the intention of gettin' the time from Southend railway station clock, what was always set right accordin' to the trains that come in.

'Well, it was hotter'n a baker's oven that day, an' I passed the river with a great reluctance in me breast, goin' at no speed at all worth mentioning. At Fowler's pond—you must've passed that on your way in—that old shire's back was all sweat and steam. "Enough's enough," I thought to meself, an' off went the shirt for a nice cool dip in the green water. Horse just roamed around on the bank munchin' grass with equal satisfaction, while I dipped me tail along with the ducks for the afternoon. Come evenin' o' course, I got a bit bothered, 'cause I still 'adn't took the time an' there was no chance of gettin' it. So I made it up . . . set the squire's watch to five exact, and up on the shire again.

'Squire give me a shillin' when I got back an' all the other folk set their timepieces to the squire's pocket watch.'

A woman appeared in the shop doorway. She had a frown on her face but by this time the stranger's interest was fully occupied and he nodded to her.

'Won't be a second, darling,' he said to her. Then to grandad, 'What happened next?'

'Happened next day I was an hour adrift, or near, 'cause come noon on the clock the sun was out apace from comin' central and Billy Figgler was just goin' in to bat. Squire looked at his watch . . . then up at the sky an' frowned a bit. Thought I was in for a lickin' arter the match. Then the squire said, "Sun's a bit slow today chaps," an' snapped his watchcase shut, just like that. Believed in mechanics did the squire, like our mum believes in God. Couldn't be wrong, no matter what. We went along happy for I don't know how long . . . till some outsider come along I suspect. Shouldn't be surprised what we 'ad a good fight in the pub over that, though I was too young for such places at the time . . . didn't like outsiders tellin' us what's what, even if they was right . . .'

The woman said, 'Arthur, we'll be late.'

The stranger looked quickly at his watch and said, 'Hell, you're right, darling.' Then he shook hands with grandad and Mr Mathews and hurried out of the shop after his wife. Grandad shook his head sadly, realizing that his parable had been wasted.

Before we left, Mr Mathews gave me a sherbet fountain and a couple of sticks of licorice.

'The lad's coming on, Rhubub,' said Mr Mathews, giving me a nod as he handed over the goods. 'Not much meat on 'm though.'

Even though grandad had told me the same himself just a few days before, he would not brook criticism from people outside the family.

'He's all right, the boy,' he replied. 'Got a body like a gypsy's dog. Lean muscle's what runs in our litters.'

'Still . . .'

'No still about it. Runs around like a rabbit with diarrhoea. Bound to be a lean 'un. Man on the flyin' horse don't mind, so why should you?'

Mathews shrugged and rested his elbows on the counter. He always wore starched, white aprons which seemed to attract all the light available within the shop to his breast, leaving the rest of the room dim by comparison. His bald head glinted occasionally in the gloom as it passed through a dusty shaft of sunlight. Suddenly there was a shout from outside the shop, followed by a stream of obscenities. Grandad clumped outside with Mr Mathews and myself close behind. He stood on the pavement with his weight on the artificial leg and his large, calloused hands on his hips. There was a painter halfway up a ladder, near where the horse was tied, and abuse still flowed from the man's lips.

'You watch your French,' growled grandad. 'I got a young lad 'ere.'

'Is that your bleedin' horse,' shouted the painter. Without waiting for an answer he said, 'I'm coming down there to boot your backside, you old coot. Soddin' horse has just eaten all my putty.'

We stared at Custard, who had her head in what appeared to be a gallon paint pot, but was obviously the putty in question. Grandad clumped forward quickly to the foot of the ladder.

'You got a good grip of them gutters?' he asked of the painter.

The man was about to descend from the eaves of the house, presumably in order to carry out his threat, when he correctly gauged the old man's intentions. He reached out just in time to clutch the metal gutter as grandad kicked away the ladder with his good leg. We left him dangling there and bellowing for Mr Mathews to get the ladder up again.

When we were out of sight grandad gave the mare a hard slap on the buttocks.

'If you're sick in the belly tonight, you strumpet, I'll beat the livin' daylights out of your greedy hide,' after which we spent the rest of the journey in silence. As we were removing the mare's tack, grandad said, without looking at me, 'Boy, keep your mind to yourself tonight. No need for the woman to know our business.'

I nodded. 'Yes grandad.'

Nan, of course, would have raised the roof had she known about the incident. She was no shrew, but she could be very upset over anything which 'lowered the family'.

That evening nan took out the family photograph album and showed me, for the first time, pictures of her and grandad in their younger years. There was one photo, which I still have now, that fascinated me. It was of grandad dressed in girl's clothes. He must have been about twelve years old at the time it was taken and the pugnacious boy's face, with its snub nose, was entirely incongruous with the long, grey skirt and white pinafore. I would have scowled, as he appeared to be doing, had I been made to wear the same outfit, but nan explained to me that custom and household economy of the time demanded that boys should wear their older sisters' clothes, where there was no older brother to pass on hand-me-down trousers. He was, she said, actually smiling, but grandad's idea of a smile was not the same as everyone else's. For me to go to school dressed as he was in the picture would have meant a fight to the death, but in grandad's day, such sights were normal.

There was one other photo which I liked, of nan and grandad on their wedding day, looking all misty-eyed (or perhaps that was an illusion created by the brown, sepia print which was, admittedly, a little fuzzy) but nan quickly turned the page when she came to this picture.

The following day nan and I went visiting my aunt Elinor in the nearby village of Canewdon. She was an eccentric old woman with a penchant for antagonizing my grandmother. Aunt Elinor had some kind of disease, one of the symptoms of which resulted in the shrinking of her skin. At that time it was stretched so tightly over her face and hands it was as clear and shiny as if she were made of bone china. There were small, almost imperceptible cracks beginning to appear on her cheeks, forehead and on the backs of her hands. The condition was painful to her, I knew, because she winced whenever she had to move. I was in awe of aunt Elinor. She had a sharp tongue which was always in use when she had company.

'Do you believe in God, boy?' she asked me that day.

'Don't know,' I said, lowering my eyes. Whatever answer I gave I would displease one of the ladies present.

'Elinor, don't you go teaching the boy your ways,' said nan. 'He's my responsibility and he don't need any encouragement to turn into a heathen . . . he's bad enough as it is. Rather go out shootin' God's creatures on a Sunday than visit His house . . .' This was rather unfair of her since she ate just as much of the rabbits we caught as anyone else.

'Stop getting on your high horse, Sarah. It's no fun being an atheist these days anyway. No one goes to church any more. I'm told more people in Russia go to church than do in England, and it's illegal there. What's the point in rejecting convention if no one gives a damn?'

'I do,' said nan, 'and I don't want you interferin' in the boy's education.'

'What's God got to do with education? And don't go tight-lipped on me Sarah. I've got as much right to opinions as you have. Perhaps if there were more people like me, who didn't approve of religion, then it might become illegal . . . then you'd get more people going to church. Sounds cock-eyed, doesn't it, boy,' she said to me, 'but that's human nature for you. Tell people they can't do something and right away they go and do it, just to be contrary. No one bothers to exercise their rights until you tell them not to. Look at the women's vote. How many of us use it and not so long ago we were killing ourselves to get the right . . .' She went on in this vein for quite some time, with nan and I sitting and listening.

Nan was never at ease in aunt Elinor's house. For one thing its contents were always changing and this gave rise to some agitation amongst family visitors. Nan and the others liked some stability in their world and nothing was constant in Elinor's house. To an imaginative boy the place was a source of mystery and intrigue. It was full of oriental curios: Chinese vases, eastern carpets, strange wooden heads and graceful-looking furniture, all of which constantly changed. Each time we went to see her, Elinor's living room had altered. A *similar* collection of objects and pieces of furniture was evident but the overall scene was never the same. To me it was a wonderful Aladdin's cave.

'Where's that hubbly-bubbly thing gone?' I would ask, pointing to the place in the corner which a camphorwood chest presently occupied, its panels decorated with carvings of leaping dolphins.

'Somebody liked it so I let them have it,' she would invariably reply to all questions of the same nature.

The room had a thousand unusual scents that struggled with one another for my attention. In the dim light I could have been in India or Pakistan or Siam, or any of those lands I had read about. In that room I became Rudyard Kipling's *Kim*, or an Afghan tribesman visiting my leader's tent in *King of the Khyber Rifles*. I could smell elephants and tigers, temple halls and jungles and the spicy interiors of a rajah's palace. I saw snakes and spiders on the carpets and thrilled to the sound of a tribal drum or brass gong. Aunt Elinor created a world for me which stirred my imagination to a feverish excitement, so that I had to be constantly told to sit still and not to touch things.

Aunt Elinor would protect me when nan chastised me in this way.

'Leave the boy alone. He's got the same restless imagination as I had as a child—it's healthy Sarah. You worry too much about things you don't understand.'

I am sure to nan the living room was some sort of appalling shrine to pagan gods that varied only in its physical appearance, never in its spiritual intent. The scents of camphorwood and tanned hide and spices were to her the evidence of evil lurking in the furnishings. She always sat bolt upright and stiff as a pole on whatever seat aunt Elinor directed her towards. Her hands would grip her bag as if to be torn from this talisman would leave her soul unprotected, while her anatomy barely touched the offensive object that attempted to support her weight. She wanted the minimum of contact with these unholy relics of an ungodly people.

'Look at this, nan!' I once exclaimed, picking up a carved wooden flower, the petals of which opened and closed whenever I turned a screw on the base. Inside the flower were three wooden balls.

'What're these for?'

'I'm sure I don't know,' replied nan, primly. Aunt Elinor was out of the room at the time.

'They've got eyes painted on them,' I cried, showing her one. She observed the object with obvious distaste.

'There's not a creature on this earth needs three eyes to see with,' she muttered. The innuendo was plain, even to me as a child. If it did not come from this world, it must be from another, a darker, more sinister place . . . a place nan wanted no part of, for herself or her kind.

In later years I realized that her house was an unofficial curio shop. This state of commerciality came about by accident. My aunt was fond of the curios she purchased and furnished her rooms with, but she believed in a functional as well as an aesthetic value. The problem was, her taste was apparently universal because many of her visitors would express their admiration of various pieces and implore her to allow them to buy the items. Thus it was that the objects that decorated her rooms tended to be transient.

Before we left she gave me two tiger cowries I had coveted. As we walked across the fields, nan and I, in the twilight of a flat sky meeting a flat landscape, I held the shells to my ears and listened to the breezes of an inner world.

'You take no notice of your aunt's talk about there being no God, boy. You've only got to be out in the fields here, with the birds chatterin' and the world still as a rabbit . . .' But I was not listening properly; my attention had been captured by distant seas, far suns and mighty winds.

# EIGHT

'How did you get your leg shot off, grandad? Tell me again.'

'Well, boy, it weren't exactly *shot* off, more like it was *crushed* off. You seen pictures of them big field guns . . . huge buggers, they was. Size of a harvester. We was draggin' one of 'em closer to the Front where the Hun was hidin' in their cosy trenches. Being' a powerful man, with these here shoulders, I was instructed to help turn the wheels, heavin' on spokes as thick and long as flagpoles. Mud up to our thighs and us with no boots on, since they'd rotted away along with our socks over the months we 'ad to wear 'em and never take 'em off. Consequences was me foot slipped and the leg went under the wheel. That great swine of a gun, weighin' heavy as a house, went right over it, crushed it like it was a banana . . .'

Cathy promised to get me a book about Amy Johnson from the library in Southend. I told her I had heard about the lady flier at school. The book was duly delivered, Dave being the postman. He viewed all books with suspicion and handed it to me as if it were thickly smeared with horse manure. I took it to my room and there I read about the wonderful solo flight to Australia and various other exploits of Amy Johnson.

The Australian flight took place in May 1930. In her Gypsy Moth named *Jason* she had flown to and over many countries I wanted to visit: Austria, Turkey, Syria, Iraq, Persia, India, Burma, Thailand, Malaya, Singapore, Indonesia . . . I wanted to see all those places one day. I had a restlessness which I found difficult to suppress when I read out the exotic names to myself. Jhansi, Insein, Tjomal, Timor, Bandar, Abbas, Aleppo. Unlike Amy Johnson, it was my intention to see them over a number of years. At the same time I could sympathize with her love of flying—it must have been romantic as well as physically demanding, to fly in a flimsy aeroplane held together with thin wires, the wind rippling along the fuselage, over the wings. The smell too, of petrol and oil, would heighten the feeling.

Amy Johnson had crashed on landing at Brisbane, when *Jason* hit a fence after she went into a steep sideslip and somersaulted in a field of millet. Amy was unhurt. One of several brushes with death before the final, fatal flight which ended over the Thames.

She died on 5 January 1941, after baling out of her plane over the estuary not ten miles from my house. She was thirty-eight years old. An eye witness said he had seen the aircraft at about 750 feet but could not hear the engine. 'Something white fluttered out and dropped into the sea. It might have been a parachute, but if it was it was a desperate jump, for the plane was less than 200 feet up. The plane skipped as it hit a wave, hung suspended for a moment, then nosed over.' It was a bitterly cold day, with fog, snow showers and an east wind. Rescue attempts from a passing convoy of ships failed to save her. Her body was never recovered, though many times over the years other victims of the river had been washed up and initially identified as 'Amy Johnson'.

The sun was hot on the back of my neck as I walked across the fields towards Milky's house. The police had visited uncle Dave that morning to talk about the fire. I had heard their voices in the parlour, low and conspiratorial, as if the police were Dave's allies, not his enemies, almost as if he and the two uniformed policemen were planning an arson attack on another farm. I even heard him laugh once, that dry, coughing laugh that I was used to hearing below my bedroom window as he said goodnight to Cathy.

All the time they were talking I sat in the kitchen, afraid that they were going to call me in to question me because I knew how weak I was with authority. If they asked me a straight question I would not be able to lie, even if I promised myself beforehand. The circumstances were always different from how I imagined they would be and I would end up stammering, blushing and blurting out the truth. Uncle Dave's anger would be the worst I would have to face.

Why couldn't he just tell them it was an accident? Because we had been poaching, I supposed, which was precisely why they were questioning him now. They knew he was often in the area and the questions would be directed away from Dave but designed to trap him.

*If he had been there, had be seen anyone? Children perhaps? Or a tramp? There was no reason why he could not walk across those fields of course. It was, technically speaking, trespassing but provided no damage was done to the property . . .*

Dave never fell into traps of this kind. His alibi was usually an activity equally distasteful to the policemen as the crime they were investigating, like lying in bed all day long or gambling on toss-penny behind the pub. Eventually the two men left and I thawed from my fear and made my way out of the back door carrying my swimming trunks and towel.

The others were waiting for me at Milky's shed. Oaky, Dinger, Jackie and Milky himself. This was Jackie's first swim with us. It would be strange sharing such an intimate activity with a girl.

Swimming in the river was a private affair, a liaison with nature in her boudoir. Even for young boys there is a sensual feeling, like that of touching a smooth stone or lying on warm grass, experienced when immersing themselves in the river. It is a meeting of two natural forms. To share it with a third did not seem altogether right.

'What kind of costume have you got?' I asked Jackie, trying to make polite conversation. I could see a piece of blue, crinkled material poking from the end of her towel.

'Mind yer own business,' she replied, glaring at me.

Somehow I was always transgressing unwritten laws when I spoke to females. My cousin Matty was forever launching adults at me with the words, '*He* said . . .' and making whatever it was that I had said sound like something underhand.

'Just curious, that's all,' I muttered.
'That's what they all say,' she snapped.
'Who?'
'Never you mind.'
I was confused. Convoluted exchanges of this kind left me feeling like a dunce. I never could understand where they were leading or what the significance was behind the banal words, which obviously meant something more to Jackie, who looked highly offended and darted glances at the others. They looked as bemused as I was, so I could not see her getting any support from that direction. I wanted to give Jackie some sort of compliment but my approaches had all been blocked now by her aggressive attitude.
We set out for the mills shortly after this and gradually Jackie's aggression towards me melted as we walked along. By the time we reached the river the gang had become its usual cohesive unit, which now included Jackie.
We found we had misjudged the state of the tide and had to wait an hour for the water to reach a depth necessary for swimming. Even then the currents were too strong for Milky and Jackie, the weakest swimmers. We had a battle with cockle shells which sprayed the water with the authenticity of bullets, or so we thought. On bare skin they stung, so we refrained from pelting Jackie, who seemed happiest when shouting encouragement to Oaky anyway. She jumped up and down, an angular, blue monkey in her swimming costume, yelling, 'Get 'im, Oaky. Get 'im,' when her favourite was on the attack, and, 'Look out! Over there, behind the corner,' when he was defending.
These extra eyes of Oaky's were most irritating but none of us complained, probably because that would have meant the end of the game. Our arguments tended to call a halt to any current activity, even after they were settled.
When the water was high we all went in and played tag. Out of the water was 'safe' and the one who was 'it' had to be a good swimmer to catch the other taunting players who tried to get as close to him or her as possible. We

outdid outselves in expending energy that day, mainly for Jackie's benefit, showing off our diving, jumping, running and thrashing around in the water, while making as much noise as we could. There was a certain amount of pretence to it because the good swimmers 'allowed' themselves to be caught when the game threatened to flag. Oaky's speciality was the aerial bomb; he would hit the water from a height, tucked into a tight ball of bone and muscle, causing the most tremendous splash and missing pursuers by a fraction. The game was full of youthful joy and daring and we all loved it. Afterwards we lay under the hot afternoon sun to dry.

'What are you goin' to be when you grow up?' asked Jackie, presumably of anyone.

'Dunno,' replied Milky, predictably.

'I want to be a newspaper reporter, like James Stewart,' I replied, too eagerly.

Dinger snorted. 'He's a film star, not a reporter.'

'I mean, like in that film we saw when we went to town. He was a reporter then. That's what I want to do.'

'M'goin' to be a P.T.I.,' mumbled Oaky.

There was a touch of shyness to his tone so I knew this was an ambition which he believed was within his grasp, unlike mine which was something I could see in the clouds but was well out of reach. Oaky knew his capabilities, which were none the less fairly extensive physically if not academically, and he worked himself to their limits. The only trouble was, I did not know what the initials P.T.I. meant and I was afraid to ask in case my query met with a barrage of scorn.

'What's that?' asked Milky. 'A P.T.I.?'

There was no derisive laughter from Dinger or Jackie. Obviously we were all in ignorance.

'Physical Training Instructor,' replied Oaky. 'Like in the Army, or Air Force.'

Jackie said, 'You want to be a soldier?'

'No. Not that, but not many places have 'em. In the services they do, and in prisons and places . . . think I'd rather be in the Army than a prison.'

'Too right,' confirmed Dinger. 'I'm goin' to join the

Army but I wanna be a real soldier. Fire a gun.'

'I can fire my uncle's shotgun,' I said. 'It's a twelve bore and it's got a kick that brings up bruises on your shoulder.'

Dinger said, 'That's 'cos you don't hold it proper. You've got to tuck the butt hard into your shoulder and *squeeze* the trigger.'

I was indignant. 'I know that. My uncle's been shooting guns nearly all his life and he taught me. It *still* hurts just the same. You want to try it.'

'I *have*,' he sneered, in a way that told me he was lying.

We lay in an uncomfortable silence after this episode until a shadow crept over our bodies. Eventually I looked up and saw that the sun had moved behind the gantry above our heads. I went up onto my elbows and Oaky followed my gaze. Then his face took on a thoughtful expression. Finally he announced, 'Today's the day!'

'What for?' asked Jackie.

'Today's the day I dive from up there. Remember, you dared me?'

My heart began to beat a lot faster.

'That was a long time ago,' I said. 'She didn't mean it anyway.'

'Yes I did,' Jackie said quickly. 'I want to see him do it.'

Neither Dinger nor Milky contradicted her. I knew what they were thinking. They did not want to become involved in case Oaky insisted we all do it. I felt it too, that fear of being exposed as a coward because I knew for sure that I could never climb up on top of the gantry and dive off. I feared it more than I feared my nightmares, that piece of architecture that protruded like a scaffold from the side of the mill.

'Well, I'm goin' to have a go,' said Oaky.

He jumped to his feet and looked for an entrance to the mill. I felt some flutterings of hope in my chest. He had to get up there first and to do so he had to enter the realms of the mill workers. Men. They would surely not allow him into the building and supposing he found a way in, they would turn him back. We followed him round the corner in his search for a door.

At the side of the mill was an open window. It looked

dark inside and the smell of grain filled our nostrils when we peered in through the opening. Oaky hauled himself up onto the ledge and dropped inside. We watched his white form move quickly into the interior, until it disappeared like a ghost in the blackness beyond.

'Better go round the back,' suggested Milky. 'Wait and see what happens.'

We waited, it seemed, for a thousand years—for as long as witches had inhabited Essex. The river had the look of a mud-coloured monster, a brown serpent whose eddies and currents were like coils winding in on themselves. It would swallow Oaky whole, devour him completely. I wanted to scream out, across the river, into the mill area, for someone to help us. An adult. Only an adult could help us now. But that was betrayal and the scream stuck in my throat, like a piece of food, lodged there.

'There he is!' cried Jackie, and we all looked up to see a small, pale figure standing on top of the gantry. A white-clay figure, terribly vulnerable, poised on the edge and, typical of Oaky, preparing for the dive like a professional. He stood, straight as a pole, his arms levelled, head up, eyes straight ahead, fixed on some part of the world hidden to us by nearer horizons.

*He was going to die. I knew it.*

He fell through the air rather than dived. It *began* as a dive but the distance between the top of the gantry and the surface of the water was too great. What started as disciplined body movements deteriorated into an uncoordinated drifting of limbs, a somersaulting of the body. Like a dead bird falls, so Oaky fell.

He hit the water, head first, with a mountainous splash, drenching us and the wharf. Several seconds later he surfaced with a breathless yell of triumph. We all yelled.

'Yeah! Yeah!' we bellowed. 'Oaky the king.' The relief came flooding to my eyes as tears, which I had to hide from the others. The elation was almost overwhelming. We were a thousand years older and Oaky was still alive. We were all alive; our hearts were still beating, our living eyes had witnessed the defeat of the river, the slaying of the serpent-monster.

'Again,' cried Oaky. He climbed out of the water, an ugly red welt along his left side. He seemed to be limping a little but he was whole. He was king.

Without waiting for an answer he ran round the back of the building again. In a few minutes he was in his position on the top of the gantry.

This time the dive was executed perfectly. He came down and entered the water as straight as an iron rod. Barely a ripple was left in his wake.

We waited, smiling.

The seconds moved like minutes and we waited.

We waited.

We waited.

Nothing.

'He'll be drowned away,' whispered Milky.

We waited for more than a thousand years, our faces hardening into granite and our hearts beating with the slow pace of stone.

Jackie began crying.

# NINE

They let me stay up very late that night, well past the time after the gas mantles had popped into brilliance. I tried to read but uncle Dave insisted on listening to his favourite programme on the wireless, *The Man In Black*, read by Valentine Dyall. I listened too, from my warm nest in the old armchair by the range, the soft, hypnotic voice holding my attention like a firm hand gripping my throat. It was impossible *not* to listen, yet terrifying to hear. When it was time for everyone to go to bed, I demanded a night light, the tenor of my voice enough to make them take heed, even though nan's concern regarding fire would normally have overridden any fear I might express. Oaky's death was on everyone's mind.

Yet it was *The Man In Black* that was the cause of my terror, not an incident that was so fresh I had had no time to assimilate it. Oaky was dead, beyond that thought was a screen as yet impenetrable. The images conjured by the soft voice on the wireless, however, were stark and vivid in my mind. I was with the narrator, by his side, as he stooped to pick up the object on the deserted shoreline. *Whistle and I will come to you.* These were the words inscribed on the object, the whistle found on the beach. Like a fool, he obeyed the words, and that night the windows of his bedroom flew inwards as if flung open by unseen hands. A strong wind lifted the curtains and in the morning he discovered to his horror that the spare bed next to him had been slept in.

If anyone thought I was going to sleep without a night light after an experience like that, they were very much mistaken. I think I would have screamed the house down first.

The next morning I awoke early, took Jessica on my

shoulder and went for a walk across the fields. Eventually we came to the huge, black scar on the landscape that I had caused and for a moment, just for a moment, I felt the wicked thrill of creative destruction. A sea of black, crisp stalks, some of it still in its original tufted shape, since it had not rained since the fire, stretched for about half a mile in each direction. There were gutted trunks pointing from the hedgerows with accusing black fingers.

Then the guilt came again, with a deepening sense of wrongdoing. There was another source of guilt too. *Oaky*. I had witnessed his death and therefore some blame for that death must have been attached to me. Why I felt that way, I could not say. It was as if I should have done something to prevent it. Just *being there* made me guilty.

Some of the mill workers had dived into the river and carried out a futile search, feeling along the bottom before the experts arrived, the police with their black-suited frogmen. By that time the river mud had been disturbed and it was impossible to see a thing in water that was never clear at the best of times. One of the frogmen said it was like having brown paper pasted over his mask.

We children stood in a group on the edge, shivering and clustered together for comfort. Occasionally a question would be asked of us; the spot where he entered the water? Whether we'd seen any bubbles afterwards and if we had, were they moving along the surface? The exact time of Oaky's dive?

We stammered out replies, more often than not contradicting each other. Sometimes, like the question regarding the time of the dive, we had no clue and shook our heads. When evening came they took us to our respective homes and informed the adults of what had taken place. Nan clung to me for a while, burying my face in the apron she wore, saying, 'Thank God it wasn't the boy. George would never forgive us . . .' George was her son, my father. I was unused to any show resembling affection from my grandmother and pulled away after a polite interval. She rarely touched me except to look behind an ear for dirt or to straighten a collar trapped by a tie. She then insisted I ate a tea I did not want.

My feet sent up clouds of black dust as I scuffed through my handiwork. When I reached the other side I discovered that Jessica had messed down the sleeve of my jacket and had to stop to wipe it off with some grass. Perhaps the smell of burnt foliage had frightened her? Even though days had passed since the fire there was still an acrid odour in the air from the cold ashes. My jacket still stank after scrubbing at it vigorously, leaving green streaks on the sleeve.

When I reached the south dyke that bordered the Crouch I climbed up the grassy bank to the path on top and looked out over the mudflats. Jessica ran backwards and forwards across my shoulders, pausing occasionally to stare in the same direction, perhaps wondering what it was that I found so interesting in stretches of mud and pools of water.

The tide was half in, the boats with their prows pointing down river. There were two long rays of water curving in from the estuary like silver horns hammered flat against the brown mud. As I watched them they grew and spread, faster than a man could walk. Eventually they would meet in a pincer movement and anyone caught inside, any bait diggers or hunters after Brent geese, would have to be very lucky to escape drowning.

I thought about Oaky and suddenly felt sick and wanted to be well away from these rivers that fractured our county. As I turned from the dyke I saw a figure in the distance, moving slowly, head down, along the edge of the mud. Whoever it was had a stick in their hand and was poking amongst the seaweed and jetsam. Probably one of the searchers, still looking for Oaky's body. I turned away quickly, realizing I could be the one to find him, by accident. I did not want to do that. There were images of dead things in my mind. It was as if the river had called me from my bed that morning, to show me something I had no wish to see, was afraid of seeing. *Whistle and I will come to you.* I began running and Jessica gripped my shoulder with her tiny claws to prevent herself from falling off.

Once home I put her in her cage and met Dave in the yard. He questioned me privately about Oaky.

'What happened?'

'He just dived from the mill . . . that crane thing. Didn't come up again. I thought he was kidding at first—you know, messing around. Thought he would pop up behind the sluice or something. He was always good at underwater swimming.'

Dave looked thoughtful. He was wearing his flat cap and his head had a squeezed look to it.

'Dived from there myself once, as a kid your age. Damn. Must have hit a stake or somethin'. There's some stumps of the old wharf in there. Never came up, eh? Can't understand that.'

'Policeman said it was the currents. Kept him under.'

'They're not that strong by the wharf. Bit spooky, ain't it? I don't like mysteries like that, without any real answers. Maybe he got stuck in the mud?'

I wished Dave had not said that. I had a horrible picture of Oaky's head buried in the sludge, of Oaky trying to breathe and drawing in that foul, black mire, filling his lungs with it and sinking deeper as the ballast weighed him down. Dave must have seen my expression because he clamped a hand on my shoulder and said, 'Don't think about it. Nothing to be done now. Just forget it . . . and stay away from those mills. If you want to swim, I'll take you into town to the baths. Just let me know. All right?'

'All right. Thanks Dave.'

I walked around the house to the road with him, to where he had parked his motorbike. He crossed his scarf over his chest before climbing onto the machine and then took his goggles out of his pocket, pulling them over his head. Suddenly, he had the look of a blind man about him, as the sun caught the glass discs and robbed his face of human character. I backed away from him, startled by the change. Then he reached to his waistband and tugged a pair of gauntlets from his belt. Once these were on his hands he began to kickstart the bike. It coughed three or four times in succession, then roared to life. This strange being that used to be my uncle gave me a little salute before moving off in a cloud of blue exhaust fumes.

In the evening I went with grandad to his allotment

where he dug some fresh vegetables for nan. I wandered off while he was at work to search for amusement in the ditch at the far end, beyond the greengage trees. The sky was the colour of beetroot and while I was idly tossing stones into the hedge I suddenly saw two small red lights moving along the bottom of the ditch. For a wild moment I thought something magical was about to occur and I started to tremble. Then I managed to make out a shape and realized the light was being reflected by a pair of eyes, like blood-beetle marbles.

It was a badger, and despite my stone-throwing he had not seen me as he scurried quickly through the bracken in the ditch. I kept as still as I could, watching him hurry along like a little old man, grunting and muttering under his breath, blowing dust from his rubbery nostrils. There was a pink scar on his snout, probably a recent fight wound, about an inch long, which crossed his nose like a Red Indian war marking. He came to a part in the bank where a hawthorn grew, its roots exposed and turned inward on themselves like thick fingers gripping the dry soil. There was a gap in the roots and he slipped between them, easily, to disappear from sight. After an interval I went to inspect the entrance to his sett and found his paw prints covering the area around the hole, hard as rock fossils. A moment later the patterned face was back again, staring out into my own. I carefully took an apple from my pocket that I had carried for two days. It was one of last year's, the skin all wrinkled, which was why I had not eaten it before. Slowly, I reached out and placed it a foot from his nose.

He shrank back for an instant, his little eyes never leaving my face and I backed off a short distance. After a long time he shuffled forward on his short legs and when he was within distance of the fruit, snatched it up and trotted quickly back to the entrance again. Then he was gone, into the underworld which was his home. I was elated! I had made friends with a wild creature! It had eaten out of my hand—almost.

Suddenly, Peter was beside me, more alert than I had ever seen him. He pushed his grizzled muzzle in between the roots, sniffing madly. I grabbed his collar and pulled hard but he was not to be deterred by a mere ten-year-old boy.

'Grandad!' I called. 'Peter's found a dead rat.' I did not want to tell grandad about the badger. He might have considered it a pest and want to smoke it out.

The old man swore and I heard the word from where I stood. Then he cleared his throat, hawking noisily, calling, 'Kee-ah bouy. Peter. Kee-ah.' Peter hesitated. To ignore grandad was quite a different thing from taking notice of me. But he still held his ground.

'Send 'im over 'ere,' came the demand a few seconds later.

'Won't go,' I complained. 'He keeps playing with the rat. S'got all maggots on,' I added, elaborating the lie.

I heard the fork being slammed into the earth and this time the deep, gritty threat in the tone was sufficient to stop Peter's claws digging away at the roots.

'Kee-ah you bliddy sod, afore I 'ave to come and get 'er.'

Peter reluctantly slunk away towards his master and a few moments later I heard the yelp which told me he had got a rap on the nose for his disobedience. I would have to watch the dog in future because I knew as soon as he got the chance he would be back and the badger would never be safe.

On the way back on the cart Peter eyed me with contrition and laid his head on my knee. His coat always smelled very strongly—just a canine smell but not pleasant—and his hair was greasy, so I usually pushed him off. However, the light was going and I had started trembling as I recalled the events of the previous day. I hugged his big bony head to my chest, taking comfort in its solid feel and the warmth that came from it. His ear twitched as I scratched beneath it, trying to repay him a little for being a dog and needing affection from me. If he could have, just once, stood up to Mick while that savage hound attacked him I could have loved him. But we were both cowards, Peter and I. We sought security in each other and found only timidity, a meek acceptance of

Mick's insane fearlessness, his utter hatred of both of us. Peter could no more understand the blind viciousness of Mick than I could fathom Dinger Bell. Peter was too gentle for the canine world and I too mild for the human one.

That night, before I went to sleep, I thought about the sett. Badgers, I knew, were clannish creatures. There would be a colony of them in the maze of tunnels and nesting chambers that formed the sett, chattering away in high-pitched voices, occasionally barking or screaming when danger was in the air. There was not much they were afraid of—dogs, I supposed, and perhaps foxes. Men, of course, which was why I was so triumphant at having made friendly contact.

I fell off to sleep with images of myself crawling through narrow tunnels, blowing dust through my nostrils and digging at the sandy soil with strong finger-claws. It was a warm, safe world under the turf and roots; there was the smell of musk and fresh earth, leaves and warm fur. I could curl up in a secure hollow and know that nothing could reach me from the outside world—no ugly deaths, no angry people, no ghosts, skeletons or undead beings. Just me and my fellow badgers, with simple thoughts and simple needs.

# TEN

'It was her what done it!' Jackie yelled into my face. 'She held 'im under.' Jackie's features were twisted into a sharp ugliness which both fascinated and terrified me. Her small fist waved under my nose. There were four of us there: Dinger, Jackie, Milky and me. We were having a council of war over Oaky, and Jackie had immediately assumed leadership of the group in Oaky's place. Dinger seemed quite happy at this; he made a good lieutenant but a poor general.

We were all clustered in Milky's shed and I could see him casting worried glances towards the door. He was afraid his parents would hear and come to investigate the noise we were making.

'You know it was her, don't you?' hissed Jackie. 'You saw the footprints.' Wet marks leading up to the front of the White House.

'Yes,' I submitted weakly. 'But what can we do?'

We had been spying on the White House ever since Milky had suggested that Oaky's death might not have been an accident, that it might have been the waterwitch taking revenge for the theft of her fruit. Oaky's body had still not been found and Dinger and Jackie were convinced of her involvement.

'Who's next? She's gonna get every one of us,' said Jackie, ''less we protect ourselves. We got to scare her, make her go away somewhere and leave us alone.'

'Maybe she's not the one? Maybe it was just an accident?' Milky was backpedalling now. He was as concerned as I was that we were getting out of our depth.

Dinger spoke. 'Look. Oaky dived into the river, right? First time he came up like a cork. *Second* time . . . second time, *nothin'*. Even if he did hit his head on somethin', he would 'ave come up. Sense, init? If he'd 'ave stuck in the mud, like what Titch says, then the frogmen would 'ave found 'im or he'd 'ave still been there when the water went away. 'Stead, nothin'. Pretty obvious somethin' strange happened and even my parents say *that*! I reckon like Jackie—that bloody waterwitch got 'im. Bet there are bits of 'im hangin' somewhere in the house . . .'

'Well I ain't going in there,' I said, emphatically.

Jackie sniggered. 'Don't be silly, none of us would dare do that. We've got to make her come out.'

'Then what?' asked Milky.

'We let her see we ain't scared of her. Shout a few things. You know, like we would if it was another gang. If she sees we ain't scared and things . . . well, that's the first bit anyway. After that we'll have another counsill.'

'I don't know . . .' began Milky.

'Look!' snarled Dinger, 'you started this anyway, so you stop makin' objections. If you go round tellin' lies then she ain't a witch an' we don't need to do anythin' . . . you tellin' lies?' His tone was threatening. Now that Oaky was gone, his personality and sense of fair play no longer around to influence the less scrupulous elements of the gang, there was nothing to curb Dinger's viciousness. Now that he had lost his leader Dinger was a little lost himself . . . we all were.

'No,' mumbled Milky. 'Weren't tellin' lies.'

'Then she must be a witch, 'cause you said she was.'

There was no argument to this and Milky nodded his head in assent. Later, we all walked to the wharf where the terrible scene had taken place. The tide was out and a thin trickle of water flowed like dribble down an old woman's chin. It glistened, wickedly attractive, yet at the same time repulsive. It seemed to me that the river, having claimed Oaky's body, had retreated with it beyond our reach. There were two hundred yards of thick, evil-smelling sludge to cross. We had no dustbin lids to use like snowshoes and in any case the desire was not there.

Immediately below us was the spot where Oaky had dived. It seemed for the first time I saw the soft-looking stakes of the old wharf nosing up through the mud like the snouts of prehistoric fish. Had he struck one of them? I looked up. The gantry was high, very high. Perhaps, as Dave had said, he had hit the mud like a spear and was buried there now, underneath . . .? I backed away from the edge.

'What's the matter with you, Titch?' asked Jackie with scorn in her voice. 'Scared of fallin' over?'

'Maybe,' I replied.

'Never known such a wet week,' she said, ' 'cept p'raps 'im.' She indicated Milky, who turned his mournful expression on her for a moment, then back to the river.

'Let's go an' find that ole waterwitch,' said Dinger, decisively.

We followed him back along the lane and then across the fields to the rear of the White House. Indian-style, we crawled through the long grasses that bordered the field until we came to the back gate. As we drew closer the house seemed to expand, slowly, until it almost filled the sky, its dirty white walls and dark roof pulsating gently. It was alive—I was sure it was alive—watching us, those shining windows glaring hatred at me. I could sense it leaning over, looking down on us as we hid in the long grass. I couldn't understand why the others hadn't noticed and anxiously studied Dinger's face for signs of panic. He looked calm, if a little grim, but there was no indication of fear.

I looked away, out into the fields behind us, trying to gain some comfort there and when I looked back the house was normal again, A house, just an ordinary house.

For a long while we just stayed there and watched. Then Dinger picked up a clod of earth and threw it at the back door. It struck, instead, the dustbin that stood just outside and the lid fell off with a loud clatter. My legs were shaking like mad. I wanted to run but fear of the water-witch seeing me, fleeing across the field alone, prevented my flight. I did not want to be singled out and marked as the next victim.

Nothing happened. Then, after a few minutes more had passed, there was a movement behind the curtains. Suddenly the back door flew open and a cardboard box was thrown out, next to the dustbin. The door closed again.

My heart was banging blood to my ears and I could see the fear in Milky's eyes as he tried to take in all four windows at once. Between us and the white clapboard wall of the house was the pond with its scummy surface. At any time the witch could enter the pond from beneath, using one of her secret passages. If we tried to sneak up to the house she might reach out from beneath and grab one of our ankles as we passed. Any journey to the house was full of peril.

'What're we going to do now?' I whispered.

'We *got* to get her to come out,' said Dinger. 'Milky, chuck a brick through the window.'

'*You* chuck a bloody brick through the window.' Milky was afraid of Dinger but the waterwitch scared him much more.

'She's probably back in the pond by now,' Jackie said. 'We'll never get her to come out from there. Come on.'

She began to crawl away despite the frown of disapproval on Dinger's face. Milky and I joined her immediately but Dinger stayed for a little while to register his protest at abandoning the place so soon. It took longer to reach the road than I thought it would and my elbows and knees were rough and sore at the end of it. We gathered in a copse, under an old yew, and Jackie took command once more.

'We got to do somethin' more drastic,' she said.

Milky shook his head. 'I've had enough of this,' he said. 'I'm goin' home. I don't want to be in this gang no more. It's not the same now anyway.' He stood up and started to walk away.

'You leave now,' said Dinger, 'an' you're out of it for good.' He shook his fist at Milky's back. ' 'N if I see you around, I'll give you one.' Milky paused, then more slowly, continued in the direction of his house.

'Chicken!' shrieked Jackie.

Half of me wanted to get up and run to join him but the other half did not want to leave Jackie. I could not bear to have her hate me as she seemed to hate Milky. When she had shouted after him her face had looked like an old woman's, all wrinkled and blotched. I didn't want to be the cause of something like that.

'We don't need him anyway,' she said. 'He's too lanky for a start. Great long streak . . .' She laughed at her own joke. Dinger and I were silent. We were both bound to her, tighter than we had ever been to Oaky. It was a different kind of friendship. Oaky had never been any more than one of the gang, although we had respected his leadership. She, Jackie, was like a witch herself, casting loyalty spells over us. I would have followed her anywhere, at that time.

We sat and talked under the yew but came to no definite plan. There were vague ideas about firing stones onto the roof with catapults but we were unsure about what to do next, even if we succeeded in getting the waterwitch to leave her house and pond.

'We got to scare her out of the village,' said Jackie. 'Scare her right away from this place. We got to find out *how*. Only way to do that is ask someone. I can't ask me auntie, 'cause she'll want to know what I'm up to. I know her. She don't like me much anyway. All of us better think about it. Don't do it so they know *why* we're askin'. Do it as if it's for school or somethin'. OK?'

We mumbled our assent.

After that we played knifey with Dinger's penknife, throwing it close to a partner's foot without actually hitting the shoe. The knife had to stick in the ground or it did not count. The victim also had a role to play in that he or she was not supposed to move or flinch when the knife was thrown.

When Dinger had gone home I tried to keep Jackie with me for a while, on her own. I wanted to impress her. For some reason I wanted her to like and admire me as she had done Oaky.

'I know where there's a badger's sett,' I said. 'Do you want to see it? It's not far away.'

'What's one of them?'

'Place where a badger lives. Its house. It's in the roots of a tree—there's an entrance hole underneath.'

She smoothed her cotton dress down with her hands

before replying. Her eyes searched my face as she spoke.

'That all it is? A hole?'

'We might see a badger. I have, three times. There's one with a scar on its nose that eats things I give it, like a pet.' I had been back to the sett since, with more food, and had managed to feed the badger twice more. He was getting closer each time, becoming more and more trusting. 'They're not dangerous, badgers.' She made me feel uncomfortable when she stared at me so hard.

She twisted round and walked a few paces, then turned again. There was something about her that made me want to run and hug her. I didn't, of course. I just stood there feeling stupid and wanting to say something clever.

'All right,' she called, suddenly. 'Show me where it is.'

I ran to her and we crossed the fields, taking the back way to the allotments. There was no one there when we arrived and I hoped grandad had not been back with Peter. Hurrying to the ditch I saw that the entrance under the hawthorn had not been disturbed.

'There it is,' I whispered.

'Where?' she asked, in a normal tone.

'Under that tree, there,' I said, pointing.

Suddenly I could see it through her eyes: just a tangle of roots and bracken.

'Can't see nothin'. What's it s'posed to be?'

I felt deflated now and wished I'd never asked her to come. She was right. It was nothing. Unless we saw the badger the whole thing would be an empty event. For a few moments I stood, willing the badger to come out but knowing it was probably hopeless. On other occasions I had waited for an hour or more and Jackie was obviously not prepared to do this.

In the silence that followed, my embarrassment grew. Finally there was a rustling sound a few yards further down the ditch. A miracle! The badger was coming back after being out foraging. But almost immediately my hopes were destroyed as I saw a small, brown shape scuttle through the grass and run into the ditch. A rat. Nothing but a rat.

'Thought that was the badger,' I said, despondently.

'What was it then?'
'Only a rat.'
Her hand whipped out and clutched my sleeve like a bird's claw, making me jump.
'What's the matter?' I asked. 'What is it?'
'Don't like rats. I'm goin' home.'
'I'll go with you to the road.'
'All right.'
She still had hold of my coat, pretending, I think, that the ground was uneven and that she found it difficult to walk. I liked being used. I felt light and warm inside, as the evening began settling in around us. Birds were finding perches for the night and in the grass around us other creatures making night-time preparations paused to let us pass. There was a greenness to it all. She did not let go of me until we reached the road and then she just said, ' 'Night,' and ran in the opposite direction to my house. There was a feeling of fullness in me which smothered the rest of the day's events and almost removed the lingering heaviness of Oaky's death. I felt I was a man, like Dave, with a man's secrets. I knew I would remember those small fingers gripping my sleeve for the rest of my life.
Before I went to bed that night I thought I ought to do the same as uncle Dave and hit my wardrobe door to get rid of the excitement in me, but I knew nan would be after me if I did, so I hit the pillow instead.

# ELEVEN

'How did my leg get took off? You keep askin' me that boy, an' I keep tellin' you. Them Huns kept swarming all over us, gettin' our positions from their aircraft—little bitty things with paper wings and held together by pieces of string, not like those you see nowadays. Anyways, we started to put up these big balloons to sort 'er see over their lines, but we had to get 'em up an' down quick like when one of their kites came over. One day we was winchin' in this monster balloon when the hawser snapped clean in two.

'I tell you boy, the tension on them steel cables is hard to imagine—stretched out like a piece of elastic it was. Came whippin' through the air like a snake gone berserk and took off that old leg as easy as cheesewire goin' through a hunk of cheddar. Used to get terrible pains in that foot and I remember thinkin' afterwards, "Edward, at least you got rid of your cramps along with that leg." Funny thing is, I still get 'em even now. No foot there but I still get the cramps . . . don't make sense, do it?'

Aunt Elinor always took me out on my birthday, a treat she used to enjoy as much as I did. She was the only relation I had who owned a car and we would drive to Southend sea front and work our way along the Golden Mile, trying all the slot machines and wasting a lot of her money. Then she would allow me rides at the fairground, and ice creams, cockles, candy floss, lemonade, hot dogs—all without a murmur about the fact that I might be sick afterwards. We would ride on the pier train, one-and-a-quarter miles to its end. It was the longest pleasure pier in the world. Sometimes it would be over mud, sometimes over water, for this was still tidal estuary country.

Then, replete, we would turn for home. Aunt Elinor's money came from a man who had died and nobody in the family talked about. All I knew was aunt Elinor and this man used to write each other a lot of letters.

In the summer of 1952, however, her illness had advanced so much she could hardly walk. Most of her hair had fallen out and even the white lines left by the wrinkles on her elbows had merged into her general colouring. She moved slowly towards the car, using a stick, still determined to have our yearly treat. I would have helped her but I knew she could not stand anyone touching her. The pain of physical contact was too much for her. So I stood by, helplessly, as she grunted her way along the path, wondering if when she bent to enter the car one day, her skin would tear all the way down her back like a shirt that was too tight. She moaned loudly while climbing into the car and I asked her if she still wanted to go. She nodded her head. Aunt Elinor had always been a very determined lady. She would enjoy herself even if it killed her.

'Right, let's go young man,' she said, putting the car into gear. Just as we were about to draw away the postman came with a letter, so I dashed out to get it for her. It was a big, heavy envelope and looked quite official.

'Open it for me please, would you?'

I tore open the seal and pulled out the contents. To my astonishment it was full of drawings and one or two poems. The sort of things I would do at school. There was a letter on top. I noticed the word SOLICITORS after a string of names. Aunt Elinor smiled as she shuffled through the contents, then she gave me the drawings to look at.

'What do you think of those?' she asked.

We were driving along by this time and I studied the pencil drawings with what I thought was a critical eye. They were the usual school stuff, vases of flowers and leaves and things, but better than I could do. The artist was probably a bit older than me, though I doubted I would ever reach any kind of standard in art. I was a man of letters.

'They look pretty good to me,' I said, knowing she

wanted me to praise them for some reason. 'Whose are they?'

'A niece . . .' she said quickly. 'You don't know her.'

'What's her name?' If I had a cousin I did not know about, it was news to me.

'Jennifer. Right, we're just coming to Warner's Bridge. You can see the aeroplanes on the airport from the top. Be ready for them because you'll have to be quick . . .'

In Southend she stayed in the car, watching me as I played the machines or purchased food for us both. I forwent my rides in the fairground, as she could not follow me in there. Finally, we drove home and aunt Elinor began talking to me about school.

'You're eleven today, coming up to senior school age.'

'Take my eleven-plus soon.'

'Going to pass?'

'Don't know. I'm good at English but I can't do Maths very well. Nor Geography.'

'What about History?'

I nodded. 'I like that. Stories. That's why I like English. You can make things up all the time.'

'Not in History you can't.'

'No, but it seems like *someone* has. The stories are all full of battles and things. And interesting. Lots of small stories about people . . .'

'Anecdotes. Yes, I suppose you're right. They are a little like fiction. Many probably *are*. How much do you know about this county . . . this area?'

I felt uncomfortable. I hoped it was not going to turn into a boring questions and answers session like it did when I visited my parents.

'Not much,' I said, warily.

She drove on for a little in silence then took an unfamiliar turning. I did not say anything, thinking she would tell me soon where we were going. At first I thought we were going to Rochford, where another aunt of mine lived but we drove straight through the high street and out the other side. A thought suddenly struck me.

'Are we going to see Jennifer?' I asked.

Aunt Elinor looked startled for a moment, then replied.

'No, she's at school, boarding school, a long way from here. I'm taking you to see a bit of history.'

'Oh.'

Finally, at Ashingdon Hill, she took a sharp right turn up a cinder track to a church.

'Here we are, Ashingdon Minster.'

'Are we going in?' I was surprised after all aunt Elinor's speeches about not believing in God.

'No, we're going round the back. It was the hill I wanted, not the church on top of it.'

She climbed from the car and I followed her painful steps through the small gate and round the back of the church.

'Look,' she said.

The land fell away from the hill in a soft curve to the plain below, before rising again to another church on an almost identical hill. To the left and right of the valley were the flatlands of the estuaries. I could see the broad back of the River Crouch moving lethargically through the plain to the north of both hills.

'That's the river King Canute came up with his fleet of Viking ships to raid Essex. Can you imagine it? Those long, sleek craft, their gunwales rimmed with bright shields?'

She sighed. I think she had forgotten I was there for a moment. Her eyes were shining but there was a faraway look in them as she stared out over the valley.

'What happened then?' I asked.

'Pardon? Oh, well, Canute gathered his army together on what is now Canewdon Hill, over there, and Edmund Ironside, the English King, on this hill. They met in the valley. Edmund was young and a good warrior but at a crucial point in the battle Edric Streona abandoned the English and joined with Canute, giving the Dane the victory.'

'He was a traitor then, this Edric bloke?'

'In a way, yes.'

I didn't like that. I hated traitors. I said so to aunt Elinor.

'Well, things are not always as simple as they may seem,' she replied. 'He may have had a very good reason for changing sides. Perhaps because he was a king in his own right he felt *he* should be commanding the English Army, and not Edmund? Perhaps his kingdom was crumbling and he needed money to support it?'

I could not agree. I thought there was no good excuse for abandoning your own kind. However, I did not argue.

'What happened to King Canute then? Did he go home with all the plunder?'

'No, he became a damnfool Christian, and built this church.'

She shot a look at me.

'Sorry, Raymond, I didn't mean to swear like that. Take no notice of me. You make up your own mind about religion. It's just that . . . well, you won't understand but I've had a clash with the Church and I'm a little bitter about it.'

'A clash with a church?'

'No, I meant with the Christian religion. Someone I loved once wanted to marry me but . . . well, it's very complicated and not very interesting to a young boy.' She laughed. 'I expect you find that strange, someone wanting an ugly old woman like me?'

I was embarrassed. 'No,' I mumbled.

She turned her attention back to the scene below us.

'1000 AD,' she said. 'A long time ago.'

I looked out, over the river and plain. It was not difficult to imagine the ships, the armies coming together in a mighty clash of steel. There were still only one or two farms to indicate human habitation, and they were a long way off. It could still have been AD 1000. Edric Streona. I saw him as a haughty knight in black armour, suddenly turning on his allies in the heat of the battle. There was no excuse. If he had intended to change sides he should have done it openly, before the fight took place. There was an anger simmering inside me. Why were there so many traitors in history? If it had not been for Edric Streona, the whole world might be a different place, though what *sort* of place I could not imagine.

Aunt Elinor grunted and when I looked at her face I

could see the strain in her eyes. She was in great pain and I said, 'Can we go home now?'

The vicar was standing outside the church door as we passed and he spoke briefly to aunt Elinor. He invited me to look inside, which I did, where a model of a Viking ship hung from the rafters. There was a Danish flag too, by one of the windows. I went outside again to hear him telling aunt Elinor that the Danes still came over to commemorate the building of the Minster, and, no doubt, their victory over the English Army.

The vicar went on to tell us that some time ago the church had taken to wearing red cassocks, instead of white, and King George, who had recently died, had written to say that only royal churches were allowed to wear red.

The vicar chuckled. 'So, I wrote back saying that was all right because King Canute had built our church and therefore we met the requirements. Never heard another word from them. Don't suppose the King was worried. Probably some fussy prelate who bothered the King's advisers until the letter was sent.' He chuckled again.

I was surprised to find aunt Elinor chatting so freely with a member of the clergy. I had expected her to ignore him or treat him brusquely, knowing her feelings, but she stayed for a few minutes chatting with him. He pointed out the gravestone of a pirate to me. There was a skull and crossbones on it, which would normally have interested me but I wanted aunt Elinor to get us home. I think I disappointed him with my reaction. He stood looking, strangely lonely, as he watched us leave the churchyard. Perhaps when he saw aunt Elinor's shuffling gait he had understood?

'Nice old boy,' she said, when we were in the car.

'I suppose so,' I replied, guardedly. I wondered if she were testing me.

She glanced across at me and then said, 'Ah, I know what you're thinking. I'm a hypocrite. Well, that's not quite true. For one thing I see no reason to be impolite to anyone, providing they're civil to me, and for another . . . well, my fight is not with individuals but with the establishment, and specifically with their damnfool rules.' She went off into a kind of reverie which I was reluctant to break. 'Especially,' she finally said in a faraway voice, 'the rule that says Catholics can't be divorced.'

'You weren't a Catholic, were you, aunt Elinor?' I said, getting lost in all this tangled talk. Our family had always been Anglicans. Dinger and Oaky were Catholics and they had different RE classes from me at school.

She looked at me sharply again. 'No, you're right. But someone I knew was. Anyway, that's all in the past. I'm getting too nostalgic in my old age . . .'

I defended her. 'You're younger than nan.'

'Only in years,' she said. 'Look at that,' she pointed out of the car window at a line of trees. 'Know what they call those? The seven witches. That's what happens to you if you meddle with someone with stronger powers. They were seven junior witches who tried to take on the top witch in a battle of spells. They lost and have stood there as trees for two hundred years.'

'Is that true?' I asked.

'Who knows? That's how the story is told.'

She looked down at me. 'Rubbish really, but it might make a good story for you one day, when you become a writer.'

I asked her what she knew about waterwitches.

'Waterwitches? Well, that's a bit of an anomaly.' Sometimes she forgot I was only eleven years old and used words that were outside my vocabulary range. I asked her what it meant.

'Well, normally witches don't like water. They hate it.'

'Milky's mum said waterwitches live at the bottom of ponds and drag children down to chop them up, to use their blood and bits as potions in spells . . .'

She laughed.

'How . . . how would you get rid of a witch, just supposing you wanted to?' I asked, taking the plunge. 'Just supposing . . .?'

Her shiny features were devoid of any expression but I could sense she was concentrating on my question. The lids of her eyes were thin films when she blinked and even though her mouth was closed I could see her long, narrow teeth behind her tautly stretched lips.

'Well, this is going to sound funny coming from me, but I'm telling you what the general belief is . . . it's said that a Christian symbol is a powerful weapon against black magic, so I suppose something like a cross would deter a witch. Make her think twice about staying in the neighbourhood. Then there's her *familiars.*'

The way she said the word sent cold fingers down my back but I asked her what it meant.

'Witches are said to have cats as familiars . . . is this frightening you?' She glanced at me. 'I don't want to give you nightmares. Your nan will be straight round to complain.'

'No,' I lied. 'I've been thinkin' of doing something for an essay at school—on witches and wizards.'

'Ah, I see.' She fell silent.

I said, 'You were telling me about familiars, auntie.'

'Oh, yes. Well, they're usually cats but they can be any animal. They spy on people for the witch. Take back reports to her. In the old days the villagers would capture the familiar and kill it. A lot of innocent cats must have been killed in those days . . . besides people.'

We drove on through the countryside without talking. I stared out at the passing scenery. It was late evening and the sun was an orange ball behind the distant thickets. *Black and orange. Black and orange.* Venomous colours to me then, and now. There has always been something a little urgent in those two very contrasting hues. I felt a quickening of my heart and trickle of apprehension in my stomach. *Witches.* I was sorry I had ever heard the word. Jackie and Dinger were determined to get rid of the waterwitch. And I was no traitor. Not like Milky. It was Jackie really. I wanted her to like me. I could not bear the thought of her sneering at me the way she had done at Milky. The names she called him would have shrivelled my heart, had it been me. I had shown her where my badger lived but that had not impressed her. Now I could tell her how to get rid of the witch.

I was dropped at the house and aunt Elinor said, 'I shan't come in. Give my love to your grandmother.'

'Yes . . . and thanks, for a very nice day. I really enjoyed it.'

'Good. Let's do it again next year.' There was a wistful note to her voice.

'All right,' I said. 'Thanks again.'

She drove off down the long, black road by the Cherry Tree. I thought of Jackie and the fact that Dinger had had her to himself all day long. I wondered what they had been doing about getting rid of the waterwitch. Maybe they had managed it without me?

I shuffled round the back of the house, forgetting for once the ever-vigilant Mick, who flew at me out of the gloaming like some terrible demon. His chain stopped him a fraction before my throat, the jaws snapping together with the sound of marble bricks. I screamed.

Nan came hurring out of the back door. Her white hair, normally tied at the back in a bun, hung down, past her shoulders. She was wearing a white shift, a nightdress.

'What is it, boy?'

'That Mick,' I whined. 'He nearly bit my throat. He jumped up at me. He's always doing that . . .' I babbled on but I could not take my eyes from her hair. It was so beautiful. A strange, unearthly beauty which had caught me unawares. She normally had the appearance of being severe but the loose hair had transformed her completely. It was like a silver mane flowing down her back.

She walked up to Mick, who cringed before her, and whacked his rump with something. Mick yelped and retreated to the back of his kennel. It was a hairbrush she held in her hand. I had interrupted her in the middle of brushing her hair. For the moment she was some avenging angel, white with holy wrath, as she strode past me into the house, the long hair flying behind her and the nightdress billowing. She confronted me in the kitchen.

'Can't I have an early night without somebody wanting something? I have a bad migraine . . .' She rubbed her temples.

'Sorry, nan.'

'Hmm. Have a good birthday?'

'Yes thanks. Auntie sends her love.'

'Well, don't be long in going to bed. Your grandad and Dave are down the . . . they've gone out.'

She turned and was going through the door to the parlour when I said, 'Nan, do I have a cousin called Jennifer?'

Nan stopped and without turning round said, 'Did your aunt tell you?'

'She just said I had a cousin called Jennifer.'

'Then she's right, isn't she? Your aunt doesn't tell fibs. Jennifer's at school. Now I have a headache . . . you get to your bed soon boy.'

'Yes nan.' There was something obviously queer about Jennifer which the adults did not seem to want to discuss so I decided to let it go. What was one more cousin to me? I had nearly a dozen up north on my mother's side.

I crept back out of the house again and went to feed my badger. The evening was still and soft with the scent of lilac. This time he ate directly from my hand, his hard snout nosing against my palm. I was a blood-brother at last! An adopted member of the badger tribe. I was happy. I belonged to every badger that lived. They were my family and I was theirs. It was a good feeling.

# TWELVE

The last time I had been by a river late in the evening, after the fall of darkness, was when I went with Dave to Tilbury. He had taken me with him when he went to collect his pay for his last voyage. I remembered being impressed by the large, white fivers that he rolled into a tube and fastened with an elastic band. The river had been the Thames of course, and as we drove up, away from the docks, I looked back to see the dark shapes of the ships, liners and cargo vessels, drifting silently along the river, encrusted with jewels. The oil refineries, too, were festooned with the same bright gems and looked like futuristic cities about to ascend into the night skies, their catcrackers—tall chimneys burning waste gases—the tails of upturned rocket engines.

Now we were lying across the levee of the Crouch, the remnants of our former gang, looking out onto the shining, slate-black surface. I had climbed out of my bedroom window and down the drain pipe once I had been sure of grandad's snores. The other two had been waiting under the street lamp for me.

'Where have you been?' Jackie had hissed at me, her arms akimbo and face and body leaning forward like an adder about to strike.

'Had to wait till grandad was asleep,' I had stammered, afraid we would be heard.

A short snort of derision from Dinger had completed my misery.

Now they were telling me about the previous day's episode, what they had been doing while I was with aunt Elinor in Southend. They had attacked the rear of the house with catapults, getting bolder all the time, until Dinger eventually broke two windows. Then they had run away, fearful of retribution either from the witch or from adults who may have seen them damaging property.

'So what now?' said Jackie. 'What did you find out, Titch?'

I was eager to do my part.

'Well, religion and familiar animals . . . no *familiars*, that's it.'

'What familiars?'

'Animals. You know witches have cats. Well, they're them . . . familiars. They're the spies of the witch but she can use any animal she wants to.

Dinger said, 'I ain't seen no cat.'

'No,' I agreed. 'Me neither, but it might be dogs, owls, bats, anythin'.'

'I see.' Jackie's features were lost in the shadows from her hair but I could see she was nodding. The moon had come up and I felt vulnerable in its spotlight. 'What about religion?' she added. 'You said somethin' about religion.'

'Yeah, what do we do there?' asked Dinger.

'We get somethin' from a church. Somethin' holy, like a cross. Witches are afraid of things like that, so my aunt Elinor says.' I remembered something. 'You remember that picture we went to see about vampires? Well they got crosses, the people in that, to keep away the vampire, didn't they? Vampires sort of crumble to dust when the shadow of a cross falls on 'em,' I explained for Jackie's sake.

Jackie shuddered. 'She's not a vampire.'

'No, but it's the same sort of thing.'

'We could probably make one,' said Jackie.

Dinger said, 'Makin' one's no good. It's gotter come from a church. One that's been blessed. It's the holiness they can't stand.'

I envisaged us creeping into a church in the dead of night, down the aisle, and stealing the brass crucifix from the altar. I was sure God would not let us get away with such a crime, whether I believed in Him or not. Being inside a church at night would be punishment enough in any case. It was bad enough being in one alone during the day. They were spooky places, churches, whatever you liked to say about them. And outside, all around, were graves filled with dead bodies. I recalled a tale of one of the villagers who had seen the side of a box tomb fall away and was chased by the evil thing that escaped from the grave. He never saw it, he had confessed, but he had sensed and smelled it all the way across the marshland to his home, where he had arrived safe but sobbing with fear.

There was another story too, about someone on their way home across the saltings after being out at the pub. On passing the graveyard he had heard something and begun running. As he ran a little old lady, about two feet high, kept popping up in front of him and screaming into his face. The man died of a heart attack not long after blurting out the story to his wife.

'We'll get a cross from a grave,' said Dinger. 'That'll be easiest. Church'll be locked at this time of night in any case. See if we can find one of those wooden ones. Be easier to carry.'

'Good idea,' said Jackie. 'What do you say, Titch?'

The idea horrified me and despite Jackie's quick agreement, I could see she was afraid too. I guessed that getting one from a churchyard was preferable to her to actually entering a church and taking it from the altar. We could get into a lot of trouble with the police that way, whereas they might not miss one from the churchyard for ages, especially if we took one from some remote corner. An old one which no one visited any more.

'Sounds like the best idea,' I said, despite my fear. There was comfort in the fact that there were three of us. Perhaps I could stand guard on the outside while the other two went in?

'Which one's the nearest?' asked Jackie.

'S'n Mary's,' replied Dinger, without hesitation.

We all peered out across the fields that flanked the river but the night was deep enough to hide our destination. The light from the moon and the stars was not strong enough to throw visibility all the way to St Mary's. Jackie jumped up and began to walk, treading carefully along the levee. I think she was anxious to get it over with. Dinger and I followed. We walked in silence for about a mile, then dropped down onto the road which touched the bank at that point.

At one point a bird flew up from the grasses at our feet—a nightjar or something. Jackie screamed and my heart stopped in mid-beat. The three of us stood, terrified, for several minutes until the full realization of what it was sunk into our minds.

'Bird,' said Dinger. He sounded as if his mouth were full of something.

We continued walking and I remembered a line or two from *The Rime of the Ancient Mariner:*

*'Like one, that on the lonesome road*
*Doth walk in fear and dread,*
*And having once turned round walks on,*
*And turns no more his head;*
*Because he knows, a frightful fiend*
*Doth close behind him tread.'*

Aunt Elinor. Why did she have to read me these things? It was one of her favourite poems but she did not realize that it kept me awake at nights. I hated it.

*The church.*

It loomed out of the night, its surrounding pines giving it an even more forbidding aspect than I had previously imagined. Even Dinger, I could see, was not anxious to go any further. We stopped and stared at the eerie architecture that melted into darkness in all its crevices and recessed corners. It seemed to be waiting for us, almost as if it had been expecting us. In the pines was a liquid blackness that dripped from their branches and gathered in pools around their trunks. I had something caught in my throat as I studied the vague shapes of tombs, gravestones and crosses that, like their lord the church, were waiting for us to enter their grounds.

'Titch, you go . . .' began Jackie.

'Never, never, never,' I blurted out, quickly. Not even for Jackie would I enter such a place full of menace. Demons, phantoms, witches, hellhounds, they were all there. The previous night I had had a nightmare about a pig with a man's face, that rushed squealing out of a dark copse and bit me on the thigh. I had run with the horrible beast still clinging tenaciously to my flesh. Somewhere its counterpart, a man with a pig's face, was waiting to drop out of the branches of a tree. Let him drop on somebody else.

'There, look!' whispered Dinger.

I followed his pointing finger with trepidation, expecting something which would confirm all my worst fears and getting ready to run like a rabbit. Instead there were some objects leaning against the churchyard wall.

'Gravestones,' I said. There were several broken tombstones propped up against the wall.

'There's a cross there, look.'

Then I saw it. A waist-high cross, broken low down the stem, and lying on its side against the rectangular tombstones.

'We'll never carry that,' I gasped.

Dinger sounded adamant. 'We *can*.'

We crept round by the side wall and reached over, hauling the heavy marble cross over to our side. Then Jackie and Dinger took an arm each while I took the stem. We began to stagger along the dark road with our load.

The cross was very heavy. The other two were stronger than I was but I could hear them grunting with the exertion. My arms felt as if they were being pulled in opposite directions by two cart horses. When we reached a canopy of trees, I asked for a halt. My fear of pig-men had gone, had been replaced by something else.

'What's the matter?' asked Jackie, but the strain was evident in her voice.

'S'too heavy,' I said again. 'We'll *never* get it there.'

'We *will*,' said Dinger. My heart sank at hearing his tone. He had set his mind on carrying that cross to the White House and I knew that this feat would be accomplished by one means or another. Dinger would not be thwarted.

We picked up the cross again and began the long trudge to the White House. I can still remember that night as being one of the worst in my life. My whole body was pushed to the limits of its capability. All fear was lost in the misery of exhaustion. Even the original purpose was pushed aside by the monotonous pain, and one foot followed another on the hard, night road. Each jarring step I took sent fresh tremors of agony up through the bones of my legs, to my spine, ribs and almost numb shoulders. My body soon disowned my arms. They became like the grafted limbs of a stranger. They still sent their pain to me but it was a second-hand pain which seemed to come from a far-off remote source somewhere out in the stars. I would never be able to stop it because I had no control over it. Even were I to release the cross, divest myself of that terrible weight, the pain would not cease because it came to me from a place I could not reach, could not influence.

Halfway to the house Jackie gave up and Dinger made me take the opposite arm of the cross. We dragged our burden along the road, the broken end of the stem grooving the tarmac and leaving a snaking line of white in our wake. We pulled like two oxen, our arms behind us and our teeth set into the night, leaning forward towards our goal. The cross made a noise against the road which screeched in my ears. All I wanted was for the journey to end. The worst of the pain was in my head. I could hardly see through its denseness.

The wash of sweat dried on my face and a fresh wetness took its place.

'Keep going. Keep going,' was all I could hear from Dinger. Jackie walked silently beside us, almost as if she knew that any words from her would cause us to stop, to break into brittle pieces which used to be soft flesh.

'Someone's comin',' said Jackie.

We pulled up, the noise of the cross scraping on the road ceasing immediately. I tried to listen but all I could hear was the singing agony of my headache.

'Quick. In the ditch,' whispered Dinger.

We turned and pulled the stone crucifix with us, heaving it into the ditch. I fell in after it and lay in the moist channel, hoping I need never have to move again. The palms of my hands felt sticky where the edge of the marble had been digging in, and I realized they were bleeding. I licked the warm blood, grateful for anything that would slake my parched throat.

Then I heard the sound. A kind of slopping walk, like someone with loose slippers on their feet. A shape passed above us, not looking down. A giant, or so it seemed. There was a flapping sound as the figure's legs passed by not a foot from my eyes and I could smell estuary mud. It had the distinctive odour of something rotting. I realized the figure was wet and the sound was that of cloth slapping against flesh. Then it was gone, into the darkness of the avenue ahead.

We stayed in the ditch for some time, regaining our strength. The pain in my head ebbed and the feeling returned to my arms in thorny waves. As I lay back, I stared at the night sky and saw a shooting star. It was so peaceful in that groove of the world I wanted to sleep but as my sense of touch returned, and the hurt in my muscles began to retreat, my awareness of our position made me sit up sharply. Something moved and scrambled along the ditch a few yards away. There were rats here and perhaps snakes.

'Let's go,' I said. 'Let's get on. We've got to get home some time.'

Dinger pulled himself wearily upright and Jackie stood up. She began to haul the cross out of the ditch on her own. I had hoped we could leave it where it was but I could see now that there was no chance of doing that.

We began the journey again and it was as if we had never rested. My muscles started screaming anew. The pain in my head revived itself. We took turns, two pulling while the other rested, trailing behind. The road seemed endless but finally we came to what was by then a mythical place, a place of which I had dreamt for a thousand years.

The house. The White House.

Without pausing to consider the danger, we opened the gate and dragged the cross along the weed-covered path. Then we let it fall onto the steps that led to the front door. It broke into two pieces, snapping just below the cross-piece. We turned as if we had just delivered something ordinary like the daily newspaper or a parcel, and walked back up the path and out of the gate. Our mission was over. The waterwitch could not possibly ignore such a powerful warning. A cross. A holy cross. The labour of transporting it over two miles from the church was so important to us, we felt she could not possibly ignore it. She would leave. We would win. Oaky would be avenged.

I did not have the strength to clamber up the drainpipe to my room. I knocked lightly on the back door and eventually uncle Dave opened it.

'Just been for a walk,' I mumbled.

He stood there in his pyjamas and looked me up and down.

'At three in the morning? You look a mess. You'd better get on up back to bed before someone else wakes up. I'll talk to you later.'

Nan called from her bed in the front room but Dave said, 'Just going out to the toilet, mother.'

I went upstairs quietly and fell into bed, fully clothed. Grandad was still snoring.

Dave never did mention the incident again.

# THIRTEEN

There were three dead chickens in the yard, three small brown heaps lying in the dust. I could see the wind fluffing their feathers. I was about to call nan, hoping the culprit was Mick, when I saw Dave coming out of the shed with his shotgun. He picked up the corpses and threw them into the corner of the yard by the dustbins. Then he saw me staring out of his bedroom window. I had gone in there to talk to him about the previous evening.

'Fox,' he called. 'Got into the yard just after dawn. Saw the bugger but I couldn't get to the gun in time.'

'Why didn't Mick get him?' I asked.

'That's what woke me, Mick barking.' He pointed to the kennel. 'He barked loud enough all right but he was on a short chain. You kept complaining he was after you so I shortened his chain.'

I hung my head. 'I'm sorry Dave.'

He waved a hand at me. 'Don't worry about it kid. Mum's upset but she'll come round. S'not your fault the dog don't like you. I don't like the beggar much either, but he's a good guard dog. I'll have to put his old chain back on, so keep out of his way.'

I nodded. I knew I was indirectly to blame for the dead hens. I had witnessed a morning of small disasters for the whole family. Firstly, one of the straps on grandad's artificial leg had snapped as he was pulling it on. He had thrown the leg to the floor in frustration, using a curse I had to guess the meaning of, and had dented the aluminium rim which his stump filled. When he had tried to push his stump inside again, it wouldn't fit, and he had cursed all the more. I had been tired after the night's escapades and wanted to sleep. Finally nan had come up to find out what all the racket was about and after admonishing grandad for using obscene language she had gone downstairs to fetch a hammer. I then had to endure about ten minutes banging, interspersed by grunts, until he had it back to the right shape for his stump.

When he had finally gone I jumped out of bed, still fully clothed, to find that every muscle in my body had seized. Hobbling to the china bowl, I filled it from the water jug, then began to wash myself thoroughly. There had been caked blood on my hands and mud just about everywhere else and it had taken some time to clean myself enough to pass inspection. The water in the bowl looked like it had come from a sewer, so I emptied it out of the window.

In the scullery nan had been pacing up and down because for to weeks she had been expecting the plumbers to arrive to fit taps in the house. For years we had had to trudge to the pump in the middle of the row of eight cottages and carry water to the house in buckets. While this had been the only method by which to obtain water, nan had been happy enough with it. However, when the farmer who owned the cottages came to tell her that he was having cold water pipes fitted to all the houses, she couldn't wait to get them in. For some reason, she had it in her head that the plumbers would start at the south end of the row, in which case we would have been second in line. They had started at the north end the day before and nan was both angry and bitterly disappointed. She knew it would be weeks before they reached our house and on top of that she would have to endure the crowing of those who had already had their taps fitted, while she still waited. I kept out of her way. She was in no mood for young boys, so after Dave had gone off with his gun I wolfed down some cornflakes and toast, and left by the front door.

After searching all our usual places I still hadn't found Dinger and Jackie. Finally I bucked up courage and went to Dinger's house. His mother was a bad-tempered woman with a face like an axe and I avoided her as much as possible.

I knocked timidly on the door and she appeared a few moments later in a housecoat and turban.

'Yes?'

'Is, er, John in please, Mrs Bellchamber?' His real christian name always sounded so false, as if it were someone else I was asking for, and not Dinger at all. It did not feel easy on my tongue.

'Upstairs,' she snapped, and nodded me inside. 'Bloody houseful in a minute.'

I went in reluctantly. I disliked the smell of Dinger's house and it always made me feel uneasy. It wasn't that the house was dirty. That wouldn't have worried me at eleven years of age anyway. It was a *strange* smell, the kind of sickly odour that old furniture often hinted at in the junk shops frequented by my grandfather. It didn't make me feel ill exactly, but I was aware of it the whole time I was in the house. It never became so familiar that I could forget it.

Dinger was in his bedroom and Jackie was there too.

'We waited for you this morning,' Jackie said, almost apologetically, which made me realize they had not done so.

'OK. My grandad broke his leg . . . his tin one. I had to wait until he'd gone.'

Jackie sniggered.

I coloured and said, 'He can't help it. It got shot off during the Great War.'

'It's just, you said tin,' she replied. 'Sounded a bit funny, breaking a tin leg.'

'Well . . .'

'Oh, stop *arguin'*,' said Dinger. He looked a little peeved and I guessed the reason for his pique was because Jackie was paying some attention to me. She realized it too and I suppose it made her feel special because she ignored him and began chattering to me about how she had managed to get back indoors in the early hours of the morning without being found out. Not many people locked their houses up for the night in our village. My nan was an exception. So both Dinger and Jackie had had an easier exit and entry than me.

'Shall we go out?' I said, during a lull in her chatter. The smell was beginning to rest uneasily on my stomach. Also my muscles still ached and I wanted to walk the stiffness out of them.

'Where shall we go?'

Dinger said, 'We could go and look at the White House. See if the cross has done any good. Must 'ave worked by now, if it was going to.' I think he felt that if he could get us out of the house he could recapture Jackie's interest. I didn't want to lose her attention but at the same time I wanted to be free of the sickly odour presented by the room we were in. It was the kind of bedroom which annoyed me. There was at least a score of model aeroplanes hanging by threads from the ceiling, all painted in garish colours and tilted at various angles of dive and flight. On the mantelpiece was a crystal set which Dinger's father had made for him and above it were some replica flintlock pistols. There were various other items of similar breed and manufacture. The only thing I really approved of was a pile of *Eagle* annuals which I had been trying to borrow ever since I had known Dinger. It had grown since our first meeting but though I was often promised a loan, those promises never materialized into anything solid. For the rest of the junk though, he could keep it. I was never a maker of models or boys' artefacts. Such activities bored me intensely as I could see no real end product, except *another* plane to hang from the ceiling, or, if it were a glider, to launch on the wind only to watch it crash to the ground in pieces a few moments later.

We left the house and began the long walk downhill from Dinger's cottage to the White House. As we reached the bottom of the slope I could see the patches of water out on the flatlands behind the houses, shining like mirrors. There would be herons out there, and hawks, and foxes. The place was teeming with wildlife. I thought about my badger and our mutual bond. There was something special about being friends with a badger.

We reached the White House.

'It's gone,' said Dinger in surprise

I think we had all expected the cross still to be there. It was the waterwitch who should have disappeared, not the sacred symbol of our power over her.

There was a small residue of white dust visible on the step. It was the only evidence that there had ever been a long journey through the night carrying an unbearable load: that and our aching muscles.

'What's she done with it?' asked Jackie, leaning over the fence. 'I bet she's thrown it in the pond.'

'She wouldn't do that,' I argued. 'She can't touch it if it's holy and the pond is where she lives for part of the time. She wouldn't want it there—that's the last place.'

'So *you* say,' snapped Jackie. 'But we've spent all that time *gettin'* it and now it hasn't worked. It was *your* idea,' she accused.

'We don't know it hasn't worked,' said Dinger. I was amazed at the time that he was siding with me, but much later I realized his concern was not for me, but himself. He, Dinger, had carried that cross to the detriment of his mind and body, and if all that suffering was a waste of time then he would have felt himself a fool.

We stood in silence for about ten minutes, staring at the windows of the house, watching for a sign. At the end of that time came the unmistakable sound of a door slamming.

'It hasn't worked,' said Jackie in a low voice. 'She's still in there. We'd better get away from here before she sees us and work out another plan.'

Dinger kicked the gate. 'Bugger,' he swore. 'I thought it would work.'

In the copse which had become our hideout Jackie told us we had to do something more powerful than just plant religious symbols on doorsteps. 'You got to fight the way they do . . . with witchcraft.'

The way she said it made my skin go cold.

'What do you mean?' I asked.

'We got to make a sacrifice,' she said. 'One of them familiars.'

Suddenly, I found myself where Milky must have stood. What had begun as a serious 'game' was now totally out of hand. There was a fanatical look in Jackie's eyes which frightened me and I knew I had gone about as far as I could.

'She hasn't got any pets,' I began, hoping to dissuade her from going any further. 'Least, I haven't seen any.'

'You said any animal would do,' interrupted Dinger.

'I did *not*,' I protested. 'I said a cat . . .'

Jackie cried, 'You get us *your* cat. You said you hated it. It'll do us as a familiar.'

'No!'

Dinger stood up, his fists bunched and his head lowered.

'You what, Titch? You what?'

'I'm not getting my . . . nan's cat,' I stammered. 'I don't care. I'm not getting it. Listen,' I pleaded, 'you can't just kill things. It's not right.'

'*She* killed Oaky,' said Jackie, simply.

'We said that, but I don't think it's true any more. I think we just *said* it. This is silly. It's only a game, really. Let's forget it now. It's going on too long. There's no such thing . . . really.'

'Yes there is,' replied Jackie, her eyes narrowing and a slight smile appearing. 'Isn't there, Dinger?' There was a sweetness to the words that chilled me.

Dinger was still in his fighting stance and he looked across at her. He lowered his arms, smirking as he did so.

'She's right,' he said.

'We got to kill a familiar,' Jackie said. 'An eye for an eye.'

I was horrified by her tone, her whole demeanour. 'You just want to kill something,' I accused her. 'Don't you? Don't you?' I found it hard to control my voice and it rose to a high pitch.

'If we got to, then we got to. I can't help that, can I? It's not cruel if you do it for a reason, is it? I don't think it's cruel. *She's* cruel.'

The tears came to my eyes. I was losing Jackie. She wanted to perpetuate a bad game which was no longer a game. It was deadly serious. I had already transgressed more unwritten laws under her direction than was comfortable for my nature. To kill someone's pet in cold blood was quite beyond me.

'He's *crying*,' said Jackie. 'What a cry baby.'

'I'm not crying,' I shouted through the tears. 'I hate you. I hate you both.' Suddenly, a slow fury that had built up inside me was unleashed, and I screamed at them. 'Don't you come *near* me! I'll smash you, Dinger Bell. I hate your bloody guts, you bloody bastard.'

They were shocked by my outburst and Dinger stumbled backwards a couple of paces.

'Don't come near me,' I cried again. 'I will. I'll punch your face in.' I was crying profusely by this time and the words were choked by the emotion that flooded out. They both stood there, white-faced, watching me wave my arms wildly. Torrent after torrent of threats poured from my lips. I hardly knew what I was saying as each word tumbled out after the next. I called them all the worst names I could think of and they stood there and took it all without a movement. Finally, I ran out of emotion and my angry tears dried on my cheeks, making them stiff. I stood watching them, feeling very awkward but determined not to unbend. Then I saw Jackie glance sideways at Dinger and almost in accord they turned and walked away. I wanted to run after Jackie, try to explain how I felt, tell her that . . . that she was a special person to me, that I liked her very much, that . . .

I turned and began to walk home.

# FOURTEEN

'Grandad, I know I've asked you before but tell me again about the time you lost your leg.'

'Ah, I think you 'ave asked me that, once or twice. Well, the frank truth of the matter is, I was in a terrible bayonet charge. Them Yanks was there by then, and o' course the Frenchies. Side by side we was, an' screamin' fit to scare the livin' shades out of those devils, when suddenly, over this ridge comes an enemy officer on a horse. I tell you boy, we was never more surprised in our lives—it was like summat out of *King Arthur*. He had a bright helmet on 'is head, I remember, shining like he was a god, and in his hand was a flashin' sabre, and he sliced the air with it as if he was cuttin' off rashers of bacon. Straight towards me he came, that mounted Hun, an' me havin' expended all me ammo. Cut me leg clean through, he did, as I stuck me bayonet into his belly—we both went down together, only he was dead, see, and I was still a good three-quarters mortal . . .'

Those fears without names or forms are the worst. On the night of aunt Elinor's death I woke with my heart in my hands and cold sweat soaking the sheets. Some nameless dread had crept into me during sleep and I knew I should be awake until morning.

At first light nan came up to tell me that aunt Elinor had died. I could see she had been crying and in the beginning that distressed me more than her news. It was only when she left me that it sunk in and then I began to weep softly. After a while I got out of bed and went to sit on the top of the stairs, not wanting to go down into a house full of grief. I could hear them talking downstairs.

'She would have suffered, poor dear,' nan was saying,

'that's why she did it of course . . .' The words were gulped rather than spoken clearly, and from my hidden seat at the top of the stairs I could hear her crying again.

Dave said, 'S'best this way, mum, You know what the doctor said. She would've died in six months anyway. Come on, don't cry. Shall I get Mrs Polonsten to come in?'

'No, no. It's all right. I'll be all right. Let's make a cup of tea. Give me something to do. As long as I keep busy for a few days, just till after the funeral. I'll be all right.'

I never knew nan when she was *not* busy, so I found this idea a little strange. What was she going to do? Work through the night as well?

Grandad said, 'Will the vicar take her?'

There was silence, followed by nan saying, 'What do you mean, dad? Of course he will. Don't matter that she didn't believe in God, does it?' The last words had an unsure note to them, as if distress were being overlaid with injuries just too horrible to contemplate.

'She committed suicide. Might not bury her regular with the others in the churchyard.'

Nan was indignant. 'Nonsense. That's just Catholics, not us. Not if I have anything to do with it.'

Grandad said, 'Well, you're the churcher. You should know, mother. Anyways, I don't think the woman would 'ave cared. She didn't believe, an' that's a fact.'

'*She* might not have done,' answered nan, her grief-stricken tones replaced by a lofty voice, 'but I do. I'm not having any sister of mine buried on pagan ground.'

I wondered at the time where they put the dead people who could not be buried in a churchyard. I had a mental picture of a solitary gravestone somewhere in a meadow, with the cows eating the grass on the mound and rabbits digging burrows round it. I could not ever remember seeing such a grave but somehow I felt aunt Elinor would have approved of it.

I heard nan say, 'Is the boy all right?'

Dave replied, 'I'll go up and look in a minute.' There was a pause, then he said, 'Do you think the boy'll get anything? She was very fond of him.'

'I don't think this is the time to be talking about such things,' said nan, 'but since you've brought it up I might as well tell you. I had a talk with Elinor some time ago. She's leaving a bit to the boy, but not to be touched till he's grown. All the rest will go to the daughter. That's only right, since *his* family will have nothing to do with her.'

Daughter? My family? What was all that about? Aunt Elinor was not even married.

Dave said, 'You're right. Jenny'll need it to finish her schooling. Pity the lad couldn't 'ave gone to a boarding school too. He's a bright little bugger. Still, that wasn't up to El. . .'

'She did make suggestions,' replied nan, 'but his dad said no. Wouldn't be fair on his brothers. George is a bit of a stickler for fairness.'

'Pity 'e don't take a fairer share in the boy's raisin' then, ain't it?' muttered grandad.

'That's as maybe,' said nan, 'but we're not all perfect. Look at little Jennifer's lot . . .'

'She's hardly little any longer,' said Dave. 'El was a country girl from a farm labouring background. That's what his family couldn't take. I tell you what, if I ever run into any of 'em they'll feel the weight of my fist. Just give me a chance to put a few of 'em straight . . .'

Nan said, 'That's enough of that talk young man. I won't have you talking violence in my house. Go up and see the boy. You're his favourite. You could do more good by making sure he doesn't suffer through all this . . .'

I quickly slunk back into the bedroom and lay on the bed but before Dave could come upstairs there was a knock on the front door. It was answered and I heard Cathy's concerned voice floating up from the parlour.

'Dave. I just heard about Elinor. I am sorry.'

'One of those things, Cath. Here, you have a word with mum, love. I'm just going upstairs to see young Titch.'

I heard his feet on the stairs.

'You all right mate?' he said, coming into the room and sitting on the bed.

'Yes.'

'Don't take it so bad. You knew she was ill, didn't you? We've all got to go some time.' He jumped up in mock disgust. 'Look at your bed, you oaf. Ain't you got any couth?'

I loved him when he clowned around like this but the confusing conversation downstairs on top of the bad news was weighing heavy on my heart.

'Have you seen my bed? Neat and taut as a drumskin. That's what military training does for you . . .' Dave had deliberately joined the Merchant Navy to get out of his conscription and while he was home he *never* made his bed.

'Man on the flying horse won't mind,' I said.

'No, but your nan will, and she's got a bigger whip. Best make it before she sees it and goes berserk, beating everybody in sight. Cath's here. She won't take kindly to a lickin' from your nan . . .' He began tucking in the sheets and blanket.

'Dave.'

'What?'

'How did aunt Elinor commit suicide?'

He paused in his actions and stared at me hard.

'You've been eavesdroppin'.'

'Couldn't help it. I was on my way downstairs when I heard grandad say it. Well, how did she?'

'You sure you want to know? Anyway, I don't think I should tell you. Dunno whether your nan would approve.'

'Someone's bound to tell me sooner or later,' I said.

He sighed and shrugged. 'She took some pills and went to sleep in the bath.' He paused, as if reflecting on something. 'If she'd have only got undressed first, they might never have guessed. But El was funny about things like that . . .' I looked at his face and realized he was talking to himself, not me. He caught my stare and seemed embarrassed. Then he directed his attentions to the bed again. I helped him and when we had finished, he said, 'Come on, let's go and see Cath. You get dressed.'

I did as I was told.

While I dressed, I said, 'So aunt Elinor's Jennifer's away at school somewhere?'

'You've got ears like an elephant,' he said, after another long searching look at my face.

'African or Indian?'

'Which one's got the biggest lugs?'

'African.'

'That's you then. Now don't go and upset your nan any more. You can talk about these things later, when you're a bit older. They'll keep. They ain't going away, that's for sure.'

We both went down to the parlour where Cathy had her hand on nan's arm. Grandad had gone out. I sat on the bed settee with Cathy while nan made some tea. We drank the tea and talked about everything except aunt Elinor. Finally nan said, 'I've got to go and see her tomorrow. You can come too Raymond.'

'See who?'

'Your aunt Elinor . . . your *great* aunt Elinor,' she corrected herself as if, now that she was dead, it was important to get her title absolutely correct. 'Pay our last respects.'

Panic began welling up inside me. She meant I would have to see a dead body. I felt Cathy's hand close around mine and I looked up into her round face with its bright red lips. Cathy knew what I was going to say.

'I don't want to,' I said, quietly. 'Please nan.'

'Does he have to?' asked Cathy, before nan could say anything.

Nan replied, 'Well, it's right he should. Family . . .'

'Mum,' said Dave in a firm voice. 'Leave the lad be. He don't need to come. No one will miss him. You'll just give him nightmares. You know what he's like . . . we'll have him screaming the house down.'

To my great relief nan shrugged her shoulders with a submissive gesture and I knew that I had been saved. I could never have gone willingly. They would have had to drag me there. The fact that I knew and loved aunt Elinor in life would have made it worse, not better. I had a mental picture of her lying in her coffin, her eyes wide and staring sightlessly at the tall, lit candles that surrounded her.

'You can let go of my girl's hand now Titch,' said Dave, after nan had left the room. 'I'll start to get jealous.' He was smiling but I felt myself blushing furiously.

Cathy still kept hold of me and said, 'Leave him alone. He's a good looking lad. I might even ask him out for a date one of these days, when he's a bit older.'

I stared at a bowl of apples on the table. Now I could understand why Dave punched his wardrobe door. The feelings in my breast were in a turmoil, as if a storm were passing through me. I did not know which way to look. I pulled my hand away quickly and said, 'Got to go and feed Jessica.'

I left the house and went to Jessica's cage. She was as pleased to see me as ever and ran backwards and forwards in her excitement. I gave her the bread and milk and left her guzzling while I sat under a greengage tree and thought about things. When she had finished eating I let her nuzzle my hand for a while but my mind was still occupied. Her apple-pip eyes looked reproachfully after me as I walked away, under the trees that afforded her partial shelter.

There was a lot to think about. Aunt Elinor had gone. Suicide. I recalled a conversation that Dave and I had had with Cathy one Sunday when she came round to tea.

Dave had stated, 'Men are stronger than women.' He was arguing with Cathy about which sex was the superior, naturally believing his own far outstripped Cathy's in all respects.

'In general they're physically stronger,' agreed Cathy, 'but women are more intelligent. There's positive discrimination towards boys taking the eleven-plus.'

I did not know what she meant and I was sure Dave didn't either but both of us were too afraid of being humiliated to ask. She explained for us.

'. . . that means, if the results weren't handicapped in favour of the boys, the grammar schools would be full of girls because boys aren't as clever as girls at that age . . .' And she added with a significant look at Dave, '. . . sometimes they never do catch up.'

So far they had ten points each.

'More women go nutty,' stated Dave. 'They're always going to the doctor for pills for their nerves and things.'

'That's a gross generalization Dave Swan, and I'm not sure it's even true. Anyway, if you take mental illness to its logical conclusion, which is suicide, then you're wrong. More men commit suicide than women.'

'Who says so?' retorted Dave.

'I saw the results of a survey in a magazine. Almost twice as many men commit suicide.' She was pretty smug and I could see Dave's face beginning to show signs of defeat. Cathy was worse than a schoolteacher when it came to facts. Then a peculiar look came into his eyes.

'More men *actually* commit suicide?' he asked for confirmation.

She nodded hard, almost as if she were sorry she had him cornered.

'That's because,' Dave said in measured tones, 'they're better at doing it than women. Don't mean the women don't try. They're just not as good at it as the men.'

They both laughed after that and I joined in with them. He was really sharp sometimes, my uncle Dave, and Cathy knew it. She somehow managed to winkle these dry witticisms from him and I could see she loved him for responding so well.

*Suicide.* Aunt Elinor was still on my mind. At least I wouldn't have to see her body. The funny thing was I saw dead animals quite often and they didn't bother me. Of course, a human was a different thing. You didn't get ghosts of animals for a start . . .

The seagulls had gathered in the middle of the field so as to have a clear sighting of any predators. One thing I could never figure out was why they always faced the same way as each other. Once upon a time I used to think it was something to do with the direction of the wind but on further investigation found that sometimes they faced to windward and sometimes to leeward. I never did find an explanation.

As I walked towards them they took to the air.

I suddenly found myself at the allotments and decided to

have a look at the badger's sett. I had never been there at that time of day before: it was almost noon. I approached the ditch cautiously, hoping to catch him nosing around in the bracken.

As I looked down into the ditch I could see something had flattened the weeds around the hawthorn and I immediately thought of Peter, the dog. Had he been after my badger? I looked for the entrance to the sett in the roots of the tree and saw that the earth had been disturbed. Where the camouflaged opening between the roots had been was a tangle of grass and twigs. Peter *had* been there. Then I noticed the snare.

I bent down and took the wire in my fingers. *Someone had set a trap for my badger.* Anger and frustration filled my breast. Who would do a thing like that? Grandad? Or maybe one of the other allotment owners? I wrenched out the peg and threw the snare into the field. Stupid, stupid people, I thought. Why did they always have to kill things? Why couldn't they leave them alone.

Suddenly I stopped. I felt a sick feeling creeping into my stomach. *Jackie had known where the badgers lived.* Surely they wouldn't do *that*? Then I remembered Dinger and the frogs . . . and all those other creatures he took a delight in torturing. They hated me, those two. They would do it to get at me. I had to find them and have it out with them. Maybe they had one of the badgers in a cage or something? Maybe they had caught it to use as bait, so that I would come looking for them? I didn't care if it was a trap. I *had* to do something about it. If they did have one of the badgers, it would be *mine* they had. He was the only one who trusted people. Any of the other badgers would avoid the scent that human hands left on a snare.

There was a time, I suppose I must have been about six years old, when rituals were a very important part of my life. In order to ward off the horrors of the night I used to go through a series of activities when preparing to settle down to sleep. These activities had to be done in the right order or the protection was flawed and the magic nullified. Firstly I would fold my clothes carefully as I undressed, always starting with my shoes and socks and working upwards. The neat pile would be placed by my bedside, with the shoes on top. Next, I would put on my pyjamas, starting with the jacket. I would chuck under the bed any toys I had left out, in case they should come to life once the candle had been snuffed. Finally, I would say my prayers and climb into bed on the *right* hand side. It had to be the right—why, I did not know but it was most important that I didn't forget this part of the ritual.

Somewhere between the ages of six and eleven I had abandoned this practice as being worthless. There were still dwarves in the cupboards and giants lying full length across the room, whatever I did, and sleep did not come any the more quickly or easily. There were some things I did still cling to however. These were mostly daytime rituals, like turning round three times before crossing a bridge over a stream in case there was a monster underneath. A more practical one was the practice of doing something dangerous before undertaking a distasteful task. In this way I would have proved my worth before attempting something else which would need courage and fortitude. I was going to have to face Dinger and Jackie in anger. It was not a task I was looking forward to without some feelings of apprehension.

There were several ways in which I could prove myself but the most practical and available one was to climb a very tall and difficult tree. On occasion, while out for a casual walk, I would note any trees that might fit my specifications for future use. One of these was a giant cedar not far from the Cherry Tree pub and I set off across the fields in the direction of my goal.

When I reached the cedar and looked up, through the shelves of its branches, my heart was beating fast. I had to get to the top or the whole exercise was useless and the highest branch seemed almost to reach the clouds. It was dark and gloomy within the leafy layers too, which did not add to my optimism.

In order to reach the first bough I had to place a dead branch up against the trunk and shin up it quickly before it broke beneath my weight. Thus I established myself at my base camp and surveyed the journey upwards. There were one or two places, about sixty feet off the gròund, where I was going to have to stretch on tiptoe between one branch and another and I knew I was going to be sick with fright when the time came to attempt it. Nevertheless, it had to be done. I began heaving myself up the first stage, cuddling the trunk of the tree as I straddled the thick, rounded limbs of the lower section. Once I had to put my hand right into a hollow knothole, praying there would not be a bird or squirrel inside that would attack my fingers. I tried not to look down the whole while, but there were situations when it was impossible not to and I could see the hard earth below, waiting to come up and knock the life from my body with one mighty punch.

When I reached the points where I had to stretch my legs were shaking so much I was in danger of wobbling myself to my death. I thought about other, pleasant things as I reached out for the next branch, all the while making decisions to turn back at the very next point of difficulty, yet never doing so. The boughs became thinner and thinner and bent under my weight. There was a strong wind near the top which made the tree sway alarmingly from side to side and I could hear my teeth chattering inside my skull. Then I was *there*, at the highest point that could possibly support my body and a feeling of exhilaration swept through my bones.

I forced my way through the thick foliage to seek a sitting position on my precarious perch and surveyed the world. My seat was at least three houses high and the flat fields stretched out below my feet taking in rivers, villages, guarded over by church spires and clumps of woodland like the gatherings of small armed bands of men. I deliberately refrained from looking directly downwards because I knew that soon I would have to embark on that journey too, knowing it was a more hazardous one than the climb upwards. I felt like the king of all the world. I was completely alone. I could make laws that all would have to adhere to or else suffer my displeasure. The feeling of achievement was easy to transmute into a feeling of power. I suddenly remembered the reason why I had originally climbed the tree. Dinger and Jackie. I had to get down and find them while I still retained that sense of confidence in my own abilities. The anger came flooding back to me.

Just as I was about to begin climbing down something caught my eye. Out by the river I could see a lone figure moving at a trotting pace along the top of a dyke. It was not hard to recognize the slightly hunched figure of the man who was looking for Amy Johnson. His characteristic spidery walk, as if one leg were trying to go in the opposite direction to the other, was accentuated by the loping run and made all the more comic by the fact that he was pushing a wheelbarrow before him at the same time. He *was* like a character out of comic cuts—a cartoon drawing that had suddenly achieved animation. I began to laugh, the mirth taking hold of my body in waves which almost reached hysteria. Tears rolled down my cheeks as I clung for dear life to the trunk, swaying like the mast of a boat on high seas. I knew I was in grave danger of falling off the branch but still I could not stop laughing. I was caught in the terrible grip of an image so humorous I was choking with mirth. Fear had me in its clutches too but my sense of the ridiculous was stronger. Twice I almost lost my hold as my body shook along with the top of the cedar. I gagged in fright both times but only had to glance towards the river for the braying to start afresh. At one point I could hardly catch my breath in between bouts. Finally the silly man disappeared down the far side of the dyke and the laughter subsided gradually.

A feeling of relief followed. My stomach ached with the spasms it had recently undergone and there was a weakness in my arms and legs not previously there. Laughter is a terrible energy drainer.

The birds that had not been frightened away by my climb up the tree had certainly been dispersed by my laughter. They had quit their branches on all sides. Now I felt truly alone. The feeling of solitude was enhanced by that of a sense of isolation. Looking out over the fields and waterways, it appeared to me that the whole surface of the earth was being drawn towards my tree as water to a waterspout. Green fields and brown flowed inward to the base of the trunk to fountain upwards in a rush of leaves and wood. I was balanced on the head of this fountain, like a buoyant piece of flotsam, dependent on the force of the flow to maintain my perch. The illusion lasted a long time and when I had exhausted my mental reservoir I began the perilous journey down.

Before I began the descent I noticed that the water in the river had reached the top of the dykes and was splashing over in places. We were due a spring tide soon. On occasion the fields nearest the river became waterlogged and our playgrounds were reduced in size. I wondered what had happened to the man with the wheelbarrow and amused myself with a mental picture of him paddling out to sea using the barrow as a craft. In this way I managed to reach the bottom of the tree without any periods of panic.

I was ready to find Jackie and Dinger, and confront them.

# FIFTEEN

A whole week went by, however, before I was to see the pair again. It was the day after aunt Elinor's funeral that I began my search for them in earnest. I tried all the usual haunts but could not find a trace of either Dinger or Jackie. After exhausting the obvious places and with my temper settling somewhat into determination rather than rage, I began to look further afield. I visited the village dump, an old wreck stuck in the estuary mud, a fort out on the sea wall and a tree den, all places we had used at one time or another.

Jackie and Dinger were not at any of them however. Nor were they at the stickleback stream where we used to catch our pets in wine bottles with the dented bottoms holed and muslin over the necks. I tried the hollow oak by the church, the bramble country and the land owned by the War Department. Finally, I found myself at the river and walked along it till I came to the mills. Milky was there on the wharf, fishing for smelt.

'Wuppa Milky,' I said, shyly. I had not seen him since he had walked away from the White House and out of the gang.

'Wuppa Titch,' he replied. He concentrated on his bottle-cork float, which was twitching on the surface of the water. The reflection of the rodless line ran between the wharves and below his dangling feet. Suddenly he gave the line a quick jerk and then began pulling in. The smooth surface broke into active silver as he whipped a twisting smelt from the water. He unhooked it and placed it by six or seven of its kin.

I sat down beside him as he baited the tiny hook with bread paste and looked out over the peaceful scene. Much of the area in and around Tenbridge was below sea level and pools of surface water lay in the fields beyond the river banks. Cattle and horses grazed on the dry patches in the meadows. In high summer farmers would take their cattle across the mudflats at low tide to uninhabited islands of pasture land, left to grow green and lush during the spring months. Everywhere the land was incised by natural or man-made canals forming a crazed pattern of islets used as sanctuaries by the shore birds. It was a bleak, desolate place but with its own particular atmosphere. It breathed medieval air, a dark, brooding environment sensitive to the incursions of modern men. Half buried in its breast were the decayed hulks of raiders and smugglers of yester-centuries, like the ribcages of giants. There were ancient keeps too, broken teeth through which came the inhalations of cold east winds.

These images were sensed rather than derived from observation. In such an emotive place it was easy to believe in supernatural forces: the land itself was a living, moody being that glowered its way through summer days. During the darker winter months it drew a cloak of mist over its back, like an old hermit without a cave into which to retreat. At night, any night, it was the source of many fears, only half understood, retrieved from racial memories.

There was a splashing sound and a glinting strip of tin foil came snaking out of the river towards me. It landed on the wharf. Milky had caught another smelt.

'How many do you need?' I asked.

'What? The fish? Enough for tea. Dozen probably.'

I nodded. 'I usually feed 'em to the cat. My nan won't cook 'em. She says they're too fiddly to clean.'

'Don't bother guttin' 'em. We just cook 'em till they're soft and mushy, then pull the tail end. The bone comes out and brings the guts with it. Same as sprats.'

I saw a crab, dark green and evil-looking, below my feet.

Milky said, 'Where's the other two? Dinger and Jackie?'

'I'm not friends with them any more,' I said. 'They've done something to . . . just been looking for them.'

'Me neither. They don't like me.'

'I know.'

'I . . .' He seemed a bit reluctant to continue, so I looked at him encouragingly. 'I been a bit lonely,' he confessed.

For some reason this statement made me feel uncomfortable. I was not used to intimate revelations from Milky. He was normally so reserved.

'Oh,' I said. 'Well . . . you know. I had to see what they were doing, that time.'

'Not blamin' you. Just be different if Oaky was here. I miss Oaky. He was a good friend.'

We stared at the river that had taken him from us.

'What do you think's happened to him?' I said. 'Maybe he's out at sea somewhere.' I looked at him, 'You don't still believe in the witch, do you?'

'Nah, me dad says he'll be shifted up and down the river by the tides. Me dad reckons the crabs and fish'll soon eat away the flesh an' the bones come apart an' get lost. Sink in the mud.'

'Poor Oaky,' I said. 'Et by the fish.'

Milky nodded, twitching his line at the same time to hook the smelt that were nibbling at the bait. We both looked at the smelt lying on the wharf and must have had the same thought simultaneously. One or two of the fish still flapped feebly in the sunlight.

'Oaky!' I whispered, appalled at what was passing through my mind. A look of horror crossed Milky's face. He was catching these fish to *eat*. We stared at each other for a moment then Milky reached down and swept the smelt into the river with his arm. There several of them floated until the gulls came down like diving stukas and snatched them from the surface.

'I'll never eat another one,' stated Milky, firmly.

'Me neither,' I said.

We strolled back towards Milky's house, through the mill yards and along the lane flanked by walls of fennel, oxeyes and bindweed.

'I got a ciggy in my shed. A real one. Want a puff?'

We went into his shed and he lifted the piping on the stove to take out a slim packet of Weights with a large '5' printed on the edge.

'Got a new swear word,' said Milky, proudly, as we puffed away. Milky collected swear words. He told it to me but it not only meant very little to me, it had none of the force and power of the words we had learned as younger members of market society. Our first word had a real gritty, gutsy sound to it, especially if you shortened the vowel and spat it out sharply. We had been six or seven at the time and had played some sort of trick on a pig farmer who had been startled into using a beautiful, two-word sentence. We likened its poetic brevity to the shortest verse in the Bible and went around for weeks, our hands on our hips, our welly-booted legs apart like miniature colossi, using it on school mates, as if the words were magic spells that would transform our enemies into stone. We soon learned that they did indeed turn adults to statues when we used them, but not for very long. One hell of a hiding usually followed a fairly rapid recovery to human form.

When I left Milky, later in the day, black clouds had begun to gather for the first time in many weeks. They were climbing on top of each other in great rolling layers to form the nebulous towers of dark, fantastic castles over my head. The world had taken on an uneasy aspect. Hedgerow shadows hardened into black rock and known trees lost their familiar identities, retreating into themselves and becoming faceless forms against the sky. I decided to hurry home before the rain came down.

As I approached the junction before the White House, I saw a movement in the distant copse: two figures appeared to be struggling with one another. The scene was disquieting. I slowed my pace. There was something rather sinister in the way the figures moved, though it was difficult for me to see precisely what they were doing. At times their dark clothes merged with the darker spinney behind them and I caught only the quick movement of pale hands and pale faces. Then, as I closed with them I saw something between them: a board on a post. They were positioning it in the soft turf by the trees.

They saw me and stopped what they were doing. Then

one of them turned and began running, across the fields and in the direction of the Cherry Tree Inn. It was Jackie. I knew then that the other was Dinger and, as he stepped back from the post he was holding, I felt a cold sickness creeping through my abdomen. Against the board was nailed a familiar black and white animal in the shape of a cross.

It was my badger.

They had found their familiar.

*They had crucified my badger.*

A cold breeze had sprung up and I had difficulty in catching my breath.

I screamed, 'Dinger!' just as the first clap of thunder cracked across the sky, my shrill tones lost in its greater voice. Dinger began walking away, looking nervously over his shoulder. I ran to the board and stared at the poor creature that was pinned by its paws, its belly round as a plumb bob and its head lolling forward. Its mouth hung open to reveal the rows of pointed, white teeth separated by a long, red tongue. There was an old, pink scar across its nose.

Various emotions vied for possession of me. I wanted to beat Dinger to a pulp, yet I knew that anything I did now would be a wasted deed. The horrible act had been committed and nothing could change it—nothing I could do, nothing they could do. Then I felt pity for Dinger and Jackie, not the badger.

The cold mists of despair entered my heart. All the trust I had ever had for a human being had been driven out by the death of that figure pinned to the board. How could Jackie do this? Jackie, who had aroused in me such feelings of tenderness, such yearning? Surely she should be the source of warm, happy emotions, not the icy emptiness that had entered my breast? I did not hate her, yet the fondness that could overlook most other faults had gone. There was nothing left. I could not forgive her. She alone had known where to find the badger. Only she.

I looked up into the dark skies. Suddenly, I wished I were like an untethered paper kite that could lose itself in the columns of black cloud, to be blown by the storm winds without a destination, without purpose. I wanted to relinquish all need to make decisions, to let some natural agent take on that responsibility.

Dinger was waiting for me to do something but I had no energy or inclination to satisfy those expectations. The lightning flashes, the thunder rolls, were increasing in intensity and the darkness was almost as dense as midnight without a moon. We were enclosed by the low, soft ceiling of the cloud. The world had shrunk to become a small, frightening place of which we two and the crucified badger were the centre.

I looked at Dinger again, wishing he would go away. Some distance behind him, the waterwitch's house stood, stark and solitary against the turbulent backdrop, like a white ship about to be engulfed by a tidal wave. The winds were flicking the branches of the plum trees backwards and forwards, like drowning sailors, fighting to stay afloat.

Suddenly a hare bolted for the open country, drawing a line between the two of us. We watched it until it disappeared into some corn. I thought about hares that Dave had killed, and the dead crows I had seen dangling from farmers' fences: were the deaths of those creatures any more terrible than that of this badger? It *seemed* that this was worse, much worse, almost like murder—but I could not say *why*. Dave killed hares to eat. The farmers killed crows to protect the crops. Dinger and Jackie had killed the badger as a ritual, in order to drive out the evil from our playgrounds. Was it any worse to kill for protection? Say the badger had been an adder? I knew I would not have cared an ounce for the death of a poisonous snake. My heart would not ache for Jackie's soul over a reptile, so why should I feel betrayed over the death of a mammal?

The answer was, of course, that she *knew* it would hurt, had done it to squeeze my heart, to give me pain.

Lightning forked above the trees and thunder punched the wind out of the clouds a second later. I ran after Dinger and caught him up. He turned defensively and I saw that his hands and face were covered in deep scratches. The snare had not been final.

'You shouldn't have done it, Dinger,' I said, trying to keep the choking sound out of my voice. 'It was only a badger.'

His hands were curling and uncurling. He said, 'That's right . . . only a badger.'

'But . . .'

'S'done now,' he stated, firmly.

'I know you did it to get at me, not the witch. Jackie told you it was my badger, didn't she?'

'You shouldn't have left the gang,' he said. 'We should-'ve all stayed together. It's no good no more. Everythin's gone bad. We had a gang. Nobody should've left.'

His face looked white and ill in the gloom of the impending storm. Suddenly it lit up, as another flash of lightning split the darkness above our heads.

'I'm sorry,' I said.

He was quiet for a long time. Then, in a voice almost too low for me to hear, he said, 'So am I.'

The thunder made me jump this time. Dinger began walking again but before he had gone far another fierce crackle of lightning stopped him in mid-stride. The hair on my head and limbs stood on end and I could feel the electricity rippling over my skin. It filled the air around us and I could see, in that suspended moment, the grasses reaching, the leaves stretching. There was a blinding streak. Then a tree within the vault of the charge was rent in two halves, down the middle, with a terrible, anguished, deafening cry. It was as if some god had taken a giant beast by the horns and had torn it from head to tail.

We watched as the tree exploded into brilliance, pieces of fiery bark flying through the air around us.

I trembled so much my legs could barely support me. Dinger came rushing back to my side and we stared as the tree was engulfed in fire, the flames reaching to a hundred feet or more above our heads. I felt the heat on my skin. The smell of burning fouled my nostrils and I choked on ashy fumes.

Before long the spinney was in flames and we had to retreat to the road as the intense heat drove us backwards.

Grasses caught alight and dead branches on the ground burst into smaller fires.

'What shall we do?' I cried. There were noises like gunshots coming from the wood and the wind rushed into the white-hot lungs of the spinney as the fire roared again and drew breath.

'Quick. The house. You go and warn the ole woman. Quick.' His face was drained of blood and his eyes were flickering feverishly.

*The old woman.*

No longer was she a witch. She was an old woman in danger.

'What are you going to do?'

'I'll get help,' he said. 'Quick.'

I began running towards the White House as the fire swept along at my heels. The smoke and bits of flaming ash billowed around me. I found it hard to draw breath. Large sparks began to rain from the sky and the thunder clapped again somewhere above.

# SIXTEEN

I found the gate in the thickening smoke, opened it and ran down to the front door of the house.

'Hi!' I yelled. 'Fire! Fire!'

The door swung open as I rapped with the knocker. I stepped tentatively inside. 'Anybody home?'

My heart was pounding and my throat felt raw from the smoke. I could hardly see through my streaming eyes and I was aware of a terrible smell coming from somewhere.

Just as I was about to turn and leave I heard a sound from upstairs which could have been an answer to my call. I thought: *perhaps the old woman is ill, bedridden*? I knew I could not leave without checking the bedrooms, yet I hesitated for a few moments. This was someone's house and I was reluctant to go upstairs. Despite the fire my inhibitions were strong enough to make me question, for a few seconds, whether I would be overstepping the mark by climbing the stairs. There was no choice. I could hear the roar of the fire outside. I climbed the stairs, calling. 'Anybody there? Where are you? There's a fire outside . . . coming towards the house. We'll be burned if we don't . . .'

I stopped suddenly. On the landing at the top of the stairs stood a tall, gaunt man. It was the same man that had accosted me on the levee and had us looking for Amy Johnson's body when Oaky was alive. In the gloom of the windowless landing I could see his rheumy eyes glistening, his long teeth behind the weathered lips. For a moment I wanted to turn and run. One of his hands rested on the worn bannister rail, as if he were about to use it to leap over and land by the door, blocking my escape. No sign of acknowledgement appeared on his face, no smile, no frown. Just that harrowed, sunken look which gave no clue to his thoughts.

'You frightened me,' I said, almost in a whisper.

'Hello boy,' he replied. 'Come to see, eh?'

I did not understand him. 'See? See what? There's a fire outside,' I stuttered. 'The old woman. I came to warn her. Fire . . . outside.'

'Old woman?'

'Yes, the one that lives here. We saw her.'

He nodded. 'Me mum. Ah! She's been taken away, long time ago. Old people's home. Couldn't look after her no more, see? Kept wetting the bed, she did. Couldn't stop her. Poor old dear. Couldn't help it, you know, but I'm not able, see? Got too much to do. Come up boy. I remember you. You're one of them what helped me look for Amy Johnson, eh?'

I shuddered involuntarily. 'Fire,' I said, weakly. 'We've got to go.'

Suddenly he reached forward and, gripping my arm with his strong, thin fingers, held me fast.

'You're hurting me,' I said. 'Please mister.'

'Poor old mum. She would've been proud of me. Her famous son. Come to look, have you? Come to see Amy?' His eyes narrowed. 'You can't have the five bob. I found her meself.'

'Don't want any five bob,' I said, near to tears. 'Let me go. I want to go home.' I wondered whether I could kick him and wrench free but he seemed to read my eyes and gripped me more tightly. Then he began pulling me towards a door on the landing. I dug my heels into a filthy threadbare mat but only succeeded in tearing a hole in it. My hand locked onto the bannister rail but he peeled away my fingers.

'Don't be silly,' he said, in a calm voice. 'I'm not going to hurt you. Just want to show you. Nobody else has seen 'er yet.'

'I don't want to see her! I don't want to!' I yelled. The house was beginning to fill with smoke and I could hear the advance of the fire outside. Somewhere downstairs windows shattered with the heat, followed by a whooshing sound and hot air that hit my face like a strong wind. His eyes took on a worried look then and he let me go. I turned to run but the fire had already engulfed the linoleum in the hallway at the bottom of the stairs. I followed the man into the bedroom and slammed the door behind me. We were going to die, I knew it. We were going to burn to death in the house.

My companion sat on the bed, a blank expression on his face. I rushed to the window and tried to gauge whether we could jump or not, but the smoke was too thick to see. The grass below was burning furiously: long grass, uncut all summer. The smell of burning mixed with another sickening odour, just as unpleasant. It added to my panic. I tore at the window catch.

'How am I going to get her out?' he said from behind me. I thought he meant his mother for a moment, then I remembered she had gone and he had been babbling about Amy Johnson. I ignored him and tried to open the window again but the catch burned my hand and the heat from the outside had warped the frame. Flames were jumping as high as the gutter.

'Help me smash it!' I cried. I looked around frantically for something heavy but there was not even a chair in the room. Just the old bed. A chamber pot! There might be a pot under the bed. I knelt down and quickly lifted the coverlet. The stench hit me first—then I screamed loudly. Someone was under the bed.

'Leave her alone,' shouted the man, knocking me out of the way. I fell into the corner of the room. He reached under the bed and to my horror pulled a body out into the middle of the floor.

*It was Oaky.*

His face was a light green colour and it wore a bloated smile. Something had been picking at his eyes and lips but I recognized the red trunks with the stripe. And the broad shoulders covered in freckles. The skin was wrinkled and white. Pieces of it had peeled off and lay in patches on the floor. The man put his arms under the putrid armpits of the corpse and tried to lift it bodily. Its belly was hugely swollen and rolled like a balloon full of water.

'Help me,' he grunted.

I screamed again, trying to get further into the corner, away from the horrible, stinking thing that used to be my friend. He let the body go again and it fell with a dull sound, the head cracking against the floorboards. Liquid began to ooze out of the ear closest to me. The jaw had fallen open to reveal a mouth full of maggots and the man closed it again with a quick movement of his hand, making the teeth snap together. He held it there.

I crawled quickly towards the door, not looking back, and found myself on the landing. The smoke and fumes made my head spin. Above me was the trap door to the attic. It was no use going down the stairs. The fire had a firm hold there, so I had to go upwards. I climbed onto the bannister, my eyes stinging and my lungs forcing coughs through my raw throat, and pushed open the trap door. Then I pulled myself up. As I did so, he came out of the bedroom, dragging the dead Oaky with him. He saw my legs dangling but before he could grab them I swung myself out of his reach.

He heaved the words out. 'Come . . . down here . . . boy . . . *help* me.'

I shook my head adamantly and he disappeared again into the bedroom. I moved into the darkness of the attic and soon I heard him grunting and wheezing below the trap door. Then his thin hands clamped like mottled claws onto the edge. A minute later his skull-like head appeared, the eyes bulging, something gripped between the teeth. He pulled himself up and then began to haul up the body from below with what I realized was a dressing-gown cord. A white arm came first, followed by the lolling, grotesque head with its ugly smile. A clown's smile, except that the redness was the gums, not make-up on the lips. When he had the body up the man began punching at the roof above him.

He made no impression at first but when he stood up and pressed his back against it, getting pressure from his legs on a crossbeam, the roof gave and light entered.

I watched him force the body through the gap, heard it

roll down the roof, its eventual fall lost in the sound of the fire. Then he climbed out after it.

A minute later the smoke became too thick to bear and I crawled to the opening myself. Climbing onto a beam, I levered myself out into the relatively fresh air. He had gone. I clung to the roof, looking down at the long drop towards the ground. Then I saw him, limping away across the smouldering grasses, his trouser legs afire and in his arms the corpse of Oaky, like an overgrown baby, its own arms hanging backwards as if in a swoon. It was the last I ever saw of either of them.

I could hear the sounds of bells ringing in the distance and shouts from people beyond the road. The slates of the roof were growing hot beneath me and the flames began licking over the guttering, around the eaves, like thirsty tongues. I would have to jump, I knew, but the ground looked so far away and I was afraid. I would break my legs or my back. Perhaps even kill myself.

Then I remembered the pond.

It looked as small as a puddle from where I sat, but was in fact a green, slick oasis in the sea of fire. Also, it was several yards out and almost the height from which Oaky took his dive of death.

A roll of thunder made me look up. There were still flashes in the sky but they were in the distance. One or two large drops of rain had begun to fall.

No longer were there thoughts of witches in my mind. I wondered about the depth of the pond. It might only be a few feet deep, in which case I would bury myself in the mud, or worse. There could be all kinds of junk, from iron bedsteads to broken bottles. Yet I *had* to jump, or burn. I climbed to the ridge in the roof and turned, then without stopping to think I ran down the slope and threw myself into the air.

That flight lasted only a few seconds in real time but to me it took so much longer. It seemed I had time to observe my progress through the air. Having had the years to ponder on those brief moments I have come to the conclusion that in times of great danger, of imminent death, one's thought processes accelerate. They gather speed until the world stands still. I could see the ground stretched out below me like a burning continent, the pond a lake towards which my body somersaulted slowly. I was a bolt of flesh and bone falling from the sky. I heard a shout, elongated yet faintly intelligible, like the moan of wind through holes in rock. Someone was calling my name. There was a folding of horizons, a gathering-up, to funnel my progress to a watery landing, as if the world had formed into fluted channels for the purpose.

I hit the scummy surface of the pond with a force that drove all the wind from my lungs, sank deep, then rose spluttering. Firm hands gripped my hair, then my clothes, and hauled me from the water. I was lifted onto a bony shoulder and while I fought for breath was carried swiftly through the smoke and flames to the safety of the road.

'Is there anybody else in there?'

It was uncle Dave. Sobbing, I gripped him round the neck as he lowered me to the road. The rain had begun to fall quite steadily now and it ran down from his lank hair in rivulets.

'Is there? Quick boy, tell me.'

I shook my head. 'I . . . I don't think so. There was . . . he got out, over the fields.' Then my head was full of bells and I was vaguely aware of people and vehicles moving around me. The wet evening was broken by shouts and the sound of running feet on tarmac. A blanket was placed around my shoulders by unknown hands. When I looked up again, Dinger was standing just a few yards away, staring at me intently.

'I got help,' he said. 'Ran to the pub. Dave was there . . . 'n some others.'

'Thanks,' I mumbled.

He continued to stare at me and I realized he wanted something.

'What's the matter?'

'The old woman. Did she get out?'

I shrugged. 'There wasn't any old woman. It was that man . . . you remember, the one that was looking for Amy Johnson?'

He looked puzzled, so I said. 'When Oaky was with us.

We went over the saltings looking for bodies.'

Dinger nodded vigorously. 'Oh, yeah. I remember now. Goofy-looking bloke. Bit loopy.'

'Well it was him. He . . . he had Oaky. Hid him under the bed. It was horrible . . .'

Dinger drew back a little. A fireman ran past, brushing him aside.

'Out of the way son,' he yelled. 'Sit by your friend.' Then the fireman was gone, a long, white canvas hose marking his trail. Dinger stayed where he was, his face pale in the near darkness. It began to rain very heavily.

'He *was* there,' I said, stubbornly. 'He was dead. I know it was Oaky. The man took him away . . .' I pointed across the fields, behind the house. 'Said Oaky was Amy Johnson. Tried to make me touch him.'

Steam filled the air and suddenly grandad had me by the arm and was leading me along the road. It seemed unreal, the events of the night, the activity that continued despite the downpour.

'He *was* there!' I yelled back, fiercely, at Dinger.

Grandad said, 'Your nan's out. Sunday. She's gone into Southend on her usual jaunt.' I nodded, hardly hearing what he was saying. 'Would 'ave to be out, tonight of all nights,' he grumbled. 'That's 'er all over. Only thinks of 'erself on a Sunday.'

As I looked back I could see the firemen clustered round the pond. They were using its water to douse the fire. I could see the hose trailing from its edge to the pump. I broke away from grandad and ran back. No one took any notice of me as I approached the pond. I stared down into its depths, almost depleted of water now and lit eerily by the light from the blazing building. I don't know what I expected to see, but I wanted to look while there were adults around to protect me from whatever was at the bottom.

It was merely a rubbish pit. There was not a witch's butcher's shop at the bottom. Only a rusty old iron bedstead, a bike frame and dozens of bottles and cans. As I watched the water go down even further an old pushchair revealed its skeleton to me. The hose made a sucking sound and began to take up sludge. There was a graveyard down there but not the one I had expected. I walked slowly back to where grandfather waited, leaning heavily on his good leg.

# SEVENTEEN

Though the rain stopped after an hour or two, the wind that had accompanied the storm increased in strength as the night went on. The firemen eventually abandoned the White House and left it to burn itself out, since every time they doused the flames the wind whipped the embers to fresh fury. I spent the night sleeping fitfully and awoke, finally, at about ten o'clock to hear strange voices in the parlour below. I soon gathered it was the police.

I could hear Dave reluctantly answering their quite innocent questions. He never ceased to be suspicious of the police and the tone of his voice was one of guarded defence, as if he expected one of them to accuse him of arson at any moment.

As I dressed, the previous evening's events seeped gradually into my consciousness and their immediate effect was one of repulsion. I wanted to erase the disturbing visions of the madman, the decomposing remains of Oaky, but they dominated my mind while I was alone. I would never again look under a bed without the chilling remembrance of that corpse entering my mind. The shock did not hit me that day, nor indeed for several days afterwards. When it did, I was standing in the kitchen of an early morning, and was suddenly seized by a fit of trembling: my teeth began to chatter and my legs shook so violently, nan had to catch me as I fell. I remember very little about what happened afterwards except that I awoke in bed with my skin tingling and with a head that felt as if it were stuffed with cotton wool balls. Years later I realized that the incident had caused a sudden purgation of my childhood fantasies (though I would still be plagued by fears of the dark and dreams). I began, from that time, to look through a glass darkly. I had put away childish things.

I joined Dave and the policemen downstairs and learned that my benign madman had presented himself to the desk sergeant at Southend in the company of the corpse of Oaky, claiming that Amy Johnson had at last been found. They took both of them away, Oaky to the undertakers and the madman to a hospital. He told the police that he had thrown the body down from the roof of the house and had himself dropped from the edge by hanging from the eaves, something I had not thought of doing. Besides, he was a tall man and would have been closer to the ground—at least that's what I told myself, in order to salve my pride.

Later, grandad and I went for a long ride with the horse and cart. We passed by Dinger's house. Dinger was on his front step but we met each other's eyes only briefly and then turned our heads simultaneously. We could never be friends again. Too much had passed between us, even for our previous ambivalent relationship to continue.

Grandad took us down by the river and the summer's events came rushing back to me, causing a flutter of panic in my breast. I looked to grandad for reassurance: his big-boned, calloused hands held the cracked leather reins with easy confidence and I followed the thick arms to the powerful shoulders, to find his blue eyes staring into mine. The skin of his face, covered in tiny creases, was like the brown leather of an old cricket ball. The expression was one of faint enquiry. After a few seconds of staring across two generations—generations in which the world had changed into a higher gear than had been possible for several thousand years—he became embarrassed and adjusted his cap.

'Grandad,' I said, 'how *did* you lose your leg?'

There was a silence during which I realized he was summoning the truth to his lips. Then he glanced at the swirling waters of the river we were passing and, again, his expression changed. He turned those bright blue doll's eyes on to me once more.

'A shark ate it off,' he said abruptly. 'Got shipwrecked in the Indian seas an' a shark got it. Big fella, he was. A gob as big as a barn door . . .'

He had not failed me. Perhaps the truth was so deeply hidden inside him now that it was impossible for him to reach it. Whatever the truth was, I did not want to hear it. I was much happier with his fiction.

'I've never seen a shark,' I said. 'What do they look like?'

He elaborated as he flicked the reins and Custard heaved forward, almost forgetting herself and breaking into a walk.

'Like one of them pike young Dave brought 'ome in the middle o' summer. All mouth an' teeth and a vicious look to 'em. Cold eyes, see. No warmth comin' through from the heart. You look at Peter there, look at his eyes . . .' Peter, in the back of the cart, wagged his tail at the mention of his name. 'Them brown eyes is warm, see. That's 'cause it's comin' through from his faithful old ticker. Dogs'll love a man to death. A shark . . . well, they just look on you or me as a plate of sausage an' mash. That cold bastard had a sausage that day all right—your ole grandad's leg. I wished I could say he choked to death on it but he swallowed it as easy as a piece of pork.'

He continued in this vein for some miles and I basked in the words as if they were the last rays of sunshine that would fall on my childhood.

The end of summer was caught in the hedges, like a trapped bird, struggling in the mesh of twigs and leaves. I was reluctant to let that season go, for there would never be another like it. There have been many since, yet not one stands out as vividly as the summer of '52, which I began as a child and finished as a . . . well, not an adult, but something in between the two.

We passed the River Roach on high ground where the broad sweep of the shorn fields flowed down to the metal gleam of its surface in a fall of green and gold. Finally, we came to the Saxon-built church on the knoll where grandad was to cut the grass and generally tidy the surrounds of the graves. Many of our ancestors were there, amongst those broken stones, nearly all of them farm labourers and their families. There were no gentry amongst us. We had cleaved the land, combed it, sown it, and shaved it for centuries. The church records only went back three hundred years but we were in them from the first. We grew out of this ancient earth, with all its dark superstitions, the faint odour of witchcraft still clinging to the scattered stones of fallen towers, its brooding aspect, its unhallowed mud. My distant cousins in their peasant dark-age dwellings had had the same nightmares as I, had passed them on to me through the chain of nights that separated our lives. They had lived in fear of magic and some had died as the result of it. There was a birthmark like a small brown bird on my chest that would have condemned me to death, had I been born one of them. They grew up, afraid of themselves and each other, moving through the atmospheric mists of this low country, toiling by day and hiding themselves by night. Lords had come and gone, safe inside the armour of their non-belief, while we had taken this earth, this shadowed landscape, these dank marshes, and used them as agents of fear, until *they* took *us*. In this place, where the leaden, dull sky came down to threaten the land with its gross belly, a cow was not always a cow, a weasel not always itself, but something more sinister, something to terrify, to chill the heart. Each fungus, each moss-shrouded alder, each wild herb, toad, snake, blindworm, bat, was a source of magic, an object of terror. They were the agents of evil which grew from the enchanted earth to plague a living man. Trees had souls, stones had eyes, the mud had mouths that sucked men down by leg and arm, by body and head. *Stay out of the shadows, cousin, and keep you clear of the night!*

I left grandad to his grave trimming and cut across the fields back to the White House to see what was left of it. The ruin was now nothing but a few charcoal staves pointing to the sky. As I stared at them I tried to recall my feelings on that evening of the fire but the whole mental picture was a maelstrom of fire, water and blackened earth.

The tree which had been struck by lightning was terribly dramatic in its new guise. The branches had been burnt away to leave the split, black trunk spread like two narrow wings; a satanic dragonfly about to take flight. The shape was awesome in its attractiveness. I could easily imagine my primitive cousins worshipping the tree as a god of dark forces.

I found the charred remains of the badger, still attached to the crumbling board that had served as its crucifix. I took it down to a backwater and pushed it out on the stagnant waters: not *exactly* a Viking funeral but the intention was there. Then I returned home.

In the evening I went to bed before the sun sank to its own resting place. Looking out of the window I could just see the burnt copse. It reminded me of a scene from *War of the Worlds* where the Martians had laid waste to the countryside around Leatherhead, blasting everything in their path with their heat rays. A few weeks previously this would have had me in an heroic role within seconds, but I found it difficult to slip into the right frame of mind to produce Martian war machines on the dykes and screaming refugees running for the sanctity of rural churches.

It had been the same during the afternoon. I had read a Ray Bradbury story, and failed in my reenactment of it afterwards. However, this had been partly due to Cathy and Dave whispering in the parlour. Dave had said something to Cathy in a low voice, too soft for me to hear.

She replied, 'No, Dave. I don't want to be tied.'

There had been silence, then her voice again.

'You look as though you've just swallowed a hedgehog. Come on, we've been through all this before. Don't let's waste what time we do have together.'

Later, Dave had gone out with his gun for a final rape and pillage of the countryside. His face had been black with anger.

The embers of the summer flared into autumn. My parents came down with my two brothers. They were all like strangers to me. My brothers initially treated me with some awe, which quickly deteriorated into contempt when they found out I knew nothing about football, cars or the nicknames of film stars. They were tough little townies. The seasons came and went through their lives unmarked except by a fall or rise in the temperature. Their world of streets and buildings was as alien to me as the countryside was to them. I pleaded with my parents to let me stay with my grandmother. I begged nan herself to let me stay. Finally, they all seemed to agree that I had matured a great deal since the episode of the fire and that my schoolwork, which was good, would be interrupted.

I kind of *drifted* during that autumn. Something inside me had died and though I did not think of it in those terms, I knew I had changed. I felt disorientated. The games of fantasy were gone and with them they took part of my reason for living. (I had not at that time learned that my writing would allow me to retain the essence of that twilight world.) I had grown up and the horrors of senior school, stretching before me, occupied my mind far more than the horrors of the night. I was a little fish in a big pond and it was full of sharks.

My parents had returned home, taking my brothers with them and I was once more left to an empty bedroom in the late evenings. Strangely enough I missed my brothers but I think that was because I was lonely, not because they were good company, or rather the kind of company I desired. I learned a new trick, which must have been dangerous, although I did not realize it at the time. I would breathe in and out, very hard, rapidly for some minutes, then, squatting down with my chest tightly pressed against my knees, puff out my cheeks without expelling air. This would cause me to black out for several seconds, during which time I would have strange and wonderful dreams. The act was like a passport to another world, where I could fly over fields of flowers, my arms outstretched like the wings of a bird. When Jenny came to stay, in late October, she soon put a stop to that.

# EIGHTEEN

Jenny's arrival at nan's house almost coincided with Dave's departure. Dave left to join his new ship on the Saturday, taking with him the sad knowledge that Cathy would probably not be waiting for him when he came home eighteen months later. Cathy was talking about going to Australia and Dave's face was set into hard lines as he said goodbye to us all. I watched him drive off in a hired car bound for Tilbury docks and once again re-affirmed my resolve never to get mixed up with women once I reached his age. Jenny arrived on Monday.

Nan said, 'Raymond, this is your cousin Jennifer. She's going to stay with us for a while before she goes to a new school.' This was the formal part, then, 'Perhaps she'll keep you out of mischief, though we can't expect miracles overnight.'

I tried to look hurt, but nan added, 'What's the matter with your face?'

'Nuthin',' I answered.

'Well, don't go out with it looking like that—the wind might change.' With that she left us, in the parlour, to get acquainted.

Before me, deep in the old armchair with its cracked leather upholstery, was a girl of about thirteen. She had a round face, pleasant enough, and long, straight blonde hair which fell to her waist. There was a stocky look to her, her shoulders were broader than those of other girls I knew and the arms thicker at the top. Yet she had the same kind of elegance I admired in Cathy. Her freckled hands—she was covered in freckles and I guessed she was teased because of them at school—lay linked in her lap. Her eyes were a kind of grey-blue.

'Well?' she said, aggressively.

'Well what?'

'Are you going to stare at me all day?'

Her voice was delightfully cultured, with rounded vowels and precise diction. No one I knew spoke like that. She could have worked for the BBC. I could have sat and listened to a voice like that all day.

'Maybe,' I replied, equally aggressively. 'Depends on if there's anything better to do.'

'I suppose you haven't met a bastard before.'

My heart almost stopped in mid-beat. What was she doing, swearing like that in the parlour? Nan would have seven kinds of fit if she heard. I had used the word myself of course, but only on rare occasions and then in the earshot only of the gang, when we had been together. Dinger swore all the time, but Dinger was not my cultured cousin from a good school, the daughter of my dead aunt Elinor. My eyes darted back and forth from her face to the door. Any second I expected the latter to burst open and an avenging angel brilliant with wrath to come hurtling into the room.

'I wouldn't . . . if I were you,' I said, timidly now. 'Nan's got a temper on her . . .'

'Well that's what I am, so why be nice about it. Don't pretend you didn't know.'

It had not occurred to me before that moment that the word actually had a meaning behind it. We used it as children because it sounded nasty and wicked, not because it actually described the recipient. It was a goad to use to bring an adversary to violence or tears. It was a weapon to use as a parting shot. It was a word used to prove that we were grown up and knew the ways of the world.

'My mother wasn't married,' continued Jenny. 'You know that. That makes me a bastard.'

'Look,' I said, panicking. 'Don't *say* that in here. I don't care what you are. You're my cousin, that's all. We'll both get a licking if you keep on. What's your school like?' I said, desperately trying to change the subject. 'Mine's rotten.'

Then she did a terrible thing. She burst into tears. Her face puckered and the water came streaming out of her eyes. She didn't make any sound, or anything like that. She just curled up tight in the armchair and let the tears flow. It was a nightmare. I had only known her for five minutes and she was turning me inside out with her strange antics. I didn't know what to do. I was like a rabbit trapped in a room with a weasel and I wanted to be a million miles away.

I sat there waiting for the crying to stop, knowing that if nan came in, blame would be cast indiscriminately in all directions and I knew where most of it would fall. Eventually she took out a handkerchief and wiped her eyes.

'I'm sorry,' she said. 'My mother . . .' Fresh tears came and I realized what it was. Aunt Elinor's death was only very recent. She was still missing her badly. There was nothing I could do to help her and I just fidgeted with my shoelace until the bout had subsided again.

'Look,' I said. 'Why don't we go for a walk? I'll show you where the fire was that I got caught in this summer.' I began to tell her the story of the summer's events and gradually captured her mind away from her grief. We went out of the front door and down the slope to the White House, still in charred ruins, and, puffed with pride at having been the centre of an adventure, I reenacted those old nightmares, taking her to the mill and along the dyke to the church where we had stolen the cross. She was a good listener and asked all the right questions. I began to enjoy her company. There was something about her that fascinated me: a kind of adultness that none of my friends had, even those of her age. She seemed a woman to me, yet approachable. She didn't make fun of my silly elaborations or exaggerations the way Dave would have. She just listened and said things like, 'Oh, how *awful*. I expect you were very frightened. I would have been.'

I shrugged at these flattering acknowledgements, delighting in the way she said *awful*, which had a melodic sound to it, like someone striking a bell with a felt hammer. I wondered how people developed sounds like that, whether they practised them late into the night until they got them exactly right.

'Where did you learn to talk like that?' I asked, candidly.

'At school I suppose. I never really thought about it before.'

'I wonder why they don't teach us that at our school?' I said, a little piqued at the lack of education I seemed to have discovered within myself.

'It's probably because you're working class,' she said simply, and she made it sound like a compliment.

'Am I?' I said, surprised. 'What are you then?'

'Oh, I'm from working-class stock, but I've been mixing with middle-class society, so my origins have been obscured. I suppose I'm aspiring middle class.'

What that all meant was beyond me, but it certainly sounded impressive. So impressive that when we came across Milky, walking his dog through the back lane, I introduced Jenny as, 'My cousin Jennifer. She's aspiring middle class at her school.'

Milky didn't bat an eyelid. 'I'll be in Form 2 next year,' he said. 'I s'pose that's pretty near the middle too.'

Jenny laughed.

As we strolled homewards, under the changing colours of the trees, a flock of geese flew overhead in a tight formation. I pointed them out to Jenny, telling her they were Brent geese coming down from Iceland to spend the winter in and around our salt marshes. It was her turn to be impressed.

'You know a lot about the country, don't you, Raymond?'

'Titch. Everybody calls me Titch,' I corrected her. 'I don't like "Raymond" much. My uncle Dave and grandad tell me lots of things. It's easy when you live here.'

'You must teach me all about the wildlife, the plants and animals and things, while I'm here.'

'Well the first thing is to stay away from Mick, the yard dog. He'll have your . . . backside,' I finished lamely. 'He's as wild as they come. Peter's all right. A bit smelly 'cause grandad doesn't wash him that much, but he's pretty hot on catching rabbits. Ginger the cat . . .'

She laughed again. 'I wasn't thinking about the domestic animals. I meant about badgers and geese and all those other things you've been talking about today. You know an awful lot about life here. It's more interesting than the kind of talk I'm used to at school.'

'What do you talk about there?'

She was vague. 'Oh, boys and things like that.'

It sounded pretty dull to be sure. But then again, I couldn't see what was *that* exciting about the village. Still, if she wanted to hear about badgers then I was willing enough to tell her. I found some fox spoor for her in the greengage orchard as we approached the house, easily definable in the soft mud. She wanted to know how I could tell the difference between them and a dog's prints. I pointed out the differences.

'They're thinner, they make a tighter pattern on the ground and the claw marks are longer.'

'Really?'

'Yes, honestly,' I said, mistaking her tone for one of disbelief. 'You can often see them on the mudflats. They go out to where the birds nest. A fox will kill a whole bundle of seagulls or knots if he can get in amongst 'em. He'll only eat one or two though. They go kind of mad when they start killing at night. Something gets into them and they just go berserk.'

'That's horrible. That doesn't sound natural to me.'

'Oh yes, it's natural. They all do it. That's why they kill lots of chickens when they get into the run. Grandad gets really mad at them. He says he wouldn't mind if they'd just take one for their supper and leave the rest alone.'

'Have you ever seen a white fox?' she asked.

The sun was going down and there was a strange light on her face. A sort of eager glow. In the distance I could hear the starlings and sparrows settling noisily into their tree colonies. One or two crows were still hopping through the furrows of the nearby fields but they too would soon be down for the night. I wanted to be indoors for some reason.

'A white fox? There aren't such things . . . are there?'

'Well, yes. You can get a white anything—an albino it's called, and they have pink eyes. But it wasn't that I was thinking of. I read a story recently, a Japanese folk tale . . .'

'You can read Japanese?' I cried.

'No, silly. It was a translation. They have these witches in Japanese folk lore that change themselves into white foxes with a small flame, like a candle flame, that travels with them just above their heads. If you chase them they disappear into the nearest rock and the rock becomes a death stone. Anyone who touches it dies. It sends out this vapour that kills all the moss and grass around it, and the creatures, the insects and birds too. The landscape around them becomes desolate and empty. The only way you can destroy a white fox is to expose it to the light of a fire which has been kindled with wood from a tree exactly the same age as the fox itself.'

'And you believe it?' I said, almost afraid to listen to the answer.

'No, not really. It's just a story of course. But it would be fun to look for a white fox this winter, wouldn't it? Even though there's no chance of finding one. It would give us something out of the ordinary to do, wouldn't it? A kind of magical quest. They say that when you see one, your whole life changes. You become a different person. Will you help, Titch?'

'Yes, I suppose so,' I replied dubiously. 'But I've had a lot of trouble through looking for witches recently.'

'I know. You told me. But these are different from waterwitches and it's only a kind of game anyway. This isn't Japan and they're not even real there. I find this place so . . . atmospheric. A game like that would give our walks a little zest.'

'Atmos. . .?'

'You know—spooky.'

'Oh, I know *that* all right. Well, if it'll make you happy, we'll look for this white fox, but I'll tell you somethin'. I hope we don't find it.' And I meant it. I had thought all that sort of thing was behind me, now that I had grown up, so to speak. It seemed that I just exchanged one set of fears for another as time went by. If it would keep Jenny's mind off the death of her mother then I was willing to risk it, but while one side of my mind told me that witches, death stones and magic were all nonsense, the other side argued that there were things that happened in this world that nobody could explain. As usual, I was caught in the middle.

That evening at tea, nan expressed how delighted she was with Jenny's table manners.

'They must teach you some nice ways at that school of yours,' she said.

She then went on to say that Jenny could teach me a thing or two about holding a knife and fork, thus embarrassing both of us, for different reasons. Grandad said nothing as usual, but I noticed he was sparing with the sauce on his sausage and mash; he usually swamped his dinner with the condiments. I could see that Jenny was going to bring some changes to the house and not all of them good from my point of view. If you had to think about every tiny move you made at the meal table it took away the pleasure of eating.

We were not usually allowed the wireless on while we ate but tonight there was soft music coming from the corner of the room. A boring classical piece. Nan was not above trying to introduce a little culture into our lives and she now believed she had an ally under her roof.

After the meal Jenny helped her to wash up while grandad smoked a pipe in front of the range fire and I did some homework. Then nan disappeared into the parlour, reappearing a little while later dressed in a fawn topcoat and matching hat. It was Sunday night, the night she always went into Southend. As she was putting on her gloves, Jenny asked: 'Where are you going, auntie?'

I stopped my work and looked up, interested in the reply. I had never thought to ask nan this: her weekly outings were so common I took them for granted, thinking I suppose that she visited one of her friends or relatives in the town.

Nan paused in the act of putting on her gloves. She looked scrubbed and groomed and her face shone, giving it an unusually rosy look. Her complexion was normally pasty through much indoor work and her white hair bedraggled by steam from the copper, but tonight she glowed and her hair, in a tight bun, had a silvery sheen to it.

'The pictures,' she said.

This was a revelation. I had no idea that nan went to the cinema.

'Can we come?' I said. 'What's on?'

Nan's mouth set into a firm line.

'No you can't. This is my one night out a week. I don't get many treats. I need to get away from you lot occasionally and I like a bit of peace and quiet on my own.'

There was a trace of bitterness to her voice which both Jenny and I caught. We exchanged glances. It sounded as though we gave her a lot of trouble between us and the only thing that kept her sane was the fact that she could get out of the house once in a while. I was a little bit hurt to find that we were such a burden to her, and bent my head over my homework again. Jenny found a book and began reading while grandad stared into the red glow of the fire, seemingly many miles away in thought, and it appeared that the whole conversation had gone over his head.

A little while later I heard the front door slam and went into the parlour to look out of the window. Nan was standing by the bus stop on the far side of the road. It was drizzling steadily with rain but she stood stiff and straight, her handbag clasped in front of her with both hands, a dumpy figure with a plain, stern face. She could have been anyone's grandmother. When I recall that image of her to mind now, I see a woman full of quiet sorrow. Not a pathetic woman, but one whose life had not had a great deal of room for frivolity. She was part of a transitional age but the changes had come too late for her. She was poor and the location remote. Elsewhere in the country people were enjoying the time-saving benefits of electricity and all the devices that it is able to run. Nan still washed clothes in a copper heated by a solid fuel fire, still skinned and gutted rabbits, bathed in a tin tub before the fire, swept the house with a broom, used a marble slab to keep the milk cool. Only in her sixties was she able to take advantage of mains water. Before that it had been buckets at the pump.

Her life had been full of hard manual labour, yet despite a certain severity about her face, she had managed to retain the appearance of something delicate, something fragile, that has come through a battering with only a few minor chips around the edges. Like a porcelain figurine that has managed to survive being used as a rugby ball by a gang of drunken louts. There was a faded look to her, like an ornament left too long on a sunny windowsill, but still she had that essential air of quality possessed by most friable materials.

The lighted bus came and took her out of the rain.

# NINETEEN

On my way home from school the next day I changed the accumulator which provided the power to the wireless. I was particularly careful with the glass battery because I knew it to be full of acid and I had seen what acid could do in a recent experiment in the chemistry laboratory. It was one of those agents which are necessary to a comfortable home life, but which are regarded by adults as something akin to the Devil's blood. When I was younger and heard that acid could burn through anything, no matter how thick, I had spilled some deliberately into the gutter to see if it would bore a hole all the way through to Australia. It didn't—all it did was hiss and smoke, and burn my nostrils with its fumes. On reaching home, Dave had immediately taken the accumulator from me and had gone storming down to the shop because the plates were exposed.

Jenny was doing some school work when I got in and she looked up and smiled as I walked through the door. I think she was pleased to see me because she was lonely for her schoolfriends. Ginger was curled up asleep in her lap.

'I stroked Mick today,' she said.

I put the battery down beside the wireless and breathed in deeply, several times.

'Did you hear what I said?' she asked. 'I stroked Mick. I just walked right up to him and patted him on the head. Then I . . .'

'Let's see you.'

'Honest, Titch. I did. Don't you believe me?'

'Yes I do. That dog would do anythin' to spite me. It hates me.'

'Oh, come on. It's probably the way you approach him. I'm sure all he needs is a little kindness. All right. I'll do it now. I wanted you to believe me *first*, before I showed you.' She put Ginger down on the floor.

She went out into the yard and began a slow walk towards Mick's kennel. When she was within his chain's length I held my breath. Surely he would rip her to pieces? No one ever got close to Mick except grandad and Dave—and nan of course. Now that I thought about it, I was the only one who couldn't get near the animal. Mick came out of his kennel slowly, his tail between his legs. Jenny knelt down and stroked his head several times. The tail didn't move but Mick made no attempt to hurt her.

I went outside and Jenny straightened, beckoning me to join her. I made one or two tentative steps towards the brute and he immediately began growling in the back of his throat. One more step and he was barking fit to wake the next village.

'It's no good, Jenny. He doesn't like me and he never will. I've . . . I've teased him too much,' I confessed.

'Ah, that's it, is it? Well, you can win his confidence back in time. Just talk to him sometimes in a normal voice and if you pass near him, do it slowly . . .'

I went indoors a little put out. Here was this girl, who said she knew nothing about country life, trying to tell me how to make friends with a dog I had known since it had been born. I was a bit huffy with her when she came back into the house and hardly spoke to her for the rest of the evening, which was a bit cruel because I could see she wanted someone to talk to, but then children will be vindictive when their pride is hurt. I hadn't grown up enough to shed that side of myself.

Later that night I was staring out of my bedroom window, looking at the stars and the night caught up in the branches of the trees, when Jenny crept in. By that time I had forgotten that I was annoyed with her.

'What are you looking for, Titch?' she whispered. 'The white fox?'

A car swept past the window illuminating her face for a moment and I was shocked to see how sad she looked.

'No. I don't believe in things like that any more. The

pond was empty. There was nothing but a load of rubbish in the bottom—old bedsteads and things.'

'I don't know what you mean.'

'The waterwitches. I told you. I believed there was a waterwitch at the bottom of the pond at the White House but when the firemen drained it there was nothing there. It was just a dump.'

She settled down beside me on the bed, her crisp white nightdress making rustling sounds.

'I used to be afraid of the dark too,' I said, 'but it doesn't seem to worry me much now. You don't believe in the white fox either, do you?'

There was a fierceness to her reply that frightened me a little.

'I *want* to, and you should too. You should try to stay scared of the dark as well. For as long as you can. When you stop believing in those things you have to grow up.'

'What's wrong with that? Dave has a fine time. He can do what he likes and nobody can tell him off or anything. He's got a shotgun and he can go to sea when he wants to . . .'

'It's not that.'

'What is it then?'

I had the feeling that she was going to divulge some horrible secret about adults. Something you didn't learn until you crossed that magical line between childhood and adulthood. Had she crossed it? She seemed to know many things that I did not, yet she was only just over a year older than I was. Thirteen. Was that the year when one was initiated into the secret? I wasn't sure I wanted to hear about it before my time came.

She said, 'Waterwitches and white foxes are just things you need. I'm going to keep looking for my white fox until I find it. I don't care if I never do . . . I just want to keep looking.'

'Why?'

'Because, because. Because the things that replace them are worse.'

The hairs on the back of my neck prickled and a cold feeling went through my stomach.

'You mean adults are scared of things too. What are they . . .?' I imagined, or tried to imagine, what creatures of the night would be horrible enough to put terror into the heart of grandad, and failed. He would just spit tobacco juice at them and tell them to 'bugger off'. I knew that he could listen to *The Man in Black* and go to bed afterwards undisturbed and sleep like a log. It was impossible to imagine what spirit would be bold enough to break that sleep.

I said, 'Grandad's not afraid of anything.'

'Oh yes he is,' Jenny said, quickly. 'You don't know, that's all.'

'Do you know?'

'I don't know exactly what it is but everyone's scared of something, and the things that grown ups . . .' She trailed the sentence to a stop and I said, 'What?'

'Nothing. I can't tell you because I don't know.'

We sat there together in silence after that, just staring out of the window at the street below. People passed very occasionally but she made no comment until we saw a shape slipping in and out of the pools of light made by the street lamps.

'Is that a white fox?' she said, her voice full of excitement. My heart jumped and I studied the creature with apprehension. It was certainly white, a rather greyish white, but then I noticed black markings too, as it paused beneath one of the lamps.

'It's a lurcher,' I said, relieved.

'What's that?' she squeaked. 'It sounds horrible.'

I was a bit scornful of her lack of knowledge and remembered Mick and her conquest.

'Just a gypsy's dog,' I said. 'They call them lurchers.'

'Why?'

'I don't know. It's just their name.'

'How do you know it's a "lurcher"?'

The skinny beast passed directly below us and I wondered what it was doing out alone at that time of night.

'I can see it, can't I?'

'Yes, but what's different about it? From a normal dog I mean. I can't see any gypsy with it.'

'Lurchers are part greyhound and part something else. Look, you can see . . . it's got greyhound in it.'

'You mean they're a crossbreed? What are they crossed with?'

'Anything. It doesn't matter what. Sometimes Alsatian, sometimes sheepdog. Anything. It makes them fast, like whippets. Don't you even know that?'

She went quiet again and then said in a small voice, 'Please don't be nasty to me, Titch.'

Immediately I felt ashamed of myself for trying to make her feel bad over Mick. I muttered something about being sorry but I was too embarrassed to make a full apology. I remembered about her missing her schoolfriends and tried to change the subject.

'Are you going back to your old school soon? What's it called?'

'St Theresa's. It's at Southwold, in Suffolk.'

'Are you going back?'

She shifted her position on the bed, moving the mattress so that the cold iron frame was against my legs.

'No . . . I don't think so. They sent me away. I did . . . something wrong.'

Her beautifully modulated voice had an edge to it that was not in keeping with the music she normally produced. I could sense that she didn't really want to talk about it but by now I was intrigued. I wanted to know more. What she could possibly have done was beyond me. She didn't seem the type to set fire to the gym, like uncle Dave had when he was at school. You couldn't be expelled from our school for anything less than trying to burn it down.

'What wrong? What was it you did?'

'It doesn't matter.'

'Oh, come on Jenny,' I pleaded. 'I won't tell anyone, I promise. Nan . . .'

'Nan . . . auntie already knows. So does gramps.'

She normally called her aunt by her correct title but grandad she never called 'uncle'—always 'gramps' for some reason.

'Please tell me.'

'I can't Titch. Not all of it.' She gave a little sigh and

bitterness crept into her words. 'If you must know, I was found with a boy. We weren't doing anything, but that didn't matter. I don't even like him very much. He was just a boy and I met him in the garden, the school grounds. It was just a dare. One of the teachers caught us sitting in the bushes and they made an awful fuss . . .'

'What was his name? Did anything happen to him?'

For some reason I identified with her companion, I suppose because we were of the same sex and it was just as likely, a few weeks before, that I might have been caught talking to Jackie.

'I don't know what happened to him. Nothing, I suppose. He was just a boy that used to deliver the newspapers to the teachers. Miss Henchel frightened him—she shouted at him—and he ran off and climbed the wall.'

'How old was he?'

'Fourteen, I think. He had nice wavy hair but he scratched his pimples. They were always red with blood. Spotty ran off and left me to take all the blame. He could have told them we weren't doing anything, though it wouldn't have made much difference. Uggh! Who'd want to kiss him anyway . . .'

'Is that what they thought you were doing? Kissing each other?'

'I suppose so.'

'So you can't go back now?'

'No. Auntie's trying to find another school that will take me. I don't care. They can send me where they like. I wish . . .' she began fervently, but then stopped.

'What?'

'I don't know. I just wish my mother was alive. Instead I've got to look for white foxes.'

She was crying now, softly, and I was alarmed that nan would come up and find her and think I had said something to make her unhappy.

'Never mind. Nan will look after you. I don't mind talking whenever you want to. Honestly.'

This just made her cry more, so I shut up. It seemed that anything I said would be the wrong thing so it was best to keep quiet and let her get rid of it as best she could. I couldn't see how white foxes were going to help us, or waterwitches, but I was willing to play along if it would make her a bit happier.

'Do you want to hear a ghost story?' I said after a while.

'Oh, *yes*. Yes please.'

'All right then.' It was against my better judgement. I knew I was going to frighten myself more than her.

'There was once two old ladies, sisters I think, that shared a house not far away from here. It was a very old house, with towers and turrets and things like that, all made out of wood that was slowly falling to bits. Because it was so old and the walls was so loose, when the wind blew at night it used to make an *awful* (I tried to pronounce it the way Jenny did) racket, creaking and moaning and grinding, so that people said it was haunted and wouldn't go near it at any price. But the sisters didn't care because they said they didn't believe in ghosts. That's what they said, but people noticed that even though the house had a hundred bedrooms they both slept in the same room.

'One night there was a terrible storm and the house was noisier than usual and one of the sisters woke up and thought she could hear a chain clanking. She lay there with the sheet pulled up to her eyes, staring into the dark and listening hard to the "Clink, clink, clink," that seemed to be coming up the long winding staircase. Then she realized that she had left the well chain—they had a well in the garden, see—left it untied and it was probably clinking against the stone sides of the well. She was just trying to get off to sleep again when all of a sudden she thought she could smell rotten flesh. She sniffed hard and, yes, there was definitely a horrible stink coming from *underneath the bed*.'

Jenny moved at this point and I could see her eyes glistening in the dark. I said, 'I forgot. You're supposed to close your eyes while I tell this.'

'Oh! I don't think I could.'

'Well, it's best, or it doesn't work as well.'

'All right then.' She did as I asked her.

'Yes, there was *definitely* a horrible stink and she thought there must be a rotten corpse underneath the bed, but she didn't dare look and was about to wake her sister when she remembered that they used the room below their bedroom to store apples in. The apples must have started going mouldy and that was why the smell was coming up, through the floorboards. Once again she turned over and tried to get to sleep. Just as she was dropping off she heard footsteps coming up the stairs and this time she was really frightened because she had no ordinary explanation for them. There was no doubt they was footsteps . . .'

'*Were* footsteps,' said Jenny, her eyes still tightly closed.

'That's right,' I said. 'And so she reached across to her sister's bed and took hold of her hand in the dark.'

I slipped my hand into Jenny's and gripped it hard. She twitched a little but she still kept her eyes shut.

'The hand felt very cold but gripped her very hard.' I squeezed Jenny's fingers. 'Just at that moment the door opened and a figure stood in the doorway holding a lighted candle. It was the second sister who had got up in the middle of the night feeling thirsty and had gone downstairs for a drink of water . . .'

Jenny's eyes flew open and she pulled her hand away quickly.

'It's best if it's winter,' I said, 'and you can put your hand out of the window and freeze it while you're talking. Works better like that.'

'I don't care, it was scary anyway. I thought I'd die when you squeezed my fingers like that. Do you know any more? I know one about a little boy who is playing hide-and-seek and he crawls into this trunk which accidentally locks itself . . .'

'I don't want to hear any more,' I said. 'Let's talk about something else.'

Jenny laughed and jumped up. 'No, I'm going to bed now, while I still feel the spooks. Goodnight Titch. See you tomorrow.'

'OK,' I said reluctantly.

Jenny went to her room, Dave's old bedroom, and I tried to settle down to sleep. Every time I closed my eyes though, I pictured a small rotting corpse inside the trunk we had in the attic. I was sure that was the box Jenny had been about to tell me of. I was glad that the birds only scraped around on the roof in the mornings and not in the middle of the night, otherwise my heart would have given out.

# TWENTY

It is strange that the clarity of my memories begins to fade from the time my disbeliefs in the supernatural world, the fantasy world of childhood, began to take firm hold of my mind. It is the nearer events that are not so clear, whereas recollections of our games, the madman, the fire, the crucifixion of the badger, and others prior to Jenny's arrival are quite vivid. Of course, they may not be strictly accurate. We tend to refurbish our memories and in doing so elaborate and alter them to suit ourselves. However, I have tried to be as honest as is possible for an adult looking back and have attempted to capture in my narrative the viewpoint of the child, rather than the man.

It seems rather perverse to me now that Jenny's insistence that we retain those early fantasies should have been the one ingredient previously missing in the mixture, that changed fantasy to concrete reality. Since she was so intensely eager that we should stay within that twilight world, it must have seemed to me that she knew something I did not and was trying to keep me from it, although for my own good. My scepticism began to dissolve and hard, cold realization took its place.

As the winter began to creep across the marshes and salt flats, brittle, white and glistening with a billion tiny crystals, Jenny and I spent less time out of doors. Mostly we sat in front of the range and read books or listened to the wireless. Around us, the earth became as inflexible as a sphere of metal. Those ponds I had feared so much in the summer were now sealed with ice, locking in any witch that inhabited their depths. Trees, once friendly and yielding, became lean and aggressive, repelling my efforts to climb them. When we did go for a walk along one of the dykes one morning we found birds huddled in frozen hollows staring pathetically at the iron circles in the sky, or scratching in solidified mud for meagre meals. Bleak enough in the summer months, the creeks were utterly desolate during the season of ice and snow. Winds that must have been born in Siberia came scything across the flats, blades intent on cutting down anyone in their path. *Life doesn't belong here*, the landscape seemed to say, *and I'm going to do my utmost to drive it out.*

The dyke we walked along that particular Saturday morning led to Rochford where the central square was used as a market, mostly during the warmer seasons, but once a month during winter too. We arrived at about noon when most activity had ceased and the farmers were finding pubs with open fires to discuss the remainder of their business. Since Christmas was not far away, chickens and turkeys dominated most of the market square and kicked up quite a din. We bought ourselves some licorice and sat on the edge of the water trough, taking in the sights and sounds that were in complete contrast to the quiet of the country we had just traversed. While we were thus occupied I noticed two people of my own age staring at us from the doorway of the Post Office. It was Dinger and Jackie. Jenny noticed them too.

'Are they friends of yours?' she asked.

Dinger was dressed, like most of us, in gumboots, overcoat and gloves, but whereas I was wearing a scarf wrapped round my head and tied under the chin to keep my ears warm, he had on a knitted balaclava. It made him look more bulky and aggressive than usual. Jackie, like Jenny, had on a woollen hat, so I was the only one with make-do headgear.

'Not exactly,' I said. 'That's Jackie and Dinger. I told you about them. They're the ones . . .' I stopped in mid-sentence as the pair began walking towards us.

As they got to us, Dinger said, 'Toothache?'

'What?' I asked.

'You got toothache, then? That stupid scarf I mean.' He smiled that old baiting smile of our gangtime days.

'No,' I said, miserable at being sneered at in front of Jenny. I made an attempt at being friendly.

'Where are you goin' then?'

Dinger looked at his feet in mock surprise.

'Don't look like I'm goin' anywhere at the moment. Me feet ain't movin' are they? Are me feet movin' Jackie? 'Cos I can't feel 'em if they are. Must have seized up or somethin'.' Jackie giggled.

'All right,' Jenny cut in with cold, precise diction. 'Don't overdo it. We can see that you're stationary without all the gabble.'

They both stared hard at Jenny, not in the least intimidated by her age or accent. As to her size, Dinger matched it and would not have been afraid of her if he did not.

''Oos she then?' said Jackie, licking steadily on a stick of candy while she regarded Jenny through narrowed eyes.

'I'm his cousin and I don't like being talked about, I like being talked *to*, especially since I'm sitting here in front of you.'

Jackie turned to Dinger. 'Talks posh, don't she? Got a plum in her mouth or somethin'.

'How would you like a smack around the face?' said Jenny.

Dinger cried, 'Cor. There's a real ladylike expression for you. Smack you round the gob, eh? That's really nice, init?' As he spoke his Essex dialect became thicker and broader. Dinger knew how to aggravate a situation. He was not even a native of East Anglia but he had a parrot's ear for accents, and could imitate old Whopper, the local tramp, to the point where he could fool friends.

Dinger was itching for a fight and I would have obliged him had I not known that he thrived on pain. You couldn't beat him when it came to violence because the harder you hit him the more it aroused him to retaliation. Nothing short of losing consciousness would prevent Dinger from winning a fistfight and we were not of the age where that was likely to happen. Now, in my later years, I can see the psychology behind his viciousness. It was not Dinger against a single opponent; it was Dinger against the world. He punished his combatants for all the ills visited upon him by his heavy-handed father and bully brother.

Jenny, however, was not afraid of anyone either, but for

different reasons. She stared hard at Dinger and said, 'Where did you crawl out from, you worm? Titch has told me all about you. Not satisfied with bullying your school-friends, you have to hurt harmless animals.'

This stung him and his face went red. I knew he was ashamed of having killed the badger, though I never understood why, since he seemed capable of any cruelty. He muttered something under his breath and pretended to see someone he knew on the far side of the square.

'Gotta go,' he said to Jackie. Then to me, 'I'll see *you* later.'

'When you like,' I replied, but my heart was beating hard in my chest. He walked away from us quickly, his breath forming plumes of steam in the cold air. I saw him pause to stamp his feet, as if to warm them, but I knew he was getting rid of some pent-up frustration at having been bested by Jenny. Jackie stood there, looking a little sheepish.

'One down, one to go,' smiled Jenny at me.

'I'm not goin' anywhere,' stated Jackie. 'I've got a right to stand here if I want to. You don't own the market square, see.'

Jenny said to me, 'What's wrong with her face?'

Jackie touched her own cheek, involuntarily, then let her hand drop to her side again. The water trough, being made of marble, was painfully cold on my backside by this time but I could not move while Jackie stood directly in front of me. Pins and needles began to invade my buttocks.

'I mean,' said Jenny, 'you would think she could wash before she comes out in the mornings.'

Her face was perfectly clean but, not being able to see that for herself, Jackie probably thought she had picked up some smuts from somewhere. I saw a muscle twitch just below her left eye and began to feel sorry for her. She looked as if she were about to cry. But Jenny had no mercy and I began to wonder whether my cousin was any better than the other two when it came to kindness.

'Peculiar smell,' Jenny continued, which indeed there was, coming from the droppings of the fowl around us.

She sniffed the air conspicuously. Jackie looked down at her own feet. Just then I could stand the pain in my bottom no longer and slid off the trough, almost touching Jackie as I found my feet. She backed off immediately crying, 'Don't you . . . don't you . . .'

'I wasn't . . .' I began, but the girl interrupted.

'You wait, Raymond Swan. I'll get you. I know somethin' about your nan, see, what my mum told my dad . . . just wait.'

After she had gone, Jenny said to me, 'What did she mean, about knowing something . . .?'

'Probably making it up,' I said. 'She's always telling lies.' But there was something about the tone she had used which made me doubt my own words. My nan was not universally liked in the village because she was considered a little too stand-offish amongst the tight-knit inhabitants. One was supposed to share all one's secrets with one's neighbours and any scandal or gossip was passed on eagerly, or was expected to be. Nan kept to herself more than most and was, in truth, a little bit of a snob, though she had no right to be since she was from the same farm-labouring stock as the rest of the people in the community. I had no doubt that if there was any truth in Jackie's words it would be something to do with dirty washing on the line or unclean windows. Nan maintained that some of the housewives elected themselves inspectors of windows and marched through the village for the sole purpose of checking the cleanliness of glass panes.

'Well, if she goes spreading any lies about auntie,' said Jenny in a firm voice, 'I'll soon give her a box on the ears. No wonder you had such a nasty time this summer with those two, Titch. They make my blood boil. Pair of scruffs. While I'm here . . .' she went on, but I wasn't listening properly. I was feeling upset that the whole business which I thought dead and buried had blown up again. I hated having enemies. It meant that wherever you went you had to be aware that you might run into them and trouble would ensue.

Not long after that we saw grandad on the far side of the square. He was leaning heavily on his good leg and had taken out his tobacco pouch to fill his pipe. His movements were slow and deliberate and I could see he had been drinking but I didn't mention this to Jenny.

'There's grandad. Let's ask him for a ride home,' I said.

Jenny nodded and we crossed the square to where he stood. He looked up as we approached but continued with his task without a greeting.

Jenny said, 'May we have a ride home, gramps?'

'Suit yerself,' he muttered. 'The cart's over yonder.' He nodded in the direction of the bank and I saw Custard tethered to a lamppost. We ran over to her and made a fuss of her before climbing up onto the cart. A little while later grandad came and heaved himself up beside us after gathering the reins. Then he clucked at Custard who began her customary slow walk home.

I wondered how much grandad had had to drink but it was difficult to tell from his face. It was red and cracked with veins but that could have been the cold weather. Jenny's face was also very rosy and I was sure my own matched theirs. It didn't matter anyway. Custard was not a horse one steered like a car. She knew the way as well as any of us and all she wanted was an occasional grunt from her master to keep her legs moving. Peter lay in the back on some straw, his eyes half closed. No one spoke. It was always like that in grandad's presence: he seemed to demand silence.

There were a few fluffs of snow in the air as we went along and the skies had darkened since the early morning. I felt a little dead inside. The summer seemed to have been several years past. I wondered whether to ask grandad about his leg, but I wasn't sure he'd play the game with Jenny there and anyway he didn't look in the mood for stories. It took us an hour to get to the house.

Nan was fixing dinner when we got in and had taken a jar of greengages that she had bottled in the autumn to make a pie for afters. Jenny went up to her straight away and began to help.

'Where have you two been then?' asked nan.

Jenny replied, 'Oh, we had a nice walk into Rochford along the dyke. It was a bit cold but I enjoyed the fresh air.'

'I see. Market day, isn't it?' Nan busied herself with the pie crust while Jenny greased a tin. I stood by, watching them.

'Yes. It was interesting—except that we met some horrible children. Former friends of Raymond's.' She always used my proper name when talking about me. 'They were quite nasty but I soon sent them packing. The girl even started talking about you. I wasn't going to stand for *that*.'

Nan paused in the act of dusting the dough with flour. She didn't look at either of us but stared out of the scullery window at grandad who was hanging the tack in the shed.

'About me? What did she say then?'

'Oh, nothing really—and that's as well for her. She was a horrible little creature and her nose kept running. Don't they own a handkerchief, some of these children?'

Nan said, 'Put some coal on the range fire please Raymond.'

'It's not down yet,' I argued, automatically.

'Do as you're told,' nan snapped, whirling on me. Both Jenny and I jumped and we were both, I think, surprised to see nan's eyes so hot with temper.

'All right, all right,' I muttered. 'I just didn't think it needed it.'

Immediately her face softened and she sighed. 'I'm sorry. I'm not quite myself today. The gas man's been and I was trying to get the washing dry. It's not easy in this weather. Goes as stiff as cardboard outside and drips all over the floor inside . . .'

'S'all right,' I said, and went to pile some more coal on the already blazing fire. It must have been hot because Ginger was almost over the other side of the room. He normally sat on the mantel in the winter to get the most out of the hot air.

Nan went back to her task and asked Jenny, 'What were the words she used then, this child?'

'Oh, she just said, "My mum told my dad something about your nan" or words to that effect.' Jenny used the same whining tone that Jackie had employed.

Nan began to lay the pie crust over the top of the basin.

'Stupid people,' she muttered. 'Why can't they mind their own business? I hate this village sometimes.'

Just then grandad came stamping in and no more was said. I didn't blame nan for being upset. I hated it when people talked about me at school behind my back.

We had dinner and then nan dressed up to take Jenny to put some flowers on her mother's grave. I didn't want to go out any more so I went up to my bedroom to read.

Grandad went out again a little while later and now that I was sure the house was empty I went to the doorway of Jenny's room. In the corner, by the jug and bowl stand, was the cupboard in which Dave kept his things while he was at sea. He had left a combination lock on the doors and I had spent many hours fiddling with the dials when I had the house to myself. At first I had tried to go through the numbers systematically but realized after a lot of labour that this was an impossible task. Then I just twiddled with it, hoping to come across the correct set of numbers by accident. Finally, I had the best idea of all. I had taken a screwdriver from beneath the kitchen sink where the tool box was kept and had hidden it behind Dave's wardrobe for such a time as this. I was going to loosen the screws on the hinges.

I paused on the threshold of Jenny's room, suddenly loath to enter. A girl's bedroom is like an empty church. There were sacred objects lying on the dressing table: a brush, a hand mirror, one or two coloured ribbons, a jar of cream. There was a sort of pinky scent to the air too, which, though it did not smell in the least like incense, aroused the same sort of feelings which that perfumed vapour engendered. To enter that room would be to trespass on holy ground. In that pastel temple the high priestess performed gentle rites which had no shape or form in my mind but which left a mystical after-odour full of the fragrance of wild flowers. Somehow the light seemed different in there; it fell on the rose-petal eiderdown as a shaft of sunlight falls on an altar cloth.

I stepped inside.

There is something sensual as well as spiritual about being in an empty church. One is aware of the tread of one's feet on well-worn floors and the smoothness to the wooden backs of the pews. Everything has been soaked in age and mystique, even the air and the coloured sunbeams passing through the stained-glass windows. The whole inner sanctum is charged with the atmosphere of the invisible Host: the smell of the dying flowers has a sickly edge to it and the dust that fills the columns of light has been stirred by His breath.

I walked across Jenny's bedroom as I would now walk down the aisle, aware of my own presence as a violator of hallowed ground. Jenny was there in all the artefacts she used and surrounded herself with; she was especially in the stuffed panda that watched my progress with glassy-eyed suspicion. It need not have worried. I no more dared to touch a part of her clothing than I would the robe of an absent priest. The bath oil she kept in a jar on her dressing table was as holy as the water in a font. To remove the panda from the plumped pillow would be steal a Bible from the stand below the pulpit. Just being there, breathing her scented fumes, was a violation in itself.

I took the screwdriver from its hiding place and began work immediately, keeping one ear tuned for the return of the others. I would have died of embarrassment if I'd been caught in that room. While I was busy I knocked over a tin of talcum powder which sent up a fine, white cloud as it hit the floor. My heart stopped for a second. The sound could not have had more impact on me if it had been an explosion. I interrupted my task to clear up the mess and spent many minutes deciding the exact position of the tin before its fall.

Finally the door was loosened enough for me to reach inside the cupboard, which I did, my hand coming to rest on the object I was after. Excitement filled my chest as I worked it out through the crack. Here was another holy artefact but one from a very different religion indeed. Dave's shotgun, lightly oiled and gleaming blackly in the dull light from the window, was in my hands. With my heart thumping I opened the breech to check that there were no shells inside. It was empty. I looked down the barrels and the shining spirals took my breath away, they were so perfect. I snapped the gun shut and ran my hand over the stock, which was polished to a light brown and slightly worn in the place where it nestled into Dave's shoulder. Such a deadly beauty that blue-black gun metal had in my eyes. The centripetal design on the barrels by the breach looked like the magic symbols cave men might have carved on their antler horn knives. I lifted the heavy shotgun to my shoulder and drew back the hammers with my thumb. They clicked satisfyingly into place. Just at that moment a Red Indian was climbing over the stockade wall and about to chop Mick with his tomahawk.

'Bang!' I shot him dead. The hammers clacked almost simultaneously and I feigned a kick from the stock. There was no blood on the corpse. He, the Indian, was as perfect in body and limb in death as he had been in life. The mangled bodies of blasted hares had taught me nothing. My dead Indians were those of the cowboy films I saw at the cinema. 'Bang, bang, bang.' I went berserk, killing right and left in the defence of my grandparents' home. Finally I got tired of the slaughter and sat on the bed, the gun across my knees. I was playing a game of fantasy. I was *aware* that it was a game, and there was little satisfaction in being aware.

I sat there, in that double sepulchre of near womanhood and death, for a long time. Somehow I had exhausted my sensual well and had nothing left in me but dry stone. Luckily I head Mick barking as nan and Jenny returned and managed to get the gun back into the cupboard in time, pushing the screws back into place, the holes now being too large to do more than just hold them. I rushed back into my own room just as the back door was being opened.

The rest of the day passed uneventfully and in the evening I went through the ritual of looking for the white fox with Jenny to satisfy some need that had built up inside her during the afternoon. Then I went to bed.

In the early hours of the morning I was awakened by a sound downstairs and crept out of bed. Grandad was asleep, snoring softly. I passed Jenny's room and went halfway down the staircase, staring into the dark room below. In the light of the embers of the fire I could see nan, sitting in an armchair in her nightdress. She was crying.

'What's the matter, nan?' I whispered. It was terribly distressing to see her weeping. I wasn't used to it. She hardly ever gave way to tears and the last time had been at aunt Elinor's funeral.

She looked up, startled, then said in a controlled voice, 'Nothing, child. Go back to bed.'

I stayed there for a second more and she added, 'I've got one of my migraines. Don't worry. I've taken a tablet. It'll soon go away.'

I went back to my room and crawled beneath the sheets again. I was too tired to think much more about it but in the back of my mind was the knowledge that nan had had one of her headaches only two days before. They didn't usually follow so closely on one another.

# TWENTY-ONE

Early in December an incident occurred which frightened us all. It was one of those really cold days when you wake up in the morning and if you had a choice, would not stir from beneath the snug, warm blankets for all the money in the world. Poking my nose out from between the sheets the air felt almost solid and it was a painful task to put my feet on lino as cold as the ice on a pond. I pulled on my clothes quickly, each garment crisp, stiff and agony on the skin. Grandad's bed was empty as usual. He would have been up at the first sign of light, if that was what you could call the dismal, grey substance that fell sluggishly on the street outside. The sky was like granite, heavy and oppressive. It matched my mood as I descended the stairs to breakfast.

Nan wrapped me up like a rag ball for my walk to school, while Jenny settled down in front of the range to do her studies. I envied her that warm position in front of the fire. I wished I did not have to go out to face the elements and did so with the air of a martyr—a Captain Oates, and a reluctant one at that. The heating at school consisted entirely of open fires which only served to warm the teachers' backsides and did nothing for the rooms as a whole. I sat near the back of the classroom and I might as well have been on the edge of a tundra in Lapland for all the warmth I got from the burning coals a million miles to my front. To write an essay, to have to *think* as well as manipulate a pen in that atmosphere, was almost asking the impossible. I think the teachers liked such days, for at least we were quiet, our normally boisterous spirits having iced over with the rest of the world.

The day passed unnaturally enough; even the playground was silent, with groups of children hunched in talk and the only activity the stamping of feet. I hurried home, looking forward to a hot meal and an evening by the fire, listening to the wireless. As usual nan had everything ready on the table and I took my place as we waited for grandad to come home.

He was late.

We hung on until six o'clock and then nan said, 'We'd better make a start.' Just at that point there was a scratching at the door and I rose to let Peter into the room.

'Grandad must be here,' I said, peering into the darkness, but after another half-an-hour he still had not appeared.

'Perhaps he's gone to the pub?' suggested Jenny.

Nan shook her head. 'He never said he would. And Peter would be with him.' The dog was lying by the fire shivering. It looked up at us at the sound of its name but made no other movement.

'Something's happened to him,' nan said, firmly. 'Peter's never come home without him before. I'm going to see Mr Beamish. You children get on with your tea.'

She put on her coat and went out to see our neighbour. Jenny and I did as we were told, but with little enthusiasm. I had visions of grandad lying ill somewhere. I didn't look at Jenny, nor she at me. I think we were both a bit afraid. A little while later a group of men appeared at the door with nan. They had torches in their hands and were talking amongst themselves.

'Don't you worry, Mrs Swan. We'll find him,' Mr Beamish was saying. 'It's probably that old nag of his. Given up the ghost—gettin' old, you know. Never was much life in the old . . .' There was a polite omission.

Jenny was alarmed. 'Who's getting old?' She had misunderstood the fragmented coversation and believed they were talking about grandad.

'Custard,' I replied, quickly. 'The horse—not grandad.'

Mr Beamish hastily came in again. 'Lord no. Not old Rhubub. He's as tough as an old . . .' I think he was going to say 'horse' but he stopped himself in time. 'Look after your grandma,' he said to us. 'We'll start in Mill Lane. Went there to do some ditchin' for farmer Alcock you say?

Well, that's where we'll start lookin'. And don't you worry. Shall I send the missus in?'

Nan said, 'No need for that. I'll be all right. The children will keep me company.'

'Can't we go and help?' I asked.

'No, you can't,' she said sharply.

So, we sat all evening while nan did some sewing and waited for news. Jenny and I tried listening to the wireless but I found I could not concentrate and turned instead to a nativity scene I was in the process of making. Even then, the pieces of balsa wood I cut out were not shaped properly. Finally I said, 'Nan, can't we go and help? I know my way as much as any of those men and Jenny will be with me.'

'It's cold out there,' she replied, but I could sense her wavering. Just at that moment there was a knock on the door. Jenny flew to open it and Mr Beamish stood there.

'We've found the cart,' he said, apologetically. 'He can't be far away. It was trottin' down Watery Lane.'

'But that's miles from Mill Lane,' said nan. I glanced at the clock on the mantelpiece. It was almost ten.

'Maybe it bolted,' he said. 'We're still lookin'. I've got PC Roseblade out there too. He's gatherin' some more men. We'll find 'im soon, don't you worry.'

I began to gather my outdoor clothes but nan said in a firm voice. 'You stay where you are, Raymond Swan. You're not going out.'

'But nan . . .'

'No buts. I don't want you lost too. One's enough. That silly old man . . .' she started but did not finish and I was surprised at her tone. It was almost as if she were blaming grandad for being lost, as if he were doing it on purpose to spite her. Mr Beamish coughed in an embarrassed way and said he would be getting back to the others. He closed the door and left.

'You two get to bed now. I'll stay up. Now.'

We saw there was no arguing with her and I lit the candle from the kitchen cupboard. We climbed the stairs together but instead of going to my room we went into Jenny's and sat by the window, staring out into the darkness. The light from the scullery window threw a beam out onto the frost covered yard. I could see Mick, lying on the straw in his kennel, his head just visible. The chickens had all gone to roost. I wondered if Mick was aware that something was wrong. His eyes were open—I could see them glinting—and he twitched his ears occasionally.

'Oh, where *is* he?' whispered Jenny, close to my head.

'I could climb down from here,' I said. 'I've done it lots of times before.'

Jenny was as sharp as nan had been.

'No, Titch. There's enough trouble as it is.'

'All right,' I replied. 'I know. But I hate doin' nothing.' I suddenly had a vision of grandad lying on the hard, cold ground, as still as a fallen tree and I shivered. 'I don't want grandad to die,' I said, my voice choking out the words.

'Who said he's going to die? Don't be silly Titch.' But there was a quaver in her tone and I knew she was as anxious as I was. I couldn't picture the world without my grandad. He didn't say a lot but his presence seemed a necessary part of a stable universe. He was like a pillar on a building which is taken for granted but which, if removed, would have the whole structure collapsing. The family, our family, needed the support his solid frame gave us. When uncle Dave came home the first person he asked for was 'Dad' and on being told that he was down the pub or out on some job somewhere Dave would nod and settle to his unpacking. He would not go and look for the old man, nor would they exchange much in the way of greetings once he came home. It was only necessary to know he was still there and functioning to realize that the world was still intact.

'Jenny,' I said. 'Do you like grandad?'

She was quiet for a long while, then she replied.

'He's a very gruff old man. I don't think he likes *me* very much.'

'He's like that with everyone,' I said. 'You don't want to take any notice of that.'

'I don't like or dislike him,' she said at last, after another long, thoughtful pause. 'He's a bit unapproachable.'

'What?' I said.

'Well, you know. You can't get close to him. He seems to reject affection. He's not the sort of gramps one can look on with affection. Not like a little Swiss toymaker with white hair and glasses on the end of his nose. He's big—and raw. Tough. I couldn't sit on his knee or anything like that, like some girls do with their uncles. You know what I mean. He's just not that sort of man.'

'I suppose so. But he's good at telling stories, isn't he? I bet when he comes home he'll have a good story to tell about tonight. Like the gypsies stole his leg or something.'

Suddenly Jenny rounded on me. 'That's it! Titch, you're a genius. *Something has happened to his leg.* Which is the shortest way home from Mill Lane?'

'Across the marshes,' I replied.

Jenny jumped away from me and ran down the stairs. 'Nan, we've had an idea,' she cried. Just at that moment there was a noise from the yard and I looked out to see three shapes: grandad, supported on either side by Mr Beamish and PC Roseblade. One trouser leg flapped uselessly beneath him as he heaved himself along on his good leg. The two helpers had to pause each time and take the strain while grandad swung himself forward. It was a slow business and the effort was evident in all three faces. Out of the darkness behind them appeared another man, carrying the tin leg. It looked bent and twisted in his hands as if a rock had been dropped on it and had crushed it.

Jenny came up a little while later and said we were to go to bed.

'Is he all right?' I asked.

'Yes, and you're a prophet Titch, aren't you?'

My eyes opened wide. 'You mean the gypsies really did steal it?'

'No, silly. He had an accident. Custard moved off while he was loading his shovel on the side of the cart and gramps slipped. His tin leg went under the wheel of the cart and bent it. The straps snapped too, I think. Anyway, he shouted at Custard but the stupid animal wouldn't stop.'

'What happened next?' I asked, a little disappointed by this unromantic tale.

'The shovel had fallen off too, so he used it as a crutch and tried to cross the marshes. It was dark though and he kept slipping on the ice. Finally he found a high spot and stayed there until someone came. He lit his pipe, he said, so that they would see it glowing. Clever, wasn't it?'

'To light his pipe? Yes, but I suppose he would have done that anyway. He's always smoking it.' I was a bit unhappy with this account. I wanted to hear that grandad had crawled to a cottage or something and saved himself, instead of waiting for others to do it. I knew I was being unreasonable but it annoyed me for some reason that he had just *waited* until someone came.

'He should have lit a signal fire,' I said.

'In this weather? Where would he have found any dry sticks? And out on the marshes?'

'I suppose so. I'm going to bed. I'll see you in the morning. Goo'night, Jen.'

'Goodnight Titch. Sleep well.'

I left her room. As I crossed the landing I heard nan and grandad talking. The other men had left.

Nan was saying, '. . . that was a stupid thing to do.'

'It weren't on purpose woman. You don't think I like hoppin' all over the country in the middle of winter, do you? The blasted pony wouldn't stay. That's all there is to it.' There was a long pause. Then grandad's voice again. 'Sorry I came home, eh? Thought you'd got rid of the old bastard did you?'

Nan's voice was full of suppressed fury.

'Don't you swear in my house Edward Swan. I live here too you know and I won't have swearing. There's children upstairs.'

'Bah. They've 'eard worse. I got a right to let rip sometimes, especially when I've spent half the night freezin' to death on the marshes. I know you woman. I know what you were hopin' for . . .'

'That's a wicked thing to say. All I wanted was for you to be found. Now you're here and none the worse for it, well, that's a different matter. But don't you go saying wicked things about me Edward. They're not true and you know it. I have as much human compassion as the next person and like it or not, you're my husband. I wouldn't wish anyone ill. I'm a good, churchgoing woman . . .'

'Bloody hypocrite, more like,' came the muttered reply. He pronounced it 'hippokryte'.

'You're a nasty-minded man.' I heard the sound of a plate being banged onto the table. 'Here, eat this while it's hot. I don't stand over a stove all day just to watch it go cold.'

'What it it?'

'Corned beef hash and if you don't like it you can go without.'

'Oh, I like it,' he replied. 'Just wanted to know what it was, is all. Nothin' wrong with your cookin' woman. I will say that. You could win prizes for your cookin' . . .'

'I don't want any prizes. I want to get to bed. How are you going to get upstairs?'

'I'll stay down here, in front of the fire. You go off woman. Leave me a blanket out. The chair'll be fine for me.'

I waited at the top of the stairs until nan had gone to bed in the front room. The conversation I had heard had not disturbed me unduly. They often argued and I had long ago put it down to old age. I guessed that all old people treated each other like that because they were naturally grumpy. When I was sure nan was asleep I called down to grandad.

'Grandad. Are you all right?'

'What? That you, boy?'

'Yes.'

'You get on up to bed.'

When he did not hear me move, he said, 'Yep. Your old grandad's not goin' to peg out just yet awhile, though that leg'll be the death of me when me time's up. Hurt's like buggery now. Must've tore the stump a bit. 'Ave a look at it in the morning.' He was speaking more to himself than me at this point.

'I thought a gypsy stole it,' I said.

'What?'

'Your leg. I thought it had been taken by tinkers and that's why you were late.'

'Get on to bed boy. Leave me to have me pipe in peace. I've got no stories for you tonight. I'm weary to the middle of me bones.'

'You didn't . . . you didn't see any white foxes out on the marsh?' I asked, hopefully.

'I won't say it agen boy. Do as you're told. White foxes . . .' he snorted. 'Damn, where did that head o' yorn come from boy? Not from me. Not from me. From your nan's side, more like. She's full of fanciful ideas. By damn, yes. Fanciful ideas all right . . .'

I left it at this and finally went to bed. As soon as I hit the cold sheets I was asleep.

# TWENTY-TWO

Sometimes, now, I wake in the darkness and feel that I am in a huge cave, a cavern deep in some mountain, and the entrance to the outside world is hidden in a maze of tunnels. Whenever this happens, which is rarely, I populate my imaginary cavern with a multitude of ethereal creatures: waterwitches, ghouls, white foxes, all those supernatural beings which haunted my childhood. I prefer them to what lies beyond the entrance, in the real world outside. I prefer them because they make me feel alive. They move in the darkness around me creating emotions in my breast which send my heart racing and have my soul folding in on itself in delicious terror. In the real world, the worries are as exotic as cigarette ash.

I can remember the details of that Sunday quite vividly still, but only the details, the small, insignificant things. When I try to recall my thoughts, my impressions, I come up with blanks. There was something there that a boy of eleven could understand, if he wanted to let it in, but I did not. I didn't want to. I had seen death, that summer, and found in a curious way that its grotesque guises, though frightening, were attractive. That is, not attractive in the beautiful sense, but magnetically hypnotizing. Life, on the other hand, unfolded new mysteries daily, and those mysteries were far from attractive. It has been that way ever since, which is why I try to cleave to childhood fears and find security in them.

The problem with adult fears, and why I prefer those of childhood and the world where magic exists, is that they are terrible only in their dullness, their drabness. There is nothing exotic in them at all. They are fears of being unfulfilled at the end of life, of not being valued, of being trapped in an unending routine of menial tasks, of being left lonely and unwanted, of being discovered trying to escape all these things in some activity which others look down upon as sordid because they too are trapped in their own depressing pits. They are petty, personal fears which, even as I voice them, seem to yawn in the face of listeners.

When adults seek to reintroduce magic and change into their lives, they normally have to step outside a code of conduct, set by time and place, from which there is no escape. Even their desperation seems sordid in itself.

But they are *real* fears. They have shapes and forms. Monotonous and colourless shapes and forms.

It was the day before Christmas Eve and Jenny and I had decided, quite late, to go to the pictures in Southend. We knew there was a *Tarzan* film on and it seemed a pleasant idea to get immersed in steaming jungles while the world was stiff with ice and heavy with oppressive skies. We took the bus into town and went straight to the cinema without telling nan or grandad. Grandad was out somewhere anyway, probably with his cronies in the market square, and nan had gone visiting, so we did not feel we would be missed until at least six o'clock that evening.

The film was a good one, something about a search for a lost idol, and the atmosphere was warm inside the cinema. We left the building at about five o'clock and walked past the Christmas tree which had been erected in the middle of the town, admiring its decorative lights. Then we strolled through the arcade on our way to the bus stop. There were other children in groups moving in the same direction. Many of us had extra Christmas money and it was a treat to be out, in the festive streets, with the lights of the shops giving the dark town an air of pre-celebration excitement. It was only one more day before we should have presents galore and the anticipation of Christmas morning filled us all with bonhomie.

Suddenly as we passed a fruit stall, I caught sight of Jackie with some friends and was relieved to see that Dinger was not with her. She caught my eye and gave me a tight little smile. Jenny had not noticed her and was talking about what we would say to nan once we got in, as we had not asked permission to go into town, which we should have done.

'We'll say we looked for her but couldn't find her anywhere. All right, Titch?'

'Yes. OK. I'm sure she won't be angry. It's Christmas, after all.'

Jackie had crossed between some stalls and now stood in front of us. Jenny's eyes narrowed.

'What do you want?' she said, as she recognized her.

'Don't want nuthin'. Got somethin' to show you. Outside.'

Jenny said, 'You can tell us. What is it? One of your silly tricks? If your friend, Dinger or whatever his name is, is waiting out there with his bully boys, he can keep waiting, because we are going home on the next bus.'

'Dinger's not there. Someone else is. Someone you know.' There was a horrible little smirk playing around the corners of her mouth and suddenly I wanted to be at home, with my grandparents. 'Come on. What'reya 'fraid of? Nobody's goin' to beat you up or anythin'. S'just someone you might want to meet, that's all.'

She began to walk off to one of the many exits to the arcade and Jenny shrugged and followed her. I trailed behind. There are few of us who can resist the chance to be let in on a secret and there was a definite secretive air to Jackie's words.

Outside the arcade the street was busy with people on their way to church and visiting those shops that had been allowed, like the arcade, to stay open on the Sunday before Christmas. Jackie went onto the pavement and started to look around. Her eyes fell on a figure standing in the light of a sweet shop some three doors down, but there was a look of disappointment on her face and she seemed to be unsure of something. The man she was staring at was tall and slim and wearing a dark overcoat. One of his hands was in his pocket, while the other scratched his cheek with a long, slim finger. He was reasonably elderly, having grey hair, but there was no stoop to his frame, He stood straight, like a military man out of uniform, and his head was held erect as if he were contemplating something in the far distance. The hand came down from the clean-shaven, gaunt face and buried itself in the right-side pocket.

'Well?' asked Jenny.

'I thought . . . wait a minute.' The smile had gone from Jackie's face, replaced by a look of anxiousness.

The man looked down at his shoes and flicked at something on the pavement with his foot. He still seemed to be lost in thought and I realized he was waiting for someone. He had that preoccupied air about him that people have when they want to go somewhere but are held fast by an appointment. Just at that moment someone came out of the sweet shop, slipped an arm into his and pecked him on the cheek.

Jackie giggled in an inane fashion and then ran off, back into the arcade, while Jenny and I stood transfixed on the pavement. I could not take my eyes from the package that the man's companion had under her arm. While her attention was taken up with the man it slipped to the pavement and she bent down to pick it up. In the light of the shop window I could see what had fallen out of the loose wrapping paper. It was two of those commercially-made stockings of red mesh, filled with a mixture of sweets: chocolate bars, wine gums. Mars bars, licorice all-sorts. I could almost read the labels from where we stood. Certainly I recognized the wrappers and my head spun. I felt giddy. They were intended for us—Jenny and me—on Christmas morning.

The man bent down and began helping nan pick up the dropped presents. He said something and they both laughed. I had never heard my nan laugh like that and have not since, and it had a peculiar effect on my throat. I made a noise to clear it and I felt Jenny's hand slip into mine at the same time.

As they stood up the man put his arm around nan's dumpy form and they prepared to move off, in the opposite direction from where we stood. I felt Jenny pulling at my hand, trying to get me into the arcade, but there was something I wanted to say to my grandmother.

'Nan!' I called.

She turned around quickly and there was a puzzled look to her face. Then it went pale and she quickly pushed the man's arm away from her. Until that point I was only aware that something unusual was going on which made me feel weak and dizzy, but which I merely needed an explanation for. Seeing her face, however, made me realize that something was terribly wrong. From being as happy as I had ever seen her, she had turned in a moment to a figure of tragic despair. She said something to the man, who hunched his shoulders and took a step away from her.

'Stay there Raymond,' she called. 'I'll be there in a minute. Jenny, is that you?'

Jenny stepped out into the light now. She said nothing and her own face had been drained of colour.

'Look after Raymond for a moment.'

A short discussion took place between her and the man, who eventually walked off down the street. Then nan came towards us and I blurted out an explanation.

'We only went to the pictures—it was—*Tarzan*. We didn't think you'd mind, did we, Jenny? We looked for you, honestly nan, but you'd gone out visiting. I'm . . . we're sorry, aren't we, Jenny? We would've asked . . .'

'It's all right, Raymond. We'll catch the bus home. That man . . . that man . . .'

'He's a friend of yours,' said Jenny.

'Yes. A friend.'

We caught the bus, none of us saying anything. I said nothing to grandad because Jenny asked me not to. I doubt whether I would have raised the subject anyway. My mind saw the incident in several different ways, none of which helped my comprehension of the scene. One part of me knew that my grandmother had a boyfriend and that what I had witnessed was wrong, yet another part of me rejected this explanation because . . . because she was my white-haired, overworked, impatient, generous nan, who was prone to headaches and who bottled greengages in the autumn. Who was gruff with my grandfather and short with the dogs. Who was sympathetic with me when I was ill and angry when I stayed up late at night. Who made my bed and complained about my muddy shoes. Who provided meals and saw that we had a fire to get up to in the mornings. She was many, many things to me, which made up the person I knew as *nan*, as my grandmother, and whatever else I had learned in life at that tender age, one of them was that grandmothers did not have boyfriends. Grandmothers did not have any life outside the home. They were white-haired old ladies who did chores and wore faded blue dresses that they covered with an apron most of the time. There was no gaiety in them that did not spring from having baked a good apple pie or having been congratulated by the vicar for raising a sum of money on a church bazaar stall. In my mind I could not take that incident any further than what I had actually seen, even in later years when the truth was less misty and explanations as to why my grandparents had separate bedrooms were obvious. At that time I did not even question the arrangement and if I had thought about it at all, I should have put it down to the reason that my grandmother had migraines and could not bear anyone near her when she went to lie down.

So I knew, but I did not know, because the two parts of my mind that held opposite views found it impossible to come together to sort out a single, rational opinion. I had seen a strange man holding my nan and kissing her on the cheek and that was all there was to it. There were no previous meetings and no liaisons afterwards, because my mind would not allow entry to such thoughts. Certainly I could never have taken the physical side of this relationship any further mentally, because I had no context in which to place such thoughts. I knew the facts of life and how couples got babies, but old people did not get pregnant, did not have babies. Perhaps that physical side was confined to kisses on the cheek? It may well have been, for all I know now. Perhaps that meeting had not been arranged beforehand and had been a single, chance thing that had been destroyed before the seed had the opportunity to grow? I doubt that now, for nan continued to go out on a Sunday evening, though I blanked the reason from my consciousness. I remember now, though the memory of it has been missing from my mind for many years, so I cannot recall when it took place and under what circumstances, a short conversation between nan and Jenny which went something like this:

Nan: *I can't expect you to understand, Jenny, but old people have wants as well as young people. I'm not so very old, either, let me tell you. It doesn't feel ugly. It may look ugly to you, but it doesn't feel ugly to us. You're just a child . . .*

Jenny: *But what about gramps?*

Nan: *Your grandfather knows. He doesn't say anything, but he knows. I could almost love him again for that. He doesn't come to me with recriminations and you've got no right to either. You're only thirteen, for heaven's sakes . . . Why am I talking to you like this?*

Jenny: *Fourteen. I'm nearly fourteen. It's horrible.*

Nan: *It isn't horrible.* Tears.

When I suggested to Jenny a little while after Christmas that we might go looking for her white fox, she said she had seen it, while I was not with her, and never wanted to talk about it again.

# TWENTY-THREE

Whatever else grandad was, he was a tough man. One of the things that impressed people most about him was that he used to pull his own teeth out when they went rotten. It surprised me therefore that after his night in the fields he developed a chill which he found difficult to shrug off. During January he spent more time at home than I had ever known him to before, nursing a hacking cough. At night he would wake me as his big chest heaved with a spasm that reverberated through the otherwise silent house and I would hear him clearing his throat of phlegm for at least ten minutes prior to his leaving the bedroom in the morning.

The incident concerning nan and her 'boyfriend' I put right out of my mind. It was not so much that it was unpleasant to dwell on it but that there was nothing I could do to influence affairs in any way and I was more anxious about the fact that Jenny would be leaving soon than something about which I could do nothing. I spent my time trying to persuade everyone that Jenny would be much happier going to a local school but people do not take a great deal of notice of a young boy's views on the education of young ladies. The fact was I dreaded being left alone once more with only the 'old people' for company. As it happened, an event occurred which would significantly part us until we met again in our early twenties when I attended Jenny's wedding.

The date was 31 January 1953. The time was ten minutes to midnight. I was awoken by nan who was holding a lighted candle in her hand which illuminated her face and I could see anxious furrows on her brow which alarmed me. Her white hair hung down over her night-dress and she looked more like an avenging angel than ever.

'Quick boy, up and dress.'

I glanced across the room and saw that grandad almost had his leg strapped on. He was trying to suppress a cough at the same time as being bent double and there was pain in his expression. He was hurrying in such a way that I knew something was terribly wrong and for a few moments thought that it was his illness that was the problem, that we had to get him to hospital quickly.

'What's the matter, nan?'

'Just up and dress boy,' grandad growled, firmly.

I jumped out of bed and looked out of the window which seemed to be attracting nan's eyes every half second. There was a strong wind blowing which howled around the corner of the house. It was not a dark night. I could see the houses opposite and the trees that lined the street. In the distance a strange sky was in turmoil.

I saw the fear that grandad and nan were displaying and it made my skin prickle. Jenny came into the room, fully dressed, and I looked at her dumbly. I pulled on my shirt and pullover together, having taken them off that way. Then my shorts. It was very cold and the bare lino was painful against my feet. I shivered, still staring out of the window. There was a noise out there somewhere, a rushing sound. I looked directly down, onto the street. White cables of water were twisting along the gutters and the whole road was full of swirling eddies that foamed and gushed around the drains.

'Grandad! There's water in the street!' I cried. I realized that nan was now hurrying up and down the stairs with items of clothing and Jenny was doing something in her room. Peter had come up to the bedroom which under normal circumstances was strictly forbidden.

'Go and get the wireless boy, quickly, the water's risin',' nan wheezed.

I did as I was told, still in bare feet, clambering down the wooden staircase. The parlour floor was awash and things were floating down into the scullery. Nan had placed a lighted candle on the mantelpiece where it gutted and spluttered in the draught coming from the open window. Ginger, the cat, was on the table. I picked the animal up and put it on the stairs where it crouched with hunched shoulders. Then I waded ankle-deep through the cold water to grab the wireless set and the accumulator. I hurried up the stairs with them where Jenny was waiting to take them from me. Ginger followed behind.

Nan was dressing. She turned her back on me but continued to pull on her clothes.

'Anything else?' I asked.

'Food. Get some food,' grunted grandad. He was still struggling with his straps and catches. 'An' my tool box, under the sink.'

'I'll get the food,' said Jenny. 'You get the tools, Titch.'

We both went bounding down the stairs again. The water was rising fast and was almost up to my knees. Jenny went to the breadbin on the windowsill after trying, unsuccessfully, to open the larder door. I rummaged under the sink and found the tool box which was full of water. I emptied it and carried it upstairs but it was very heavy and I had to let it crash to the floor when I reached the bedroom. Jenny was explaining that the weight of the water rushing into the house had jammed the larder door shut but she had bread and cheese from the breadbin.

I went to the window again. The water was halfway up a car parked on the opposite side of the road. I could also see something in the distance, a white-topped wall of water which started near Milky's house and moved swiftly across the countryside, parallel to our road.

'Grandad!'

As I shouted the wave began to turn, sweeping round in a crescent shape, like a mighty arm about to brush the village clear of houses. There was a brief explosion and a shower of sparks as it toppled a pylon in a nearby field. The sky was lit up for an instant as if a wizard had cast a handful of fiery lights into the air above the water. The tall, long shape raced towards us.

Grandad was beside me, looking over my shoulder.

'Dyke's given way,' he said. 'Must be twenty, thirty foot high.'

'Can the house stand up to it?' cried nan, from behind us. 'Oh God!'

We watched it moving towards us, magnificent in its grand approach and cruel in its murderous white aspect. It looked solid, unyielding, deliberate, like a monster let out of its cage and determined to crush all in its path to freedom. Then we felt the shock as it hit the house and I was thrown to the floor with Jenny. The whole cottage was engulfed in water for a few moments. It smashed the windows and came pouring into the bedroom. Nan was crying something but I could not catch what it was. I thought of what Dave had told me about ships and terrible storms and realized that this was what it was like to be at sea in mountainous waves. I clutched at nan's clothes and held her for a few moments as we were all rolled around the bedroom floor. Grandad heaved himself to his feet at the first opportunity, gripping the windowsill for support. Then the water began to drain away, down the stairs and nan, Jenny and I were able to stand up again. Ginger was on top of the wardrobe but I could not see Peter. Then he came through the door, shaking himself vigorously, having been swept down the staircase. A terrible thought struck me.

'What about Mick?' I cried. 'And Jessica?'

'Nothin' we can do,' said grandad. 'Have to take their chances.'

'But Mick's chained.'

Grandad did not look at me and I knew I should have kept quiet. Both animals were either dead or beyond reach. Then I thought of all the cattle, horses and sheep out in the meadows, and possibly a tramp or two, and the gypsies in their flimsy caravans. I felt ill. All the badgers, in all the setts, for miles and miles around, had died in a single onrush of water. My own badger had preceded them by only a few months.

Nan got us some dry clothing from the wardrobe. I had to wear a pair of Dave's old trousers rolled up to the knees. We continued to stare out of the window as the water level rose steadily. It was less violent than before, although I could see currents snaking around corners in the moonlight. I was very afraid and I think Jenny was too. It seemed as though we were all going to drown. I felt Jenny shiver next to me, violently.

She said, 'What do you think has happened, gramps? Where has all the water come from? It's not even raining.'

'Don't know girl, but we'll be all right. Spring tide, no doubt. She'll start to go down soon, when 'er turns.'

'But the sea is half a mile away.'

'It'll have breached the estuary wall, yonder.' He pointed to the east. 'An' the rivers've doubtless bust their banks. We lie a bit low 'ere.'

There were objects floating by us. Huge buoys that had broken free from their moorings in the shipping lanes of the Thames. Once I saw something dark and flat in the distance with people clinging to the top of it.

'What's that?'

'Looks like a prefab or some such,' replied grandad. 'Family's got onto the roof.'

It was floating out towards the sea and I was glad I could not see the expressions on the small, pale faces of the passengers. The bungalows at the bottom of the road were already covered and I realized that Dinger's house was even further down there somewhere in the dip. And Jackie's too. It seemed so unfair that such a gradual slope should determine the difference between life and death for the occupants in the buildings around us.

Despite grandad's assurance that the water level would soon begin to descend, it rose steadily until it was almost to the top of the staircase.

'It'll be in here soon, dad,' said nan. 'What're we going to do?' She was wringing her hands and Jenny clutched at her dress. They took hold of each other and stared at grandad, looking for some sign of hope in his big-boned face.

'We'll have to go up in the attic,' he said. 'Pull the bed over 'ere boy.' The trap door to the attic was on the landing. Nan had regained her composure and Jenny too began to relax. We had something to do. We were not helpless and waiting for death to overcome us.

They helped me drag the bed through the doorway and then I climbed up and pushed open the attic door. Standing on the headboard I heaved myself up into the dark interior. Grandad put a small table onto the bed and nan and Jenny were helped onto it one after the other. I pulled nan up first as Jenny helped from alongside her. Once up, one of her feet slipped from a wooden beam and went through the thin plaster ceiling, but she eventually found a secure place. Then Jenny passed me up the candle which I gave to nan to hold. Jenny followed. Next came the tool box, Ginger and Peter. Finally, grandad climbed laboriously onto the bed, then stopped while he was racked by a coughing fit. I could see his pink scalp through the white, cropped hair below me as his head shuddered.

I said, 'What's the tools for, grandad?'

He did not answer. Instead, he gripped the edge of the attic hatchway with two big, calloused hands and began heaving himself up with only the strength of his thick arms. His legs dangled, unable to get a purchase on the table. I took one of his muscled arms in order to help him but he growled, 'Leave me be boy. I can manage better on me own.' But it was no use. Perhaps the weight of his tin leg was too much because he had to drop back down onto the bed below. Then he was gone for a moment, returning with a pile of clothes with which he proceeded to make a small hill in the middle of the bed. By this method he managed to get onto the table, which wobbled precariously until he took his weight off it and hauled himself into the attic.

He sat there, on the edge of the hatchway, panting heavily and gulping down large draughts of air. His coughing started again. When it had subsided he began rummaging in his tool box. Nan asked him what he was doing.

'Got to go through the wall, into next door,' he explained. 'Cottages slope down to our'n, so we'll move up through the attics to the top of the road. If nobody else 'as thought to do it, we'll take 'em all with us as we go.' He handed me a four pound hammer and a cold chisel. 'Here boy, bring 'un along. You two sit awhile,' he said to nan and Jenny. 'I'll shout you when I get through. These old houses ain't got but a few bricks atween 'em.'

He began crawling the length of the attic and I followed, careful to remain on the beams, otherwise I would have gone crashing through the ceiling. We found the dividing wall in the dark and grandad asked for the tools. Then he began chipping away at the bricks. Once I felt the wind of the hammer as it went past my face and moved back a little. It was a slow business, made slower by the fact that grandad was weaker than usual and kept pausing to cough.

While he was hammering away I heard something.

'Grandad, stop a minute. Listen.'

'What?' he asked, pausing.

There was a shout from the other side of the wall.

'Who's that?' cried a voice.

Grandad answered and then said to me, 'It's Beamish.'

'Mr Beamish,' I yelled. 'We're coming through the wall. Can you help from your side?'

'What? What's that?'

I explained again at the top of my voice, and eventually he must have understood because there came the sound of hammering. Beamish was in his mid-thirties, with two small girls, and like most men in the cottages he was a farm labourer. He was strong and that strength would be supplemented by an urgent desire to get his family to a safer place. Finally the first brick came out and we were able to talk to each other properly.

'What've you got there, Beamish? What tool you using?' asked grandad.

Beamish said, 'Just a piece of iron bedstead. Tools are still in the shed.'

'Well stand back a bit then. I've got a four pounder 'ere. I'm about to knock a few bricks out with it. Now one's gone, others should come easy. You start on t'other end of your attic.'

'Why? What's the idea?' asked Beamish. 'The wife an' kids are goin' daft here. What're we doin', for God's sake? The water's . . .'

Grandad interrupted. 'We got to move up the slope. The water'll be over this end of the cottages soon. Top house is at least twenty foot higher up. Come on man, don't waste time.'

He began hammering at the bricks again almost immediately and true enough they gave way with remarkably less resistance than they had previously shown. Even before the hole was two feet wide the two animals slipped through, careless of the swinging hammer. Grandad was panting with exertion, having to kneel on the beam and smash at the wall without toppling off.

When the hole was big enough we got nan to squeeze through, then Jenny, me and finally grandad. Nan went immediately to Mrs Beamish and her children and they began whispering in the far darkness of the attic. The Beamish attic had been boarded over for use as a storeroom which made everything that much easier. Jenny was near to me and put an arm around my shoulder. Beamish took the hammer from grandad and began repeating our former exercise. In this way we moved up, through the cottages, to the Cunninghams' at the end, gathering people as we went.

The water stopped rising before it entered the Cunninghams' bedrooms. Dawn crept over the placid lake that surrounded us, peaceful and unassuming. Nan started a sing-song—hymns, of course. Almost everyone joined in but me. I did not feel like singing. I stayed by the window.

Still, shining waters stretched as far as I could see. In the distance the mills rose out of the lake looking like grey, squared battleships. An hour earlier I had watched the water creeping up the sides of those buildings with fear in my throat. Now the whole world was a calmer, safer place. I could see the tops of trees and houses all around, and there was still a lot of flotsam winding its slow way between them, some getting caught on snags. What a strange place it looked. Not my village at all. I did not recognize it as any place I knew. The water had claimed so much. Even the remains of the White House and my lightning tree would be covered. I wondered if the water would ever go down again.

Grandad's rugged features came between me and the scene outside.

'You all right, boy?' he asked.

'Yes.'

'Fine.'

Suddenly, I wanted to ask him something.
'Grandad?'
'What?'
'How did you lose your leg, truly?'
He looked at me with tired, rheumy eyes.
'By God boy, you never give up, doz'un? This is God's honest truth, as sure as them hymns is holy songs, are you listnin' boy?'
'Yes.'
'I coffed the bugger off in me sleep one night. Came off's clean as a ploughshare takin' a slice o' turf. Bugger me, I says, that were a sharp coff—cut right through me bleedin' leg . . .'
Nan looked across at him keenly and he stumped away to the corner of the room asking if anyone had a dry light and some tobacco. Then I heard Jenny saying to nan, 'It'll be different now, won't it? I mean, gramps is a hero, isn't he?'
Nan just looked at her with a helpless expression on her face and I wondered why Jenny seemed so upset afterwards.
Of course, now I am able to ponder on it with the dubious wisdom that age brings, I know full well what that bleak expression meant and Jenny's subsequent distress. Heroism does not impress old ladies the way it does young girls. Old ladies favour gentleness, tact and loving kindness over feats of valour, and they are inclined to be less forgiving over past misdemeanours, like lying about one's true age before the wedding ceremony is over and consummated. The grudges of old ladies are like rocks, having had time to set hard over several decades.

When the water had descended about seven feet, small boats began to appear and the evacuation began. I knew I would be going home to my parents, at least for a time, but I was glad. Tenbridge would never be the same for me again.
Later, I was to hear of ghastly stories, and wonderful ones too. Of a father who tried to keep his baby warm on the roof of his house and suffocated it accidentally; of

people in bungalows who had survived a night at sea; of miraculous rescues from the roofs of floating prefabs; of families in small boats swept out to sea and lost forever; of terrified animals plucked from the water as they passed by bedroom windows; of stranded steam trains whose passengers cannibalized carriages to use as fuel and escape the flood. The Witchwater Country claimed life indiscriminately: here one was allowed to live, there one was snatched by death. Sorrow and relief were companion emotions on that night of nights, when East Anglia was swallowed, masticated and regurgitated by a wild beast we thought we had caged and tamed.

Amy Johnson had company, wherever she lay.

# TWENTY-FOUR

A neap tide coupled with high onshore winds had been responsible for the flooding. It was not until we had been evacuated that I found out that the floods had been on an international scale. Billions of cubic feet of water from the Atlantic Ocean had been forced into the North Sea by gales and thence onto the lowlands of Britain and Holland. In Britain, rivers had burst their banks and had swept across the countryside claiming lives and property, sometimes slowly and insidiously, at other times with a thunderous roar as barriers and walls gave way before the pressing weight of water. The East Anglian coastline had been drastically reshaped. The Witchwater Country had a new face.

In our village thirteen people lost their lives. Most of the terrible stories we heard came from places like Canvey Island, Foulness and other lower-lying areas of the estuary, but we had our share of watery visitations too. Like Milky's family, Dinger's had managed to reach the mills and were able to get above the level of the flood waters, but Jackie and her family were all drowned. Cathy had been staying with relatives, inland, but three members of her family had not been so lucky.

Mick, that tough and angry brute, turned up on grandad's doorstep three weeks after the waters had subsided and they were busy clearing the mud from the house. He had snapped his collar, no doubt in a fit of frenzy, and had managed to swim to high ground. Nan wrote that they were never going to chain him again. It did not seem fair, she said, that he should survive such a night just to become a prisoner of the yard once more. Jessica was never seen again.

There were stories that lived on even when the village

was back to normal: of the stubborn bull that refused to give ground, while other cattle around it froze and went down one by one as their legs went from under them, and which was finally rescued after a whole day up to his shoulders in the flood water by a crane and harness; of the farmer who went out at midnight to investigate something shining at the top of the dyke near his farm, and who had to race the water back to his house as the dyke gave way; of the squire whose estate was on a slope and who made his way to high ground by walking along the top of his estate wall as the waters rose alarmingly around him, defeating death with an amazing balancing act.

Jenny went to a new school and I was sent to my parents to be turned into a city gentleman. The games of fantasy were finally over. Where does childhood end? It ends with the death of fantasy, when fear of the dark is replaced by fear of the light. When you see and know the object of your fear then you enter that adult world you yearn for so much as a child.

A year after the flood grandad died, weakened by the chill that never left him after that night in the fields. You could say his leg had killed him after all. I fully expected that the cause of his death would be a fight in a pub or a heart attack brought on by a bout of cursing, but he passed away quietly, in his sleep. I returned to Tenbridge for his funeral but his removal from the Witchwater Country changed the whole landscape for me. It moved back the horizons and intensified its bleak aspect more surely than any physical agent could have done. The sea had torn open the land and had reshaped it: grandad's death left it as empty and desolate as the first morning the world had ever seen.

Some time later nan's gentleman friend asked her to come and live with him, which she did. I visited them once, not long before my grandmother died. I cannot say they were blissfully happy, for nan seemed too anxious when he was out of her sight. Whether she thought he would drop dead in the street once he was out of her caring gaze, or worse still, that he would be attracted to some other woman, I do not know. I only know that her manner was forever agitated when he was out of the house alone, and her relief, on his return, too evident. She fussed over him with a frown on her forehead, not a smile on her lips and she never left me alone with him so that we could talk about her. He was a pleasant enough man, with gentle manners and a kindliness that would have been as out of place on grandfather as the Crown Jewels. There was nothing in common between the two men she had disproportionately shared her life with.

It seemed to me that her life was just as clouded with one man as it had been with the other, only in a different way, possibly known only to her. I do not doubt she would have argued with me had I raised the subject with her, saying she had been happy with both partners. She was that kind of woman; everything internal was private and that which was shown was what she felt people would approve of, not condemn. I left her, standing on her doorstep and watching after me, with disturbed feelings in my breast. If she was unhappy even in happiness, was the state of bliss a myth which could only be found between the pages of books?

Jenny had been quite right to question nan's feelings once grandad had led us to safety. His heroism had been exemplary. He was an old man with an imperfect body and strength failing through illness. Now that I look back on it, his actions seem to me to be superhuman. Not only would no one have blamed him for doing nothing, they would have expected an aged cripple to behave in such a way as not to make younger, healthy men look like panicking fools. In short, I see him now as someone magnificent and unapproachable (though not unimpeachable), like a knight from the pages of *The Faerie Queene*. Someone who made all the demands on his spirit and body that a knight would make in order to carry out his duty according to his sense of honour. That such a man should be rejected, as she saw it, was unthinkable to Jenny.

Yet what she did not see was the weight of all the years hidden to her which nan had had to carry and perhaps subconsciously balance against that single night. Nan had had to make her choice many years before and nothing that grandad could do would alter that. Both my grandparents were noble, in their individual ways, but they had each a different concept of nobility. Grandad's heroism was of high action. Nan's, that of long suffering. *She never left him.* Therein lay the only connection between their separate viewpoints. It has taken me many years to accept this and even now I see that grand old man, standing like a giant on one of the knolls overlooking the Witchwater Country, in my mind's eye, and feel a pulse of pride mingled with resentment at my grandmother's failure to allow this picture through the haze of bitterness with which she surrounded herself. But then I am a man and my cowardice is that I readily identify with a male ancestor who stood above other men when it came to physical prowess and heroic deeds. Of the two sorts of courage, I grasp at the one which is illuminated by splendour and glory, rather than the one hidden in the shade.

She never left him. It was her request that we buried them together, on the Canewdon knoll, overlooking the Witchwater Country. The earth shapes those who once shaped the earth.